Before *Stranger in the Moonlight,* there was the shimmering promise of

Moonlight in the Morning

Praise for the first wonderful *New York Times* bestseller in Jude Deveraux's thrilling new Edilean trilogy. . . .

"Deveraux delivers a modern romance addressing relatable relationship obstacles. . . . Tristan and Jecca's chemistry jumps off the page."

—*Publishers Weekly*

"Lots of tender moments . . . with embers of realism throughout. . . . I eagerly await the second offering in the Edilean trilogy."

—*Goodreads*

"An engaging, charming tale . . . with a surprising final twist."

—*Genre Go Round Reviews*

Uncover more romantic secrets of Edilean in these "exquisite and enchanting" (*BookPage*) bestsellers

Scarlet Nights

"Deveraux brings to life the sort of sweet and spunky heroines who attract the muscular men her fans expect and enjoy. . . . *Scarlet Nights* will hook readers and leave them with a smile."

—*Booklist*

"Readers will delight in immersing themselves in the comfortable world of Edilean. . . . Deveraux's colorful cast and easy way with words shine."

—Publishers Weekly

"Deveraux is a master storyteller, and her books fairly shimmer with excitement and adventure, making her one of the most popular women's fiction writers today. *Scarlet Nights* is no exception. With strong characters, down-home charm, and an intriguing story, fans will enjoy catching up with the folks from Edilean."

—Wichita Falls Times Record News

Days of Gold

"Deveraux has a sure hand evoking plucky heroines, dastardly villains, and irresistible heroes, as well as a well-rounded supporting cast. . . . The pace moves quickly and the romance sparks with enough voltage to keep readers turning pages."

—Publishers Weekly

Lavender Morning

"Sweet and salty characters . . . entertaining . . . one of her most fun and pleasing tales."

—Booklist

"Quick dialogue, interesting settings, and plot twists."

—Deseret Morning News

More bestselling sizzle from Jude Deveraux, whose novels are "just plain fun to read . . . she keeps readers on the edge of their seats" (*The Baton Rouge Advocate*)

The Scent of Jasmine

"A delightful adventure romance. . . . [An] enchanting heroine and engaging hero. . . . This is a tale to read for the simple joy of a well-crafted romance."

—*RT Book Reviews* (4½ stars)

Secrets

"A sweet love story filled with twists and turns."

—*Booklist*

"The deceptions will keep readers trying to guess the next plot twist."

—*RT Book Reviews*

Someone to Love

"Fabulous. . . . Fast-paced. . . . Delightful paranormal romantic suspense."

—Harriet Klausner

Have you ever wanted to rewrite your past?
Get swept away in the magic of

The Summerhouse and Return to Summerhouse

"Marvelously compelling. . . . Deeply satisfying."

—*Houston Chronicle*

"Entertaining summer reading."

—*The Port St. Lucie News*

"Deveraux is at the top of her game."

—*Booklist*

BOOKS BY JUDE DEVERAUX

Jude Deveraux

Stranger in the Moonlight

a novel

Pocket Books

New York   London   Toronto   Sydney   New Delhi

Pocket Books
A Division of Simon & Schuster, Inc.
1230 Avenue of the Americas
New York, NY 10020

This book is a work of fiction. Names, characters, places, and incidents either are products of the author's imagination or are used fictitiously. Any resemblance to actual events or locales or persons, living or dead, is entirely coincidental.

First Pocket Books paperback edition September 2012

POCKET and colophon are registered trademarks of Simon & Schuster, Inc.

For information about special discounts for bulk purchases, please contact Simon & Schuster Special Sales at 1-866-506-1949 or business@simonandschuster.com.

The Simon & Schuster Speakers Bureau can bring authors to your live event. For more information or to book an event, contact the Simon & Schuster Speakers Bureau at 1-866-248-3049 or visit our website at www.simonspeakers.com.

Manufactured in the United States of America

10 9 8 7 6 5 4 3 2 1

ISBN 978-1-4165-0975-2
ISBN 978-1-4516-7460-6 (ebook)

Prologue

Edilean, Virginia

1993

In all of her eight years, Kim had never been so bored. She didn't even know such boredom could exist. Her mother told her to go outside into the big garden around the old house, Edilean Manor, and play, but what was she to do by herself?

Two weeks ago her father had taken her brother off to some faraway state to go fishing. "Male bonding," her mother called it, then said she was *not* going to stay in their house alone for four whole weeks. That night Kim had been awakened by the sound of her parents arguing. They didn't usually fight—not that she knew about—and the word *divorce* came to her mind. She was terrified of being without her parents.

But the next morning they were kissing and everything seemed to be fine. Her father kept talking about making up being the best, but her mother shushed him.

It was that afternoon when her mother told her that while her father and brother were away they were going to stay in an apartment at Edilean Manor. Kim didn't like that because she hated the old house. It was too big and it echoed with every footstep. Besides, every time she visited the place there was less furniture, and the emptiness made it seem even creepier.

Her father said that Mr. Bertrand, the old man who lived in the house, had sold the family furniture rather than get a job to support himself. "He'd sell the house if Miss Edi would let him."

Miss Edi was Mr. Bertrand's sister. She was older than he was, and even though she didn't live there, she owned the house. Kim had heard people say that she disliked her brother so much that she refused to live in Edilean.

Kim couldn't imagine hating Edilean, since every person she knew in the world lived there. Her dad was an Aldredge, from one of the seven families that founded the town. Kim knew that was something to be proud of. All she thought was that she was glad she wasn't from the family that had to live in big, scary Edilean Manor.

So now she and her mother had been living in the apartment for two whole weeks and she was horribly bored. She wanted to go back to her own house and her own room. When they were packing to go, her mother had said, "We're just going away for a little while and it's just around the corner, so you don't need to take that." "That" was pretty much anything Kim owned, like books, toys, her dolls, her many art kits. Her mother seemed to consider it all as "not necessary."

But at the end, Kim had grabbed the bicycle she'd received for her birthday and clamped her hands around the grips. She looked at her mother with her jaw set.

Her dad laughed. "Ellen," he said to his wife, "I've seen that look on your face a thousand times and I can assure you that your daughter will *not* back down. I know from experience that you can yell, threaten, sweet talk, plead, beg, cry, but she won't give in."

Her mother's eyes were narrowed as she looked at her laughing husband.

He quit smiling. "Reede, how about you and I go . . . ?"

"Go where, Dad?" Reede asked. At seventeen, he was overwhelmed with importance at being allowed to go away with his dad. No women. Just the two of them.

"Wherever we can find to go," his dad mumbled.

Kim got to take her bike to Edilean Manor, and for three days she rode it nonstop, but now she wanted to do something else. Her cousin Sara came over one day but all she wanted to do was explore the ratty old house. Sara loved old buildings!

Mr. Bertrand had pulled a copy of *Alice's Adventures in Wonderland* out of a pile of books on the floor. Her mom said he'd sold the bookcase to Colonial Williamsburg. "Original eighteenth century and it had been in the family for over two hundred years," she'd muttered. "What a shame. Poor Miss Edi."

Kim spent days reading about Alice and her journey down the rabbit hole. She'd loved the book so much that she told her mother she wanted blonde hair and a blue dress with a white apron. Her mother said that if her father ever again went off for four weeks her next child just might be blonde. Mr. Bertrand said he'd like a hookah and to sit on a mushroom all day and say wise things.

The two adults had started laughing—they seemed to find each other very funny. In disgust Kim went outside to sit in the fork of her favorite old pear tree and read more about Alice. She reread her favorite passages, then her mother called her in for what Mr. Bertrand called "afternoon tea." He was an odd old man, very soft-looking, and her father said that Mr. Bertrand could hatch an egg on the couch. "He never gets up."

Kim had seen that few of the men in town liked Mr. Bertrand, but all the women seemed to adore him. On some days as many as six women would show up with bottles of wine and casseroles and cakes, and they'd all laugh hilariously. When they saw Kim they'd say, "I should have brought—" They'd name their children.

But then another woman would say how good it was to have some peace and quiet for a few hours.

The next time the women came they'd again "forget" to bring their children.

As Kim stood outside and heard the women howling with laughter, she didn't think they sounded very peaceful or quiet.

It was after she and her mother had been there for two long weeks that early one morning her mother seemed very excited about something, but Kim wasn't sure what it was. Something had happened during the night, some adult thing. All Kim was concerned with was that she couldn't find the copy of *Alice's Adventures in Wonderland* that Mr. Bertrand had lent her. She had *one* book, and now it was gone. She asked her mother what happened to it, as she knew she'd left it on the coffee table.

"Last night I took it to—" The sentence wasn't finished because the old phone on the wall rang and her mother ran to answer it, then immediately started laughing.

Disgusted, Kim went outside. It seemed that her life was getting worse.

She kicked at rocks, frowned at the empty flower beds, and headed toward her tree. She planned to climb up it, sit on her branch, and figure out what to do for the long, boring weeks until her dad came home and life could start again.

When she got close to her tree, what she saw

stopped her dead in her tracks. There was a boy, younger than her brother but older than she was. He was wearing a clean shirt with a collar and dark trousers; he looked like he was about to go to Sunday school. Worse was that he was sitting in *her* tree reading *her* book.

He had dark hair that fell forward and he was so engrossed in her book that he didn't even look up when Kim kicked at a clod of dirt.

Who was he? she thought. And what right did he think he had to be in *her* tree?

She didn't know who or what, but she did know that she wanted this stranger to go away.

She picked up a clod and threw it at him as hard as she could. She was aiming for the top of his head but hit his shoulder. The lump crumbled into dirt and fell down onto *her* book.

He looked up at her, a bit startled at first, but then his face settled down and he stared at her in silence. He was a pretty boy, she thought. Not like her cousin Tristan, but this boy looked like a doll she'd seen in a catalogue, with pink skin and very dark eyes.

"That's *my* book," she yelled at him. "And it's *my* tree. You have no right to them." She grabbed another clod and threw it at him. It would have hit him in the face but he moved sideways and it missed.

Kim had had a lot of experience with older boys and she knew that they got you back. It didn't take much to set them off, then you were in for it. They'd chase you, catch you, and pin your arm behind your back or pull your hair until you begged for mercy.

When she saw the boy make a move as though he meant to get down, Kim took off running as fast as she could. Maybe there'd be enough time that she could reach what she knew was a great hiding place. She wedged her small body in between two piles of old bricks, crouched down, and waited for the boy to come after her.

After what seemed like an hour of waiting, he didn't show up, and her legs began to ache. Cautiously and quietly, she got out from the bricks and looked around. She fully expected him to leap out from behind a tree, yell "I got you!" then bombard her with dirt.

But nothing happened. The big garden was as still and quiet as always and there was no sign of the boy.

She ran behind a tree, waited and listened, but she heard and saw nothing. She ran to another tree and waited. Nothing. It took her a long time before she got back to "her" tree, and what she saw astonished her.

Standing on the ground, just under her branch, was the boy. He was holding the book under his arm and seemed to be waiting.

Was this some new boy trap that she'd never seen before? she wondered. Is this what foreign boys— meaning ones not from Edilean—did to girls who threw dirt at them? If she walked up to him, would he clobber her?

As she watched him, she must have made a sound because he turned and looked at her.

Kim jumped behind a tree, ready to protect herself from whatever came flying, but nothing did. After a few moments she decided to stop being a scaredy-cat and stepped out into the open.

Slowly, the boy started walking toward her, and Kim got ready to run. She knew not to let boys she'd thrown things at get too close. They prided themselves on the quickness of their throwing arms.

She held her breath when he got close enough that she knew she'd not be able to get away.

"I'm sorry I took your book," he said softly. "Mr. Bertrand lent it to me, so I didn't know it belonged to anyone else. And I didn't know about the tree being yours either. I apologize."

She was so astonished she couldn't speak. Her mother said that males didn't know the meaning of the word *sorry*. But this one did. She took the book he was holding out to her and watched as he turned away and started back toward the house.

He was halfway there before she could move. "Wait!" she called out and was shocked when he stopped walking. None of her boy cousins *ever* obeyed her.

She walked up to him, the book firmly clutched against her chest. "Who are you?" she asked. If he'd said he was a visitor from another planet, she wouldn't have been surprised.

"Travis . . . Merritt," he said. "My mother and I arrived late last night. Who are you?"

"Kimberly Aldredge. My mother and I are staying in there"—she pointed—"while my father and brother go fishing in Montana."

He gave a nod, as though what she'd said was very important. "My mother and I are staying there." He pointed to the apartment on the other side of the big house. "My father is in Tokyo."

Kim had never heard of the place. "Do you live near here?"

"Not in this state, no."

She was staring at him and thinking that he was very much like a doll, as he didn't smile or even move very much.

"I like the book," he said. "I've never read anything like it before."

In her experience she didn't know boys read anything they didn't have to. Except her cousin Tris, but then he only read about sick people, so that didn't count. "What do you read?" she asked.

"Textbooks."

She waited for him to add to that list, but he just stood there in silence. "What do you read for fun?"

He gave a slight frown. "I rather like the science textbooks."

"Oh," she said.

He seemed to realize that he needed to say more.

"My father says that my education is very important, and my tutor—"

"What's that?"

"The man who teaches me."

"Oh," she said again, but had no idea what he was talking about.

"I am homeschooled," he said. "I go to school inside my father's house."

"That doesn't sound like fun," Kim said.

For the first time, he gave a bit of a smile. "I can attest that it is no fun whatever."

Kim didn't know what *attest* meant, but she could guess. "I'm good at having fun," she said in her most adult voice. "Would you like me to show you how?"

"I'd like that very much," he said. "Where do we begin?"

She thought for a moment. "There's a big pile of dirt in the back. I'll show you how to ride my bike up it then race down. You can stick your hands and feet straight out. Come on!" she yelled and started running.

But a moment later she looked back and he wasn't there. She backtracked and he was standing just where she'd left him. "Are you afraid?" she asked tauntingly.

"I don't think so, but I've never ridden a bicycle before, and I think you're too young to teach me."

She didn't like being told she was "too young" to do anything. Now he *was* sounding like a boy. "Nobody teaches you how to ride a bike," she said, knowing she was lying. Her dad had spent days holding her bike while she learned to balance.

"All right," he said solemnly. "I'll try it."

The bike was too short for him and the first time he got on it, he fell off and landed on his face. He got up, spitting dirt out of his mouth, and Kim watched him. Was he one of those boys who'd go crying to his mother?

Instead, he wiped his mouth on his sleeve, then gave a grin that nearly split his face in half. "Huzzah!" he said and got back on the bike.

By lunchtime he was riding down the hill faster than Kim had ever dared, and he jerked the front wheel upward, as though he were going over a jump.

"How'd I do?" he asked Kim after his fastest slide down the dirt hill. He didn't look like the same boy she'd first seen. His shirt was torn at the shoulder, and he was filthy from head to toe. There was a bruise forming on his cheek where he'd nearly crashed into a tree, but he'd pulled to the left and only grazed it. Even his teeth were dirty.

Before Kim could answer, he looked over her head and stiffened into the boy she'd first seen. "Mother," he said.

Kim turned to see a small woman standing there. She was pretty in a motherly sort of way, but whereas Travis had pink in his cheeks, she had none. She was like a washed-out, older, female version of him.

Without saying a word, she walked to stand between the two children and looked her son up and down.

Kim held her breath. If the woman told Kim's mom

that she'd made Travis dirty, Kim would be punished.

"You taught him to ride a bike?" Mrs. Merritt asked her.

Travis stepped in front of Kim, as though to protect her. "Mother, she's just a little girl. I taught myself to ride. I'll go and wash." He took a step toward the house.

"No!" Mrs. Merritt said, and he looked back at her. She went to him and put her arms around him. "I've never seen you look better." She kissed his cheek then smiled as she wiped dirt off her lips. She turned to Kim. "You, young lady . . ." she began, but stopped. Bending, she hugged Kim. "You are a truly marvelous child. Thank you!"

Kim looked up at the woman in wonder.

"You kids go back to playing. How about if I bring a picnic lunch out here for you two? Do you like chocolate cake?"

"Yes," Kim said.

Mrs. Merritt took two steps toward the house before Kim called out, "He needs his own bike."

Mrs. Merritt looked back, and Kim swallowed. She'd never before given an adult an order. "He . . ." Kim said more quietly. "My bike is too small for him. His feet drag."

"What else does he need?" Mrs. Merritt asked.

"A baseball and bat," Travis said.

"And a pogo stick," Kim added. "And a—" She broke off because Mrs. Merritt held up her hand.

"I have limited resources, but I'll see what I can do."

She went back to the house and a few minutes later she brought out sandwiches and lemonade. In the afternoon she returned with two big slices of freshly baked chocolate cake. By that time Travis had learned to do wheelies, and she watched him with a mixture of awe and terror. "Who would have thought that you're a natural athlete, Travis?" she said in wonder, then went back in the house.

In the early evening, Kim's uncle Benjamin, her cousin Ramsey's father, yelled, "Ho, ho, ho. Who ordered Christmas in July?"

"We did!" Kim yelled, and Travis followed her as she ran to her uncle's big SUV.

Uncle Ben wheeled a new shiny, blue bicycle out of the back. "I was told to give this to the dirtiest boy in Edilean." He looked at Travis. "I think that means you."

Travis grinned. He still had dirt on his teeth, and his hair was caked with it. "Is that for me?"

"It's from your mother," Uncle Ben said and nodded toward the front door.

Mrs. Merritt was standing on the step, and Kim wasn't sure but she looked like she was crying. But that made no sense. A bicycle made a person laugh, not cry.

Travis ran to his mother and threw his arms around her waist.

Kim stared at him in astonishment. No twelve-year-old boy she knew would ever do something like that. It wasn't cool to hug your mother in front of other people.

"Nice kid," Uncle Ben said, and Kim turned back to him. "Don't tell your mom but I went over to your house and did a little cleaning. Any of this look familiar?" He pulled a box toward the back of the car and tipped it down so Kim could see inside. Five of her favorite books were in there, her second-best doll, an unopened kit for making jewelry, and in the bottom was her jump rope.

"Sorry, no pogo stick, but I got one of Rams's old bats and some balls."

"Oh thank you, Uncle Ben!" she said, and followed Travis's example and hugged him.

"If I'd known I was going to get this, I would have bought you a pony."

Kim's eyes widened into saucers.

"Don't tell your mom I said that or she'll skin me."

Travis had left his mother and was looking at his new bike in silence.

"Think you can ride it?" Uncle Ben asked. "Or can you only handle a little girl's bike?"

"Benjamin!" Kim's mother said as she came out to see what was going on. Mr. Bertrand was still inside. As far as anyone knew he never left the house. "Too lazy to turn a doorknob," Kim's father once said.

Travis gave Kim's uncle a very serious look, then took the bike from him and set off at a breakneck speed around the house. When they heard the unmistakable sound of a crash, Uncle Ben put his hand on Mrs. Merritt's arm to keep her from running to the boy.

They heard what sounded like another crash on the other side of the house, and at last Travis came back to them. He was dirtier, his shirt was torn more, and there was a streak of blood across his upper lip.

"Any problems?" Uncle Ben asked.

"None whatever," Travis said, looking the man straight in the eyes.

"That's my boy!" he said as he slapped Travis hard on the shoulder. He closed the lid of the SUV. "I've got to get back to work."

"What work do you do?" Travis asked in an adult-sounding voice.

"I'm a lawyer."

"Is it a good trade?"

Uncle Ben's eyes danced with merriment but he didn't laugh. "It pays the bills, and it has some good points and bad. You thinking of trying the legal profession?"

"I rather admire Thomas Jefferson."

"You've come to the right place for him," Uncle Ben said, grinning as he opened the car door. "Tell you what, Travis ol' man, you get out of law school, come see me."

"I will, sir, and thank you," Travis said. He sounded very adult, but the dirt on him, the twigs, and the bruises, made what he was saying funny.

But Uncle Ben still didn't laugh. He looked at Mrs. Merritt. "Good kid. Congratulations."

Mrs. Merritt put her arm around her son's shoulders, but he twisted away from her. He didn't seem to want Uncle Ben to see him so attached to a woman.

They all watched Uncle Ben leave, then Kim's mom said, "You kids go play. We'll call you in time for dinner and afterward you can catch fireflies."

"Yes," Mrs. Merritt said. "Go play." She looked as though she'd been waiting for years to say that to her son. "Mr. Bertrand is going to teach me how to sew."

"Lucy," Kim's mom said, "I think I should tell you that Bertrand is using you for free labor. He wants his curtains repaired and—"

"I know," Lucy Merritt said, "but it's all right. I want to learn to do something creative, and sewing is as good as anything else. You don't think he'd sell me his machine, do you?"

"I think he'd sell you his feet, since he rarely uses them."

Lucy laughed.

"Come on," Kim's mom said, "and I'll show you how to thread the machine."

For two weeks, Kim lived in her idea of heaven. She and Travis were together from early until late.

He took to having fun as though he'd been born to it—which Kim's mom said he should have been.

While they played outside, inside the two women and Mr. Bertrand talked and sewed. Lucy Merritt used the old Bernina sewing machine to repair every curtain in the house.

"So he can get a better price when he sells them," Kim's mom muttered.

Lucy bought fabric and made new curtains for the bathrooms and the kitchen.

"You're paying him rent," Kim's mother said. "You shouldn't be paying for them too."

"It's all right. It's not as though I can save the money. Randall will take whatever I don't spend."

Mrs. Aldredge knew that Randall was Lucy's husband, but she didn't know any more than that. "I want to know what that means," she said, but Lucy said she'd told too much already.

At night the children reluctantly went inside their separate apartments. Their mothers got them washed and fed and into bed. The next morning they were outside again. No matter how early Kim got up, Travis was always waiting for her at the back of the house.

One night Travis said, "I'll come back."

Kim didn't know what he meant.

"After I leave, I'll return."

She didn't want to reply to that because she didn't want to imagine him being gone. They climbed trees together, dug in the mud, rode their bikes; she tossed the ball, and Travis hit it across the garden. When Kim brought her second-best doll out, she was nervous. Boys didn't like dolls. But Travis said he'd build a house for it and he did. It was made of leaves and sticks and inside was a bed that Kim covered with moss. While Travis made a roof to the house, she used her jewelry kit to make two necklaces with plastic beads. Travis smiled when she slipped one over his head, and he was wearing it the next morning.

When it got too hot to move, they stretched out on the cool ground in the shade and took turns reading *Alice* and the other books aloud to each other. Kim wasn't nearly as good a reader as he was, but he never complained. When she was stumped by a word, he helped her. He'd told her he was a good listener, and he was.

She knew that at twelve he was a lot older than she was, but he didn't seem to be. When it came to schooling, he seemed like an adult. He told her the entire life cycle for a tadpole and all about cocoons. He explained why the moon was different shapes and what caused winter and summer.

But for all his great knowledge, he'd never skimmed a rock across a pond. Never climbed a tree before he came to Edilean. He'd never even skinned his elbow.

So, in the end, they taught each other. Even though he was twelve, and she only eight, there were times when she was his teacher—and she liked that.

Everything ended exactly two weeks after it began. As always, as soon as it was light outside, sleepy-eyed Kim ran out the back door, past the back of the big old house, to the wing where Travis and his mom were staying.

But that morning, when Travis wasn't already outside and waiting for her, she knew something was wrong. She started pounding on the door and yelling his name; she didn't care if she woke the whole house.

Her mother, in robe and slippers, came running out. "Kimberly! What are you shouting about?"

"Where is Travis?" she demanded as she fought back tears.

"Will you calm down? They probably just over-slept."

"No! Something is wrong."

Her mother hesitated, then tried the knob. The door opened. There was no one inside, and no sign that anyone had been there.

"Stay here," her mother said. "I'll find out what's going on."

She hurried to the front of the house, but Mrs. Merritt's car wasn't there. It was too early to disturb Bertrand, but she was too concerned about Lucy and her son to let that stop her from going inside.

Bertrand was asleep on the sofa—proving what everyone suspected, that he didn't climb the stairs to go to bed. He came awake instantly, always glad for a good gossip. "Honey," he said, "they tore out of here at two this morning. I was sound asleep and Lucy woke me. She wanted to know if she could buy that old sew-ing machine."

"I hope you gave it to her."

"Nearly. I charged her only fifty dollars."

Mrs. Aldredge grimaced. "Where did they go? Why did they leave in the middle of the night?"

"All Lucy would tell me is that someone called

to say her husband was returning and she needed to leave. She said she *had* to get there before he did."

"But where? I want to call her to see if she's all right."

"She asked us to please not contact her." He lowered his voice. "She said that no one must know that she and Travis were here."

"That sounds very bad." Mrs. Aldredge sat down on the couch, then jumped up. "Heavens! Kim is going to be heartbroken. I dread telling her. She'll be devastated. She adores that boy."

"He was a sweet one," Bertrand agreed. "Skin like porcelain. I do hope he keeps it, and doesn't let the sun ruin it. I think my good complexion comes from a lifelong belief in staying out of the sun."

Mrs. Aldredge was frowning as she went to Kim to tell her that her friend was gone and it was likely that she'd never see him again.

Kim took it better than her mother thought she would. There were no tantrums and no tears—at least not that anyone saw. But it was weeks before Kim was herself again.

Her mother took her into Williamsburg to purchase an expensive frame for the only photo she had of Travis. Kim and he were standing by their bikes, both of them dirty and smiling hugely. Just before Mrs. Aldredge clicked the shutter, Travis put his arm around Kim's shoulders, and she clasped his waist. It

was a sweet portrait of childhood and it looked good
in the frame Kim chose. She put it on the table by her
bed so she could see it just before she fell asleep and
when she awoke every morning.

It was a month after Travis and his mother left that
Kim brought down the house. The family was just sitting down to dinner when Reede, her older brother,
asked what she was going to do with the bike Travis
had left behind.

"Nothing," Kim said. "I can't do anything because
of Travis's bastard father."

Everyone came to a halt.

"What did you say?" Mrs. Aldredge asked in a whisper of disbelief.

"His bas—"

"I heard you," her mother said. "I will *not* have
an eight-year-old using that kind of language in my
house. Go to your room this instant!"

"But, Mom," Kim said, bewildered and already close
to tears, "that's what you always call him."

Her mother didn't say a word, just pointed, and
Kim left the table. She barely had the door to her
room closed before she heard her parents burst into
laughter.

Kim picked up Travis's picture and looked at it. "If
you were here now I'd teach you a dirty word."

Sighing, she stretched out on her bed and waited
for her dad to be sent to "talk" to her—and to slip her

some food. He was the sweet one while her mother did the discipline. Kim thought it was very unfair that she was being punished for repeating something she'd heard her mother say several times.

"Bastard parents!" Kim muttered and held Travis's picture close to her chest. She would never forget him and she would *never* stop looking for him.

One

New York

2011

The big office sprawled across a corner of the sixty-first floor. Full-length windows went along two sides, offering breathtaking views of the skyline of New York. The other two walls had tasteful paintings chosen by a designer, but they gave no hint of the occupant. In the middle was a desk of rosewood, and sitting in a steel and leather chair was Travis Maxwell. Tall, broad shouldered, and darkly handsome, he was bent over papers and frowning.

Another damned merger, Travis thought. Another company his father was buying. Did his desire to own, to control, never end? When Travis heard the door to his office open, he didn't look up. "Yeah? What is it?"

Barbara Pendergast—Penny to him, Mrs. Pendergast to everyone else—looked at him and waited. She didn't put up with bad moods from anyone.

Travis looked up at the silence and saw her. She was twice his age and half his size, but she intimidated the hell out of everyone but him. "Sorry, Penny, what is it?" She had worked for his father until just a few years ago. Together the two of them had gone from owning nothing until Randall Maxwell was one of the richest men in the world. When Travis joined the business, Penny decided to help him out. It was said that Randall Maxwell's protests could be heard six blocks away.

Penny waited a moment to give the full weight to her announcement. "Your mother called me."

"She what?!" Travis forgot about the merger as he leaned back in his chair and took a couple of deep breaths. "Is she all right?"

"I'd say she's better than all right. She wants to divorce your father because there's a man she wants to marry."

Travis could do nothing but stare. Penny wore her usual boring, but expensive, suit. Her hair was pulled back, and she was looking at him over her reading glasses. "My mother is supposed to be in hiding, keeping a low profile. How can I protect her if she's out in public? And she's been *dating*?"

"I think you should see this," Penny said and handed him a photocopied newspaper article.

It was from a Richmond newspaper and told of a fashion show for kids that had taken place in Edilean,

Virginia, where his mother was staying, or more accurately, hiding. He scanned the article. Some rich woman had thrown a lavish birthday party for her daughter and there were some clothes designed by a Jecca Layton and—He looked up at Penny. "Sewn by Ms. Lucy Cooper." He put the paper down. "That's not so bad. Cooper is an assumed name, and there's no photo."

"It's not bad unless your father decides to go looking again," Penny said. "Her love of sewing is a dead giveaway."

"What else did Mom say?"

"Nothing," Penny said. "Just that." She looked at her notepad. "To quote her directly: 'Tell Travis I need a divorce because I want to get married,' then she hung up. You know she thinks you, her precious son, makes the world spin on its axis."

"My one unconditional love," Travis said with a half grin. "Did she say who she wanted to marry?"

Penny gave him a look. Travis knew there had always been great animosity from his mother to Mrs. Pendergast. For many years, Randall left his wife and child home, but he never went anywhere without Penny. "Of course she didn't tell me," Penny said. "But to answer before you ask, I don't think she would have been stu—uh, unwise enough to let this unknown man in on who she is currently married to. So no, I don't think the man is after her money."

"Would that be the money she stole from Dad, or the money she could get in a divorce settlement?"

"Since I don't believe in fairy tales, I'd say the three point two million she stole."

"I watch her accounts pretty carefully, and there have been no unusual charges. In fact," he said proudly, "she's been self-supporting for years now."

"Are you referring to the living she's been earning with the hundred grand in equipment and supplies she bought with the embezzled money?"

Travis gave her a look to let her know he'd heard enough. "I'll take care of it." Even as he said it, he dreaded what he saw as the future. His father would make a war of a divorce. It wouldn't matter if his wife relinquished all claim to his assets and paid back what she ran away with—a pittance to him and legally half hers—he'd still use everything in his power to make his wife's life a living hell. The deal Travis had made with his father four years ago was that he'd work for him if his father would leave Lucy alone. He wasn't to move heaven and earth to find her, and if he did find her, he couldn't torment her. It had been a simple bargain. All Travis had had to do was sell his soul to the devil—i.e., his father—to obtain it.

"Anything else?" he asked Penny.

"Mr. Shepard has asked to have dinner with you tonight."

Travis groaned. He was doing the legal work needed to buy Mr. Shepard's company out of bankruptcy. Since the man had started his business thirty years ago, it wasn't going to be a pleasant meal. "Helping

Dad destroy a company will be a picnic after today."

"What do you want me to do?" Penny asked, her voice with a hint of sympathy in it.

"Nothing. No! Wait. Don't I have a date tonight?"

"Leslie. This will be the third one in a row that you've canceled."

"Call—"

"I know. Tiffany's."

For all his complaining, when Travis glanced at the newspaper article on his desk, he couldn't help smiling. Edilean, Virginia, had been the site of the happiest memories of his life—which is why when his mother ran away, she went there. Kimberly, he thought and couldn't help the feeling of peace that came over him. He was twelve and she was just eight, but she'd taught him everything. He didn't know it then, but he was a boy living in prison. He hadn't been allowed to be with other children, had never watched TV or read a work of fiction. He may as well have been living in a cave—or a past century. Until he met Kim, he thought. Kim with her love of life. On his desk was a little brass plaque, the only personal item in the room. It read: I'M GOOD AT HAVING FUN. WOULD YOU LIKE ME TO SHOW YOU HOW? Kim's words to him. The words that had changed everything.

Penny was watching him. She was the only person he trusted to know the truth about his life. "Shall I make your plane reservations, or do you want to drive?" she asked quietly.

"Drive where?" When she didn't answer, he looked at her. "I . . ." He wasn't sure what to say.

"How about if while you're at dinner tonight I buy a normal car—something that's legal to drive on the streets—and you pack a bag full of normal clothes? Tomorrow you can drive down to see your mother."

Travis still wasn't sure what to say. "Leslie . . ."

"Don't worry. I'll send her enough diamonds that she won't ask questions." Penny didn't like Leslie, but then she didn't like any of the girls Travis dated. "If you can buy her off, it's not love," she'd said several times. Penny wanted him to do what his dad had done and find a woman who loved her family more than the contents of any store.

"All right," Travis said. "Get Forester to handle this merger."

"But he can't—"

"Do it?" Travis said. "I know it but he doesn't. Maybe it'll fall through and Dad will fire the ambitious little twerp."

"Or maybe he'll succeed and your father will give him your job."

"And you said you didn't believe in fairy tales," Travis said, grinning. "All right, where's this reunion?"

She gave him the time and address.

He stood up, looked at his desk, and all he could think of was seeing his mother again. It had been too long. On impulse, he picked up the brass plaque of Kim's words and slipped it in his pocket. He looked back at Penny. "So what do you call a 'normal' car?"

As she left, she gave him one of her rare smiles. "Wait and see."

That evening a Town Car and driver were waiting downstairs for Travis. It stopped at his apartment building, the doorman opened the door, and the elevator was held for him. He spoke to no one.

His was the penthouse apartment, with views all around. The same decorator who'd done his office had filled his apartment with her idea of good taste. There was a huge antique Buddha in an alcove, and the couches were upholstered in black leather. Since Travis was in the apartment as little as possible, decorating it had never interested him.

There was only one room that held truly personal items, and he went to it now. It had originally been a walk-in closet, but Travis had requested that it be filled with glass shelves. It was in this small room—which he always kept locked—that he put his trophies, awards, certificates, those symbols of what Kim had taught him about having "fun."

It was those two weeks in Edilean, spent with feisty little Kim, that had given him the courage to stand up to his father. His mother had tried, but her sweet nature was no match for a man like her husband.

But Travis had found that he could hold his own. The first time he saw his father after having met Kim, Travis said he wanted physical instruction as well as academic. Randall Maxwell had looked at his young son in speculation and saw that the boy wasn't going to give in. An instructor was hired.

As Lucy had said about her son, he was a natural athlete. For Travis, the strenuous activity was a release from the grueling academic work he was given to do, and as Travis learned what they had to teach, the instructors left and a new one arrived. By the time Travis was college age, he was trained in several martial arts. His nose had been broken twice, once in boxing, once by an instructor's foot in his face.

His father had wanted Travis to continue being tutored for college, but Travis said that the minute he was of age, he'd leave and never return. At that time his mother was still living at home. Her life was as isolated as Travis's, but then, she'd never been a very social person.

Travis went to Stanford, then Harvard Law, and it was while he was away from the prison that was the only home he'd ever known that he discovered life. Sports—extreme sports—drew him. Jumping out of planes, being dropped by helicopter onto a snow-covered mountain, cliff diving. He did it all.

He passed the bar exam but had no interest in spending his life in an office. Even though his father demanded that his son work for him, Travis refused. In anger, his father shut down his trust fund, so Travis got a job as a Hollywood stuntman. He was the guy who got set on fire.

When his father saw that his ploy didn't work, that

he hadn't made his son knuckle under to him, he turned his attention to his wife and made her miserable. One afternoon Lucy accidently saw a way to intercept a business transaction of her husband's. With only a moment's hesitation, she sent $3.2 million into her own account. She then spent about ten minutes packing a bag, took one of her husband's cars, and fled.

Randall told his son he wouldn't go after Lucy if Travis would stop trying to kill himself and work for him.

Travis would have done anything for his mother, so he left L.A., went back to New York, and worked for his father. Whenever possible, Travis relieved his stress by participating in any violent sport he could find.

Now, he looked about the room at the trophies, the medals, the souvenirs. On the wall behind the shelves were many framed photos. The Monte Carlo races. His face was dirty and the champagne he'd sprayed when he'd won had made streaks, but he'd been happy.

There were pictures of some of his more outrageous Hollywood stunts with fire, explosions, leaping off buildings. Interspersed among the pictures of the sports were the ones with the women. Movie stars, socialites, waitresses. Travis hadn't been discriminate. He liked pretty women no matter where they were born or what they did.

He closed the door, leaned back against it for a moment, and looked around him. He would turn thirty this year and he was tired from all of it. Tired of being under his father's control, tired of making money for a man who had too much of it.

His mother had been right to run away and hide, but he knew how guilty she felt that Travis was protecting her. But the way he saw it was that she'd spent a lifetime protecting him, so he owed her.

Right now Travis's worry was that his mother was marrying some man just to release her son. His fear was that his mother's guilt was overwhelming her, and she was going to start the divorce proceedings just to give her son freedom.

But Travis knew that his mother had no true idea what she was asking for if she went for a divorce from Randall Maxwell. *Ruthless* was too mild a word for the man.

On the other hand, there was no way Travis could describe how much he'd like to have his own life back. Even though the last four years had worn him down, before he got out, he wanted to make sure that his mother wasn't walking into something just as bad as her marriage had been.

Travis left the trophy room and locked it securely. Only he knew the combination, and none of his many girlfriends had ever seen inside it.

He went to his bedroom, a sterile place with no personality, and into his closet. One side contained his sports clothes, the other his work suits. At the end were what Penny would call "normal" clothes, jeans and T-shirts, a leather jacket. It took only moments to throw them into a duffle bag.

He stripped down to his briefs and glanced at his body in the mirror. He had almost no fat on him and he worked to keep his muscles strong. But his skin was marked with scars from burns, punctures, surgical repairs. He'd broken his ribs more times than he could count, and under his hair was a deep scar from where a misfired piece of steel had come close to killing him.

Minutes later, Travis was dressed and ready to go to dinner with a man who needed some reassurance that the business he'd started from scratch would continue. Travis knew that what the man really needed was a shoulder to cry on. With a sigh, he left the apartment.

It was 8:00 P.M. and Travis had been driving for hours to reach Edilean. The car Penny had bought for him was an old BMW. The engine sounded good, but he could barely get eighty out of it. No doubt that was Penny's idea of how to keep him from exceeding the speed limit. She'd put a packet of hundreds in the glove box, and he'd had to smile. If Travis used a credit card, his father would know where he was. He well knew that his father kept close watch on him. It was one thing to have charges in Paris but another to have little Edilean, Virginia, show up on the statement.

"Just until Mom is safe," he said aloud as he down-shifted. At least Penny hadn't insulted him by getting an automatic. She'd let him have some fun!

At the thought of that word, Travis thought of last night. Trying to comfort a man nearing seventy hadn't been easy. But Travis knew that if he didn't attempt it, no one else would. His father often said in disdain that Travis didn't have a shark's heart. It had been meant as a put-down, but Travis took it as a compliment.

He'd managed to get away from dinner by eleven. He wanted to sleep because he planned to leave early for Edilean.

But the next morning, just as he was ready to leave, his cell rang. It was his father. It was 7:00 A.M. on a Saturday morning but his dad was at work.

"Where are you?" Randall Maxwell demanded.

"Leaving town," Travis said in a cold voice that matched his father's.

"Forester can't handle this deal."

"You're the one who hired him."

"He's a good number cruncher and he sucks up to the clients. They like him."

"Then when he tells them their jobs are gone, he can hold their hands," Travis said. "I have to go."

"Where is it this time?" Randall muttered.

"Watch the sports pages."

"If you get yourself killed," Randall said, "I'll—"

"You'll what, Dad? Not attend my funeral?"

"I'll say hello to your mother."

For a moment Travis froze in place. Why had his father spoken of her *now*? Had he heard something? That a Lucy Cooper had been mentioned in a Richmond newspaper hadn't been enough to alert him, had it?

Travis decided to brazen it out. "You're pulling out the big guns this morning. You must want something bad."

"I need you to go over this deal. There's something wrong in this contract, but I can't figure out what it is."

One thing Travis knew about his father was that his instincts were infallible. If he thought there was something wrong, there was. In the last four years there'd been a hundred times when Travis had wanted to say there was nothing wrong, that no one was trying to put one over on him. Travis couldn't help thinking that if he screwed up, his father would let him out of his devil's deal. But he knew that wouldn't happen.

Randall knew when he was pushing his son too far. "Give me this morning and you can take a couple of weeks off."

Travis was silent as he thought that his father knew him too well. But then, Randall Maxwell was a brilliant judge of character. Many years ago he'd rightly judged that Miss Lucy Jane Travis would be too afraid of him to do anything but comply with whatever he told her to do.

"Take three weeks off," Randall said. "This deal will take that long. Just figure out what they're trying to put over on me in this contract and you're free."

The last thing Travis wanted was to leave his father in anger or suspicion. The rage would come later when

Travis helped his mother in the divorce. "Send the contract to me."

"There's a man waiting outside your door now," Randall said.

Travis couldn't see his father's smile of triumph, but he felt it. The only thing in life that really mattered to the man was winning.

It had been two in the afternoon before Travis got away. He'd wanted to call his mother and tell her he was coming, but he didn't have a throwaway phone, and he didn't dare use his cell.

In the end, the second he finished with the contract, he left. He called his father from the car. "That old man is as big a crook as you are," Travis said. "Page 212, last paragraph, says that if you don't agree to his terms you're in default and the company goes back to him."

"Terms?" Randall shouted. "What *terms*?! What's he talking about?"

"I have no idea. You'll have to ask old man Hardranger that."

"You have to—"

"No I don't," Travis said. "Get Forester to find out what the old man wants. Or sic Penny on him. Anybody but me. See you in three weeks," he said, then clicked off the phone. "Or not," he added.

It was difficult for Travis to imagine that possibly—maybe—he was about to get out from under his father's thumb. If his mother had had enough time to get up her courage to actually go through a divorce, Travis would be free.

The thought made him smile for most of the drive down to Edilean.

It was eight o'clock on a Saturday night, and as far as he could tell, the town was dead. Every store was closed, no all-night drugstore, no one sauntering by walking a dog. All in all, he thought the little town with its old buildings was a bit eerie, rather like a sci-fi B movie where all the inhabitants had been abducted by aliens.

It wasn't easy finding Aldredge Road, but when he saw the sign he smiled more broadly. He knew Kim didn't live on the road but her relatives did, and the ancestral home, Aldredge House, was there.

But Aldredge House wasn't where he was going. His mother had rented an apartment in the home of Mrs. Olivia Wingate, which was just behind where Kim's cousin lived. Travis's original plan was to arrive there in the afternoon and see his mother. Since he didn't want anyone knowing who she was or who he was, he planned to park along the road and call her on the cell phone Penny had sent him that morning. After he'd seen her and made sure she was all right, he'd find a hotel.

He hadn't changed his plan, but it was growing dark and he didn't like her walking out alone. He'd have to meet her close to the house.

Travis was thinking about this as he drove down the

tree-lined road when a big teenager wearing a yellow reflective vest and carrying a flashlight stepped out of the bushes in front of him. As Travis slammed on the brakes, he thanked his years of race car driving for his quick reflexes.

There was a tap on his window and another kid was motioning for him to put down the window.

"You wanta slow down, mister?" the boy said. "There are kids around here, and besides, people are leaving. Park over there by the Ford pickup."

"Park?" Travis said. "I wasn't planning on going to—" He didn't finish, as he didn't want to tell anyone his business. He could hear music and see lights through the trees to the left. It looked like there was a party going on. Travis thought of turning around and leaving, but there was a car behind him. A U-turn would draw too much attention to himself.

"You take any longer, mister, and the place will be empty. You already missed the wedding cake," the kid said.

"Yeah, sure," Travis said and pulled in beside the truck. Wedding? he thought and couldn't help grimacing. Was it Kim who was getting married? After all, it was the Aldredge House so it could be.

As he got out, he put his hand up to block the light from the next car, and also to hide his face.

A very large man was standing outside a truck that unless Travis missed his bet, had been revved up to illegal street use. He was looking at Travis as though trying to figure out who he was.

"You with the bride?" he asked as he opened the door to help his pregnant wife out.

"Colin!" she said. "You're off duty now, so stop interrogating people." She looked at Travis. "Welcome to Edilean," she said, "and please go inside. Let's hope there's some champagne left. Not that I'll be having any."

"Sure, thanks," Travis said.

As the two of them walked toward the house, the big man gave Travis a look up and down.

"Great," he mumbled. It looked like he'd raised the suspicions of an off-duty cop. More people walked past, most of them leaving, and looked at Travis. It was then that he realized that all the people he saw were in their finest. He was wearing a gray shirt and a pair of jeans.

For a moment Travis contemplated what he should do. Leave? See his mother tomorrow?

On the other hand, he thought that it was possible that his mother was at the wedding. He didn't think so, as she had always been a quiet, retiring woman, but maybe so. It was even possible that the man she was thinking of marrying would be there too.

He had a vision of the two of them sitting in a corner holding hands and whispering sweet words to each other. It might be a nice thing to see.

And maybe Kim would be there—if she wasn't the

bride, that is. Not that he could introduce himself to her again. Not that he hadn't seen her as an adult, but it had been a while. She'd been a very pretty little girl and she'd grown into an even prettier woman. The vision of her riding down the hill, her auburn hair flying out behind her, would stay with him forever.

Maybe he could change into some more appropriate clothes and maybe he could go and see the wedding. Not stay. Just look, then leave.

He opened the trunk of the car.

Two

❧

"*So how are* you and the new boyfriend—Dave, is it?—getting along?" Sara Newland asked as she sat down across from Kim. Each table had a different color cloth on it, what the bride called "Easter colors." The band was taking a break, and the big dance floor was empty. Overhead, the tent was strung with tiny silver lights that cast pretty shadows everywhere.

Sara's twin boys were now a year old and were at home with a babysitter. The wedding was a rare night out for her and her husband, Mike.

"We're doing great," Kim said. She had on her bluish purple bridesmaid dress, with its low, square neckline and swishy skirt. Jecca, who was the bride as well as Kim's best friend, had designed it for her, and Lucy Cooper had made it.

"Think it's permanent between you two?" Sara asked.

"It's too early to tell, but I have hope. How are you and Mike doing?"

"Perfectly. But I'm not making much progress in taming him into a domestic life. I wanted him to help with the garden. Know what he did?"

"With Mike, I can't imagine."

"He chased off the guy who runs the backhoe, taught himself how to use the big machine, and he's cleared a strip about two acres long for the new fence. You should have heard him and the owner of the backhoe yelling at each other!"

Kim smiled. "I would have liked to have been there. I spend most of my life with salesmen. Every word they utter leads back to me buying more from them."

Sara learned forward and lowered her voice. "So how was Lucy Cooper with your dress?"

"I never saw her," Kim said. "Jecca did the one and only fitting."

"But you saw her dancing with Jecca's dad a few minutes ago, didn't you?"

Sara and Kim were cousins, the same age, and they'd played together since they were babies. For the last four years they'd talked about how odd it was that Lucy Cooper, an older woman staying at Mrs. Wingate's house, ran away whenever Kim appeared. Other people saw her at the grocery, the pharmacy, even in Mrs. Wingate's shop downtown, but when Kim showed up, Lucy hid. One of her cousins had snapped a photo of Ms. Cooper and shown it to Kim, but she saw nothing familiar in the face. She couldn't imagine why the woman avoided her.

"I couldn't miss something like that, could I?" Kim said. "Down and dirty. Raunchy. More than a little embarrassing at their age."

"But did you see Lucy's face?"

"Yes and no. She had it buried in Jecca's dad's body parts, so I'd see an eye here, and an ear there. I'd have to get one of those police artists to draw a full face for me."

Sara laughed. "When I saw her, she looked like the happiest woman alive."

"No, that would be Jecca."

"It was a beautiful wedding. And her dress was divine! She and Tris are a stunning couple, aren't they?"

"Yes," Kim said with pride. She and Jecca had been roommates all through college and had remained BFF, even though Jecca lived in New York City and Kim in Edilean. A few months ago Jecca had come to Edilean to spend the summer painting, had met the local doctor, Kim's cousin Tristan, fallen in love, and had married him today.

"How's Reede doing?" Sara asked, referring to Kim's brother. Reede had volunteered to help Tris while he recovered from a broken arm, but now it looked like he was going to have the responsibility of Tris's medical practice for the next three years.

"Reede is not a happy camper," Kim said. "I didn't know a person could complain as much as he does. He's threatening to jump a freighter and leave town."

"He wouldn't do that, would he? We *need* a doctor on call here in Edilean."

"No," Kim said. "Reede has too much of a sense of duty to do that. But it would be nice if he didn't look at this as a three-year prison sentence."

"Everyone will be glad for Tris to come back and be our doctor again."

"Especially the women," Kim said, and they laughed. Dr. Tristan Aldredge was a truly beautiful man, with a sweet temperament, and he genuinely cared about people.

"Who's that man who keeps staring at you?" Sara asked, looking behind Kim.

She turned but saw no one she didn't recognize.

"He stepped outside just as you turned around," Sara said.

"What's he look like?"

"Your typical tall, dark, and handsome," Sara said, smiling. "It looks like his nose has been broken a few times—or maybe I see that in all men since I met Mike." Her husband was a master of several forms of martial arts.

"My secret admirer, I guess," Kim said as she stood up.

"Is Dave here tonight?"

"No. He had to cater a wedding in Williamsburg."

"That must be difficult for you," Sara said. "He's gone every weekend."

"But home during the week," Kim said. "His home, not mine."

"Speaking of which, how's your new house?" Sara asked as she also stood. It hadn't been easy, but she'd managed to lose the baby weight and now had her slim figure back.

"Wonderful," Kim said, and her eyes lit up. "I turned the big garage into a workroom, and Jecca helped me decorate the inside. Lots of color."

"Does Dave like it?"

"He likes my kitchen," Kim said. "When I get more settled, we'll have you and your three kids over. But tell Mike he can't bring his new toy, the backhoe, with him."

"I'll do that." Smiling, Sara said good-bye and left. The band was returning, and she wanted to get away where she could talk.

Kim stood there for a moment, looking at the friends and relatives around her. There were also some newcomers in attendance, meaning people who weren't descended from the seven founding families, and they'd come to see Dr. Tris get married. He was beloved by everyone, and she wondered how many people were there uninvited because they wanted to see Tristan again. He had saved many lives in their small town.

It had been Kim's hope that Jecca would marry her brother, Reede, but she'd fallen for Tris almost the day she met him. Because of job changes, Kim's dream of having her best friend live in the small town of Edilean had been postponed for another few years.

Kim couldn't help thinking that by that time she would be almost thirty. I'll be a statistic, she'd often thought but had said to no one. She was successful in business, but her personal life didn't seem to be going anywhere.

The bridal couple had left some time ago—Kim hadn't caught the bouquet—but some of the guests were hanging around to dance as long as the band played.

As she walked toward the side of the tent, she again thought how much she wished she could have had a date tonight. She'd met Dave six months before, when she'd gone into Williamsburg to talk to a nervous bride about the rings she and her fiancé wanted. The girl had been maddeningly indecisive and her groom was even worse. Kim had wanted to start giving them orders, but she could do nothing but make strong suggestions.

After an hour, and still no decisions, the girl's father had come in, instantly sized up the situation, and told his daughter which rings to get. Kim had looked at him in gratitude.

When she went out to her car, her way was blocked by a big white truck with BORMAN CATERING written on the side. A good-looking young man came running toward her.

"Sorry," he said as he pulled out his keys, but then he saw that the bride's father had blocked him in. Since the father was locked inside his study on a conference call, Kim and the man had introduced themselves. The first few minutes they'd exchanged complaints about the bride's inability to make a decision.

"And her mother is just like her," Dave said. He was David Borman and he owned the elegant little catering company.

By the time the father got off the phone and moved his car, she and Dave had a date. Since then, they'd gone out twice a week, and it had been quite pleasant. There were no fireworks, but it had been nice. The sex was good, nothing outrageous, but sweet. Dave was always respectful of her, always courteous.

"So where are the bad boys when you need them?" Kim mumbled as she took a flute of champagne off a tray and went outside.

She knew Tristan's house and grounds as well as her own, so she headed toward the path that led to Mrs. Wingate's house. To her left was the old playhouse. She'd spent a lot of time there when she was a child. Her mother and Tris's were good friends, and when they got together, Kim would go to the playhouse. It was in bad shape now but Jecca had plans to restore it.

Kim sat down on a bench at the head of the path. The moon was bright, the lights from the big tent twinkled, and the air was moist and warm. She closed her eyes and let it all seep into her. Was there a way to make jewelry that looked and felt like moonlight on your skin? she wondered.

"Do you still teach people how to have fun?" asked a man's voice.

Abruptly, she opened her eyes. A tall man was standing in front of her, looming over her. She couldn't see his face, as the moon formed a circle behind his head. His question was so suggestive, so provocative, that she couldn't help feeling uncomfortable. There was no one else around them, just this stranger and his creepy question.

"I think I should go," she said as she got up and headed toward the tent with its light and people.

"How long did the house I built for your doll last?"

Kim halted, then slowly turned back to him.

He was taller now, and from what she could see of his face in the low light, he was no longer choirboy-pretty as he had been when he was twelve. There were lines at his eyes and, as Sara'd said, his nose looked as though it had been hit a few times. But he was very handsome, with dark eyes as intense as the night around them.

"Travis," she whispered.

"I told you I'd come back and I have."

His voice was deep and strong, and she liked the sound of it. As she took a couple of steps toward him, she felt as though she were looking at a ghost.

"I thought maybe you wouldn't remember me," he said softly. "You were so very young then."

She was reluctant to tell him the truth, of the depth of her despair after he left. She'd cried herself to sleep many nights. The photo of the two of them was still her most prized possession, the thing she'd grab if the building caught on fire.

No, she thought. It was better to keep it light. "Of course I remember you," she said. "You were a great friend to me. I thought I was going to lose my mind from boredom, but you came along and saved me."

"Saved you by being someone who knew nothing. You were a good teacher."

"You on that bike!" she said. "I've never seen anyone learn as fast as you did."

Travis had an image of the things he'd done on a bicycle since then, of leaps and jumps, and turns in the air. He wondered if Kim had any idea how good she looked. The moonlight on her hair, still with a hint of red in it, and the color of that dress in the silvery light—it made a beautiful picture. Had she been any other female in the world, he would be making a pass at her right now. It had never mattered to him if the woman was the wife of a diplomat or a barmaid, if Travis was attracted to her, he let her know.

But Kim had lived all her life in a small town where everyone knew her. She wasn't the type of woman he could make a move on five minutes after seeing her.

Kim felt the awkward silence between them and thought that he hadn't changed. When he was twelve, he hadn't said much, just watched and listened and learned.

"Would you like to go back to the wedding?" she

asked. She was still holding her champagne flute. "Get something to drink?"

"I . . ." Travis began, then seemed to hear himself say, "I need help." He doubted if he'd ever before said those words. His life had made him fiercely independent.

Immediately, Kim went to him. "Are you hurt? Should I call a doctor? My brother, Reede, is here and—"

"No," he said, smiling down at her. She was even prettier up close. "I'm not hurt. I came to Edilean for a reason, to do something. But now that I'm here I don't know how to go about it."

Reaching out, Kim took his hand in hers. It was a large hand, and she could feel calluses on it. It looked like he did something in his life that required physical labor. She led him over to the bench and had him sit down beside her. The light from the wedding celebration was behind her and she could see him better. He had on a dark suit that looked as though it had been tailored for him. His cheekbones reflected the moonlight, and she saw lines between his eyes. He looked worried. She bent toward him in concern.

When she leaned forward she unintentionally gave Travis a view down the top of her dress. Kim had told Jecca the neckline was too low, but she'd laughed. "With a set of knockers like yours you should show them off." With a compliment like that, Kim couldn't insist that the bodice have a modesty panel put in it.

Travis was so distracted by the view that for a moment he couldn't speak.

"You can tell me anything," Kim said. "I know we haven't seen each other in a long time, but friendship lasts forever, and you and I are *friends*. Remember?"

"Yes," he said, swallowing. He had to take his hand out of hers or he'd be pulling her closer to him. Why hadn't he used the drive down to think about what he'd say if he did see Kim again? Instead, he'd spent most of the time on the phone planning the rock climbing trip he was going on in six weeks. Equipment had to be purchased and Travis needed to do some training. Wonder if there was a cliff he could climb in little Edilean? And did this backwoods town have a gym? He didn't want his body turning to mush while he was here trying to figure out his mother's problems.

He saw that Kim was still waiting for his answer. He hadn't planned to ask for help, hadn't even planned to see her again, but seeing her inside the tent, in that figure-hugging dress, had been too much for him. When she'd slipped out and disappeared into the woods, he'd followed her.

Now, he couldn't keep sitting there in silence. Kim was going to think he was a moron.

"It's my mother," he said. "She's living here in Edilean." He fell silent again, not sure what to tell and what to keep back. He didn't want to scare Kim away.

"What about her?" she coaxed as she tried to remember what she knew about his mother. When it had all happened, Kim had been too young to understand what was going on, but over the years she'd figured out some things. Lucy Merritt had been hiding from her abusive husband.

At the memory of the name, Kim gasped. "Lucy! Your mother's name was Lucy. Is she Lucy Cooper, the woman who runs away every time I get near? She's lived in Edilean for four years, but tonight was the first time I saw her, and even then it was only a partial view."

Travis was genuinely surprised. He'd asked his mother about Kim a couple of times, but she'd always said that they traveled in different circles, then changed the subject. "I didn't know that she hid from you, but I'm sure she would feel that she needed to. She didn't see many people when we were here before, just that old man and your mother. And you."

"Mr. Bertrand died the next year, and my mother would never tell anyone that Lucy was here."

"What about you?" Travis asked. "If you'd recognized her, would you have told?"

"I—" Kim broke off. If she'd seen Travis's mother here in Edilean she would have been on the phone to Jecca two minutes later. And she would have told her cousin Sara and maybe her new relative by marriage, Jocelyn, and she rather liked her cousin Colin's new wife, Gemma, so maybe she would have told her. And she would have *had* to tell Tris, as he was Mrs. Wingate's friend.

"Maybe," Kim said in a way that made Travis smile.

"If this is your cousin's house and Mom lived next

door, it must have been difficult for her to hide from you."

"She managed it," Kim said but didn't elaborate on the many times Lucy Cooper had escaped her view. Jecca had lived in Mrs. Wingate's house for a while, and every time Kim visited, Lucy would magically disappear. Now Kim wondered if the poor woman had slipped into a broom closet. Whatever she did, Kim knew one thing for sure: Her mother had told Lucy not to let Kim see her.

Kim wanted to get the focus off her. "Is your mother here because of your father?"

"Yes," Travis said as he leaned back against the bench. He was silent for a moment, then turned to smile at her. "I'm keeping you from your friends—and your relatives. Mom said everyone in Edilean is related to one another."

"It's not that bad, but close," Kim said.

"Is that dress one of those . . . bride things?" He waved his hand.

"I was the maid of honor."

"Oh," he said. "Doesn't 'maid' mean that you're not married?"

"I'm not. What about you?"

"Never married. I work for my father," Travis said. "The deal is that if I work for him he won't pursue Mom." He was telling her things that he never told unless necessary, but the words seemed to pour from him.

"That doesn't sound pleasant," Kim said and again wanted to reach for his hand, but she didn't. She couldn't imagine being in such a situation, but she thought how . . . well, how noble, heroic even, it was of him to sacrifice himself for his mother. Who did that today?

"It seems that now my mother wants to get married, but she's still legally married to my father."

Kim didn't understand the problem. "She can get a divorce, can't she?"

"Yes, but if she files that will let my father know where she is and he'll do what he can to make her life unpleasant."

"There are laws—"

"I know," Travis said. "I'm not worried about the divorce. It's the aftermath that I fear."

"I don't understand," Kim said. The band was playing their last set, and she could hear people laughing. She wondered if Travis had ever learned to dance.

Travis turned to her. "Can I trust you? I mean, *really* trust you? I'm not used to confiding in people." Every word he said was from his heart. This was Kim, the grown-up version of the little girl who'd changed his life.

"Yes," she said and meant it with great sincerity.

"My father is . . ."

"Abusive," Kim said, her jaw set.

"He is to anyone who is weaker than he is, and my mother is a delicate woman."

"Jecca adores her."

"Mom mentioned her. She's the young woman who lived in the apartment next door."

"And she's the bride. I guess you know that Jecca and your mother became great friends. They worked out together, sewed together. There was a point when I was becoming downright jealous."

Travis was looking at Kim in shock. He talked to his mother once a week—even if he was out of the country—but he'd heard nothing of this. He'd seen the article that said she'd made clothes for some woman, but he'd thought that meant his mother stayed in her rooms and sewed.

"Jecca is Joe Layton's daughter," Kim said when Travis was silent.

"Joe Layton?"

"I assume that's the man she wants to marry, isn't it? Tonight the two of them were dancing together as though they were about to tear each other's clothes off. Jecca said Lucy was very flexible, but I had no idea she could do a back bend like *that*. I hope that when I'm her age I can—" She broke off at Travis's look. "Oh. Right. She's your mother. I feel pretty certain that the man she wants to marry is Joe Layton."

"What's he like? What does he do?"

"He owns a hardware store in New Jersey, one that's been in his family for generations. But he's turning it over to his son and opening a store here in Edilean."

"Can the small population of this town support a hardware store?"

"We are near some large cities," Kim said coolly.

"I didn't mean to insult Edilean. I was thinking in terms of money. My mother stands to make a profit by the divorce."

"I've known Jecca for many years," Kim said tersely, "and I can assure you that her father is *not* after your mother's money." She really and truly did *not* like what he was insinuating. She stood up. "I think I'll go back to the reception now."

Travis didn't say a word. Just as he'd known he would, he'd blown it with Kim. But then, he always messed up when it came to good girls. He didn't call when he was supposed to, forgot birthdays, didn't send a gift that she'd expected. Whatever he did seemed to be wrong—which is why he tended toward women like Leslie. Give her something shiny and she was happy.

Kim got to the end of the path before a strong sense of déjà vu hit her. She was eight years old again, she'd just let her temper override her and thrown a clod of dirt at a boy. She then ran away and hid, waiting for him to come after her. But *that* boy hadn't come. She'd had to go after him. In the weeks that followed she'd found out that the boy didn't know how to do much of anything. Couldn't skip rocks, couldn't ride a bike. He knew lots about science but couldn't put a blade of grass between his thumbs and make a whistle. He didn't know anything about the really important stuff in life.

She turned back to Travis. Just as he'd done so long ago, he was sitting there, not moving. She didn't know what was in his head now—probably something he'd learned in a book—but it was obvious that he was as socially awkward now as he was then.

Slowly, she walked back to the bench and sat down beside him, her eyes straight ahead. "Sorry," she said. "My temper sometimes gets the better of me."

"Then you haven't changed."

"And you just sat there, so neither have you."

"Maybe as children we're the purest forms of ourselves."

"In our case, I think so." She took a breath. "Joe Layton isn't after your mother's money. As far as I know, no one knows she has any or will receive any. I don't mean to reveal a confidence, but Jecca said that her dad knows little about Lucy, whether she has kids or not, anything. Whenever he asks about her personal life, Lucy starts kissing him and—I guess you don't want to hear the rest of that."

"I would prefer your descriptions to be less graphic."

She smiled at the way he spoke. His extensive schooling was in every syllable. "I understand. I think you can rest easy that they are together for love, not money."

When he said nothing, she put her hand on his arm—and Travis put his hand over hers. He had almost forgotten how caring she was. When they were kids she was appalled at the things he didn't know. She seemed to have a checklist of what each and every kid in the world *must* know and she'd set about teaching him.

Right now there were a few things he'd like to teach

her. She looked so good in that dress in the moonlight that it was difficult to keep his hands off her. But she was looking at him as though he were a stray dog that she needed to rescue. He had to work to keep desire out of his eyes, but she seemed to want to give him a bandage.

He knew he should let go of her hand, but her long fingers were— He lifted her hand. "Is this a scar?"

She pulled out of his grasp. "Very unfeminine, I know. But it's a hazard of my trade."

"Your trade?" Thanks to the Internet, he knew all about her jewelry shop. He'd followed her all through school, then back to Edilean, where she'd opened her own business. Kim never knew it, but Travis attended every one of her one-man shows while she was at school. One time, he'd barely escaped being seen. She'd come in with two other girls, a tall, slim, dark-haired one, and a short blonde girl with a figure that had every male in the room staring.

But Travis only had eyes for Kim. She'd grown up to be as pretty as she'd been when they were children. And he liked the way she laughed and seemed to be so happy. Travis didn't think he'd ever been that happy in his life—at least not since he'd left Edilean and Kim so many years before.

"I make jewelry," she said.

He turned on the bench to look at her. "The jewelry kit!"

She smiled. "You remember that?"

"You had me open it. You got it . . . ?"

"My aunt and uncle had given it to me for Christmas, but I wasn't interested enough to even open it. I was an ungrateful child! It was in that box Uncle Ben brought to us."

"With my bicycle," Travis said, his voice softening with the memory. "You were very creative with everything in that kit. I was amazed."

"And you were an excellent model," she said. "No boy I knew would have let me put a necklace of beads around him." She didn't tell him that the pleasure of those two weeks and the jewelry kit were all tied together. Travis and jewelry and happiness were synonymous to her.

"I still have that necklace," he said.

"Do you?" she asked.

"Yes. Kim, that was the best two weeks of my childhood."

She started to say it was for her too, but she didn't. "What are your plans about your mother?"

"I don't really have a plan. I just heard of this yesterday. She called . . ." He thought it best not to say "my secretary." "And left a message saying she wanted to get married, so she needed a divorce. That's all she said. It was a total shock to me. I thought she was living in an apartment in a house owned by a respectable older widow and they were sewing children's clothes.

Now I find out that Mom is doing back bends in front of the whole town." He looked at Kim. "So, no, I haven't come up with a plan. Mainly, I want—"

"What?"

"I want to know if this man Joe Layton is good for my mother. Forget love—she thought she was in love with my father. I want to know if he's a good person and that he's not going to browbeat my little mother."

Kim drew her breath in sharply. Jecca's mother had died when she was young, and she'd been raised by her father. Joe Layton was a very strong-willed man who liked things done his way. All through college, there had been hundreds of girlfriend sessions where Jecca was tearing her hair out about some maddening thing her father had said or done. While the man could be very sweet, he could also be a serious pain in the neck. And he was *very* possessive! When Jecca fell in love with a man in Edilean, Virginia, Joe Layton had moved there to be with her—and his stunt had almost caused Jecca and Tris to break up.

"What is it?" Travis asked.

"I, uh . . ." She didn't know exactly what to say. She was saved from replying by the sound of voices coming their way.

Kim could tell from Travis's expression that he didn't want to be seen. At least not yet, before he saw his mother. "Follow me," she said as she stood and lifted her long skirt to start running down a narrow path through the woods.

"Gladly," Travis murmured as he followed her. It was dark in the heavily wooded area, but there was enough moonlight to see Kim's pale skin and the silvery blue of her dress. He loved watching her run.

His eyes were so focused on her that he almost collided with what looked to be an old playhouse. The tall turret, shadowed in the moonlight, looked like where the evil witch in a fairy tale would live.

"In here," Kim said as she opened the door, then locked it behind them.

Travis started searching for a light switch, but Kim caught his wrist and put her finger to her lips indicating he should say nothing. She motioned for him to get out from in front of the window.

He leaned back against the door, close beside Kim.

Outside they heard the voices of what sounded like teenagers.

"Come on. I'm over here," came a loud male whisper.

"We'll get caught." It was a girl's voice.

"By who? Dr. Tris? He's already on his honeymoon." There was the sound of kissing. "I'll bet that right now he's doing what we want to do."

"I'd trade places with her," the girl said in a dreamy voice.

Kim looked at Travis, and they grimaced. The girl had said the wrong thing.

"So now I'm not good enough for you?" the boy asked.

"I just meant . . ." the girl said. "Oh, never mind.

Let's get back to the tent. My mom will be looking for me."

There was a loud turn of the door handle on the playhouse. "The damned thing is locked anyway," the boy said.

"Good!" the girl said and footsteps ran down the leafy path.

When it was silent again, Kim let out her breath, looked at Travis, and they laughed. "Tomorrow the entire teenage population of Edilean will be wondering which couple got to the playhouse first."

"But it was just us oldies," Travis said.

"Speak for yourself. You're the one about to turn thirty. I have years and years to go." She moved to the right. "Come through here, but duck. The doorway is low."

He followed her into a very small second room, with a short daybed built into the wall.

Kim motioned to the bed. "You are now looking at the love capital of Edilean. Well, the indoor one."

"If you have two in a town this size that must make Edilean the romance capital of the world."

"You have to have something interesting to do in a town that doesn't have a Walmart."

Travis laughed as Kim sat down at one end of the bed and motioned for him to take the other. He had trouble fitting his long legs into the small space.

"Here, stretch out. See how we fit?" she said. Their legs went to the sides of each other.

"You and I always have fit together rather well," Travis said.

Kim was glad that the lack of light hid her expression. We're friends, she reminded herself.

"So tell me about Joe Layton," Travis said and his voice was serious.

"I don't know him well, but he did boss Jecca around a lot while we were in school. But to be fair, all our parents did. My mother never let up on me. She wanted to know who I was dating, when I got in, and if I'd applied for a job yet."

"Sounds like she cares about you. How is she now?"

"She demands to know who I'm dating, when I got in, and what the weekly gross for my shop is."

Travis laughed. "And your dad?"

"My father is made of sugar. He truly is the sweetest man alive. My parents and my little sister, Anna, are on a long cruise right now. They won't be back until the fall."

"So you're in town alone?"

"My brother, Reede, is here, and I do have a few relatives." She thought he was being polite to ask so many questions about her when what he wanted to hear about was the man his mother wanted to marry. "I think Mr. Layton is a good man, but it depends on your mother, doesn't it? From what you've said, she doesn't seem to stand up for herself very well."

He took his time answering. "When I was growing up, my mother was a very quiet woman. I think she'd learned that to stand up to my father just made him worse. If she stayed in the background, it gave him the illusion that everything was under his control, so he didn't need to reassert his authority."

"And what about you?" she asked. "What was *your* life like?"

Travis tried to move on the little bed, but there wasn't room. "I'm about to fall off this thing. Your feet are . . . Do you mind?" he asked as he picked up her feet and put them on his thigh.

Kim would have died before she protested his movement.

"Ow! Sorry, but the heels on your shoes are rather sharp and . . ."

It took her about a quarter of a second to flick her pretty high-heeled sandals off and put her feet back on his thigh. He made it seem natural when he began to massage them. Kim thanked the Spirits of the Spas that yesterday she'd had a mani-pedi. Her heels were as smooth as glass.

"Where were we?" he asked.

"Uh . . ." Kim couldn't remember. No man had ever given her a foot massage.

"Oh yes, you asked about my life. The truth is that you changed everything."

"Me?"

"I didn't grow up like other kids. We had a big house on a hundred acres in upstate New York. The place was built by a robber baron around the turn of the last century and it was a testament to his greed. Very high ceilings and lots of dark paneling. It suited my father perfectly. My mother and I lived there with a houseful of servants—all of whom became like family to us. We hardly ever saw my father, but his presence was always there."

Travis's thumbs caressed the ball of her left foot, his fingers sliding between her toes. It wasn't easy for her to comprehend what he was saying.

"Until that summer when my father went to Tokyo and my mom drove us to Edilean, I had no idea that my life wasn't like other people's. You taught me how other kids lived, and I'll always be grateful to you for that."

"I think you're making it up to me now. Travis, where in the world did you learn to do that?"

"Thailand, I think," he said. "Or maybe it was in India. Somewhere. You like it?"

"If I pass out from ecstasy, pay me no mind."

"Can't have that, can we?" he said and tucked her feet to the side of him. "Tell me more about Joe Layton."

Kim let out a sigh of disappointment that he'd stopped rubbing her feet, but she sat up straighter. "I don't have any answers. Jecca complained a lot about her father, but she also loves him very much. I know she's the light of his life. When she was younger, he wanted her with him every minute. The first summer she went back home from college, she had to beg and plead to get to visit me for just two weeks. And Mr. Layton scrutinized every man Jecca so much as looked at. She said that Tristan—the man she married—paid a bride price by giving her dad a building."

"For his hardware store?"

"Yes," Kim said.

"Is the store open yet?"

"No. There was a lot of remodeling, rebuilding actually, that had to be done. Mr. Layton had some friends of his come down from New Jersey to do it. He and Jecca had a big fight, as she said there were good contractors in Virginia, but he wouldn't listen to her."

"Sounds like a man who likes to have his own way," Travis said, frowning. "My father is like that. He has to rule over every situation."

"You think your mother said yes to Mr. Layton because he's . . . He's what's familiar to her?"

"That's exactly what I'm afraid of. I wish there was a way I could see them together—but only if he didn't know who I was."

"You're right," Kim said. "If you're introduced as Lucy's son, Mr. Layton will be on his best behavior with you. You'd never see anything close to the truth." Her head came up. "Would your mother agree to—"

"Not telling him who I am?" Travis asked. "That's what I'm wondering. I don't know. I find women extremely unpredictable. My mother could laugh and agree, or she could get angry and ask how dare I think I know more about people than she does."

Kim had to laugh. "Spoken like Mr. Spock."

"Is he someone in Edilean?"

"No," she said. "He's someone from TV. My parents' generation. Do you often find missing pieces in your education?"

"Whole decades," he said with sincerity. "People make references to things I've never heard of. I have to watch other people to see whether to laugh or not. However, I've learned to *never* ask what the hell they're talking about. That gets me branded as something akin to being an alien."

Kim laughed more because that's just what she had done. "You can ask me anything and I'll do my best to answer it."

"I'll take you up on that." He paused. "So tell me, are Dr. Spock and Mr. Spock the same person?"

"No. Far from it. My dad has DVDs of *Star Trek* episodes, so I'll lend them to you."

"I'd like that very much," Travis said as he suppressed a yawn. "Sorry, but it's been a very long day. I meant to be here this afternoon so I could talk to my mother right away. But my father had something he wanted me to do, so I got a late start."

Kim turned around and put her bare feet on the floor. "Have you eaten? And where are you staying?"

"Unless Edilean has a hotel and a restaurant open

past—what is it now? Nine-thirty?—I'll be going into Williamsburg."

Kim decided not to think too hard before she spoke. "I have a guesthouse and a refrigerator full of food. It's really just a tiny pool house that the previous owners made into a place for their son to stay when he visited. When I bought the house, my brother, Reede, said he would move in there, but it's too small for him. He took over Colin's—he's the sheriff—old apartment, but he hates that too. Reede does, not Colin, although Colin hated the apartment too."

She stopped before she made a complete fool of herself.

"I would be honored to accept," Travis said softly. "As for dinner, I'd take you out, but . . ."

"The old cliché: We roll up our sidewalks at nine."

"When did you get sidewalks?"

"I am wounded!" Kim said. "We've had sidewalks for three years now. Next year we're getting electric streetlamps."

"I bet the lamplighter is crying over the loss of his job," Travis said.

"We married him off to the cobbler's daughter, so they're happy."

They laughed together.

Three

As *she drove* home, Kim marveled at the fact that Travis had returned. She kept checking the rearview mirror to make sure she hadn't lost him. He was driving an old BMW that didn't even have an automatic transmission. Maybe she could teach him that he didn't need to shift gears.

She was dying to ask him thousands of questions about what he'd done in the last years, but she thought it would be better if he told her at his own pace. She knew he worked for his bastard of a father—the word made her smile in memory—and his father had money. But if his car was any indication, it looked like he didn't share it with his son.

Kim thought about the horror of what Travis's current life must be like—and why he was doing it. To give up his own life to protect his mother! How heroic was that?

As she pulled into her driveway she remembered

that he'd asked for her help, and she vowed to give it.

Travis parked beside her and got out. "You don't use your garage?"

"I have it set up as a workroom." She fumbled for her house key on the ring.

"So when it snows or rains or gets really hot, your car is outside?" He took the keys from her and unlocked the door.

"Yes," she said as she went inside. She switched on the lamps by the couch she and Jecca had chosen. The room was done in shades of blue and white. One wall was bookcases and a TV, a fireplace below. The ceiling went up to the roof, with big white exposed rafters.

"Nice," Travis said. "It looks like a home." He was wondering why his expensive decorator couldn't have done something like this. But then, he'd not given the woman any help by telling her what he liked.

"Thanks," Kim said and turned away so he wouldn't see her grin. "Kitchen's this way."

"Kim, you don't need to feed me," he said. "That you're giving me a place to sleep is enough. I can—" He stopped talking at the sight of her kitchen. It opened into the dining area, and all of it was warm and cozy. There was a big pink granite island, with copper pots hung along one wall. The dining table was big and old, with cut marks from hundreds of meals.

"I like this," he said. "Have you had this house long?" He knew the answer to that because he'd followed the sale every inch of the way. He'd even had

Penny make a couple of calls to the bank where Kim was applying for a mortgage. He wanted to make sure everything went through smoothly.

"Less than a year," she said.

"And you made it look like this in that time?"

"Jecca and I did it all. We . . ." She shrugged.

"You two are artists, so you knew what you were doing. What can I do to help with dinner?"

"Nothing," Kim said, but she wondered how he knew that Jecca was an artist. Had she told him? "Just sit down and I'll get you something to eat."

He took a seat on a stool on the far side of the counter and watched her.

Kim could feel his eyes on her as she started going through the refrigerator. She felt guilty that everything in there had been made by Dave and his catering crew, but there didn't seem to be any need to tell Travis that. To say that she had a fairly regular boyfriend would be to assume that something could possibly happen between her and Travis. Foot massage aside, he didn't seem to be interested in anything besides friendship. And he was looking at her as though she were still eight years old.

She put a place mat on the counter in front of him, then a plate and the matching knife and fork. Her mother had tried to get Kim to save money by using her grandmother's dishes, but Kim had refused. "You just want to get rid of the old things," Kim had said, and her father had suppressed a laugh. In the end, her mother gave the whole set to Colin and Gemma Frazier for a wedding gift, and they'd loved them.

"What's that look for?" Travis asked, and Kim told him.

"Gemma is a historian and she knew the history of the company that made the dishes. She treated them like they were treasure."

"But not you?" Travis asked.

"I like new. What would you like to eat?"

"Anything," he said. "I'm a pure omnivore."

She put spoons in each of the nearly dozen plastic bowls she'd taken from the fridge and let him help himself. She couldn't help sitting on the stool next to him and watching him. He ate European style, with his fork turned over in his left hand, his knife in his right. His manners were those of a prince.

Without the sharp contrast between shadows and harsh white light on him, she could now see some of the angelic look that he'd had as a boy. In adulthood, his hair was midnight black, his eyes were as dark as obsidian, his cheekbones angular, and his jaw strong. It looked like he hadn't shaved in a day or so, and the whiskers further darkened the look of him. All in all, she thought she'd never seen a better looking man in her life.

Travis saw the way she was leaning on her elbow and looking at him. If he didn't distract her he was going to put his hand on the back of her neck and kiss her. "Aren't you afraid of getting something on that dress?"

"What? Oh yeah, sure." She broke her trance of staring at him. "I guess I should put on something more comfortable."

Travis gave a little cough, as though he nearly choked on his food.

"You okay?"

"Yes," he said. "I'll just finish here while you . . ."

Reluctantly, she got off the stool. "Sure, of course." She hurried down the hall to her bedroom and closed the door. "I am making a fool of myself," she whispered aloud.

It wasn't easy to reach the zipper in the back of her dress, and for a moment she thought of asking Travis to unzip her. That thought made her giggle—which disgusted her. "You *are* eight years old," she said aloud and began to undress.

In the kitchen, Travis breathed a sigh of relief. Kim, so beautiful in her low-cut dress and sitting there watching him, had been too much for him. Had he been in a normal situation, he would have given her looks to let her know how interested he was in her. He knew from experience that girls who looked at him as Kim did were an easy make.

But then what would happen? he thought. Would she start talking of *their* wedding?

The truth was that Travis didn't think he'd mind that. So far, everything around Kim had felt like he was coming home. Her, her house, even what he'd seen of her friends, had been pleasant and welcoming.

But what happened when she found out more about him, about his past, about who his father was? He'd see the stars fall out of her eyes—and he couldn't bear that. No, it was better that he let her keep her ideas that he was noble, someone who had done only good deeds in his life. Better to never let her find out the truth.

He'd finished eating by the time Kim returned wearing jeans and an old T-shirt. Unfortunately, Travis thought she looked even more desirable than before. It hit him that it had been a mistake to accept her invitation to stay at her house. He stood up.

"Ready to go to bed?" she asked.

Travis didn't dare answer that question. He just nodded, but when Kim started toward the back door, he halted. He wasn't going to be in the same room with her and a bed. "Why don't you give me the key and point me in the right direction?"

"But I need to show you where things are."

"I'm sure I can find everything." He smiled at her in a way that said he wouldn't take no for an answer.

Kim handed him her key ring.

There was an awkward moment at the back door when they parted. Kim bent forward, as though she meant to kiss him on the cheek, but he pulled back. For a moment she thought he was going to shake her hand, but then he gave her a brotherly pat on the shoulder and left the house.

As Kim put away the leftovers, she couldn't help grimacing. She was the one who'd said they were friends, so she had no right to complain when Travis stuck to that.

The next morning she awoke to the smell of cooking, and her only thought was *Travis!* She rapidly dressed and put on a bit too much eye makeup, but then her brows and lashes had always been too pale. She cursed herself for not having them dyed before the wedding. But then, she had an idea that Travis liked women who could pull off the no-makeup look. It took three shades of brown to achieve that look.

She had on nice black slacks and a crisp linen shirt when she went into the kitchen. Pausing in the doorway, she saw Travis with his back to her as he cooked something on her new Wolf range. He had on jeans and a denim shirt. She wasn't sure, but he looked to have a truly magnificent body under his clothes.

"Good morning," she said.

Travis turned, skillet in hand, and smiled at her. She so badly wanted to put her arms around him. For a moment he seemed amenable to that idea, but then he broke eye contact.

"It's my turn to feed you," he said and nodded toward the island that had one place setting.

"You aren't eating?"

"I got up a couple of hours ago and ate then. I hope you don't mind that I did laps in your pool."

Kim was very, very sorry that she'd missed seeing him in swim trunks. "I'm glad someone is using the pool. That was my only hesitation about buying this house. I liked the layout and I loved the three-car garage for my work, but I don't know how to take care of a swimming pool."

He slid an omelet onto her plate. "I thought maybe that was the case, so I did a little cleaning for you and checked the pH. There were some chemicals in a closet, so I used some of them. I hope I wasn't being presumptuous."

"Presume all you want," Kim said as she looked at her plate. There was an omelet with peppers and onions in it and two pieces of whole wheat toast. "I'll put on weight eating like this," she said, then waited for him to say something nice.

But there was no way Travis was going to comment on the state of Kim's body. She looked great! She'd grown taller than he'd expected; she was the perfect height for him. Her white blouse clung to her, and the black pants curved around her bottom half.

His silence at her hint made her tell herself that Travis really didn't know how to act around a woman. "So what are you planning to do today?" she asked.

This morning, Travis's first thought had been to call his mother and tell her he was in Edilean. He should arrange to meet with her somewhere private where they could talk about the divorce, the man she wanted to marry, and what she planned to do with her life. He should then spend the next three weeks getting ready for the divorce case that would, no doubt, make all the newspapers.

But as he looked at Kim, he tried to think of a reason to take as long as he could to postpone all the bad that was coming. "What were you going to do today?"

"Church if I got out of bed early enough." She looked at the clock. She still had time to get ready and go, but that would mean leaving Travis behind. She thought it was entirely possible that when she returned, he'd be gone. He'd probably talk to his mother, be reassured that Joe Layton was a good man, then Travis would go back to . . . to wherever he lived. To whomever he lived with but wasn't married to.

She searched her mind for a reason to make him stay—and for her to be with him. "I'm sure you want to see your mother, but maybe you should see Mr. Layton's new hardware store before you do."

Travis smiled as though she'd said something brilliant. "I think that's a great idea. You can tell a lot about a man when you see where he works." Which is why Travis's office had no personal items in it, he thought but didn't say. "Would you mind going with me? If you're too busy to go, you could draw a map. I could—"

"I would love to!" she said. "We'll take my car. Could you excuse me for a little bit? I have to make a phone call first, then I'll be ready to go."

The minute Kim closed her bedroom door, she called Carla, her assistant.

"Hello?" Carla asked, obviously half-asleep.

"It's me," Kim whispered as loudly as she could. "I need you to finish the Johnson rings today."

"What? I can't hear you."

Kim went into her closet and shut the door. "Carla, please wake up. I need you to finish a couple of rings for me today."

"Kim, it's Sunday. I was at the wedding until after midnight. I drank too much."

"I did too," Kim said, "but those rings need to be done today. The wedding is tomorrow."

"But you were going to do those and—"

"I know," Kim said. "I'm a rotten, lazy boss, but something's come up. An emergency. I need for you to come over here to do them. They've been cast. They just need sanding and polishing."

Carla groaned. "That's hours of work, and it's Sunday."

"Time and a half."

Carla was silent.

"Okay," Kim said. "Double time. I just need them done today. All right?"

"Sure. Fine," Carla said. "But I want Friday the eighteenth off *and* double time for today."

Kim glared at the phone. Oh how she used to dream of being the boss, of setting her own hours, and having employees to follow her orders! "All right," Kim said. "You know where the key to the garage is, so come over here and get it done."

"Do you have a hot date?" Carla asked. "Dave planning to pop the question? You design your own ring yet?"

Kim wasn't about to tell Carla about Travis. "I have to go. And remind me to order more rouge tomorrow."

"For your face or the jewelry?"

Kim grimaced. Carla's humor often left people groaning. "See you tomorrow," she said, then hung up. Minutes later, she was in the living room. Travis was in the big navy blue chair with the matching ottoman and reading the Sunday paper. Jecca had chosen that chair. "It's for the man in your life," she'd said.

"Which one?" Kim had asked sarcastically.

"The one that's going to come along and sweep you off your feet."

"Like Tris did to you at Reede's Welcome Home party?"

"Yes," Jecca had said with a dreamy sigh, and Kim knew she had managed to get the conversation away from her.

Kim quietly sat down on the couch and picked up the Sunday magazine.

Minutes later, he asked, "Ready?" without looking up.

"Any time," she answered, but she wasn't in a rush to leave. Usually on Sunday morning she was hurrying to get ready for church, answering the phone to her mother's calls, and thinking about the work that needed to be done that week. Sunday afternoons were quiet for her. Her past boyfriends, the ones with the normal jobs, would sometimes come over to visit, but Dave was always busy on weekends. Since she'd met him, her weekends had been solitary.

"You look like you're miles away," Travis said.

She smiled at him. "I was thinking how I usually work on Sundays."

"That doesn't sound like fun," he said.

He was repeating her words of long ago. "I can attest that it is no fun whatever," she said, quoting his response, and they laughed together.

"Shall we go see what my mother is getting herself into?"

"Since you don't want to be seen, how about if we take a back way? There's an old forest road, but I don't know what shape it's in. I'll try not to lose us in any potholes."

Travis still had her keys from last night. "In that case, how about if I drive? And we'll take my old car so we don't hurt your pretty new one."

"All right," she said, but there was caution in her voice. The area around Edilean was rough. It was a wilderness preserve, maintained by the state of Virginia, but she knew that her cousins often took care of the trails. The question was whether anyone had looked at that particular road in the last few years.

A few minutes later, she and Travis were in his old Bimmer and sitting at the head of a trail that looked like it hadn't seen any traffic in years. There were holes, ridges, fallen rocks, and a dead tree was taking up half the roadway.

"Looks like we should turn around and go by the

road," Kim said. "I'll tell Colin about this and he'll get it fixed."

"Colin?"

"The sheriff. You may have seen him at the wedding. He's big, dark hair."

"Pregnant wife?"

"That's him. Did you two meet?"

"Sort of," Travis said, and he thought about the risks of what Kim was saying. The sheriff would ask why she wanted the road cleared, and how she'd discovered it was a mess. And then there was what would happen if they didn't go in this way. A ride through town with Kim seated beside a stranger was bound to cause comment—and he'd be damned if he'd hide in the back!

"We could walk," Kim said. "It's only about two miles to the building."

"Those are awfully pretty sandals you have on," he said.

"Thank you. I just bought them. They're made by Børn and I love the soles. They're—" She broke off. "Oh right. They'd be destroyed walking through that."

"Kim . . ." he said slowly as he looked into her eyes.

She could almost read his mind. He *wanted* to drive down that old road. If they went slowly and carefully, they might be able to do it. If it got to be too much for him to drive, they could walk—and maybe Travis would give her a piggyback ride. She checked her seat belt to see if it was securely fastened.

"Once I get going, I can't stop," he said in warning. "This car isn't four-wheel drive, so if I slow down we'll get stuck."

"Then you'd have to call a Frazier to get you out."

"A Frazier?"

"The sheriff's family. They know about cars."

"Do they?" From Travis's perspective, the road was easy. It would do some damage to the undercarriage of the car, but he might be able to avoid that. The question was whether or not a girl like Kim could stand it. "The sheriff would drive over that?"

"Colin? Are you kidding? He'd drive up the mountainside. He's nearly always the first person to arrive if someone needs rescuing. I keep telling him what a great team he and Reede would be. My brother goes down on helicopter cables to save people. He—"

Travis was looking at her in such an odd way that she stopped talking.

"This is like the bicycle, isn't it? You need to do it even if you fall on your face."

He smiled at her because she understood so completely. On the other hand, her talk of what other men could do was crushing his ego.

"I'm game if you are," she said.

"If we do this, you have to trust me," he said, his face serious.

"Didn't I ride on your handlebars when you rode up that dirt hill?"

He smiled at her in such a way that Kim wanted to

kiss him. There was gratitude as well as pleasure in his eyes.

"All right," he said as he glanced out the windshield, his hand on the gearshift. "Put one hand on the armrest and one here and hold on. And don't scream. Screaming distracts me."

At that last, Kim's eyes widened and part of her wanted to say, Let me out of here! But she didn't. She put her hands where he told her, braced her feet on the floor, then nodded. She was ready.

With a grin, Travis put the car in low and took off. To her shock, he started out going fast and he didn't slow down for anything. With lightning reflexes, he went around potholes, or straddled them precisely. When a fallen tree blocked the way, Travis went up onto the side of the road. The car banked left at what Kim was sure was a forty-five-degree angle, and he was heading straight for a giant oak. Kim wanted to scream. She wanted to warn him that they were about to crash, but she held her breath—and kept her eyes open.

Travis swerved to the left and missed the tree by no more than an inch. It was so close that Kim's intake of breath sounded like a mouse's squeak.

He never let up speed as he put the clutch to the floor and upshifted. When he hit a hillock made by years of overgrown weeds and a rotten tree trunk, all four wheels left the ground.

As they sailed through the air, Kim thought it could

be the end of her life. She glanced at Travis, the last person she'd ever see alive.

He turned his head a bit, his dark eyes wildly alight—and he winked at her.

If Kim hadn't been terrified, she would have laughed.

When the car hit the ground, her body jolted hard—but he kept going at what seemed to be warp speed.

Travis took the car to the side again, riding on the bank, then twisting hard to the left, then to the right and back again.

Finally, before them loomed the back of the huge building that used to be a brick factory. But Travis didn't slow down. He went around, over, and across three more big holes.

The solid wall of the brick building was straight ahead and Travis was flying toward it.

When she saw a pile of dirt in their way, Kim again had to work not to scream.

"Hold on, baby," Travis said, then hit the hill at full speed. They went through the air and landed hard on the other side, but they were still heading toward the building.

He turned the steering wheel so hard to the left that he looked like he was about to wrench his shoulders out of their sockets. The car skidded to a halt so close to the building Kim could have put down the window and touched it. But she didn't move. She was frozen into place. Her body was rigid from what she'd just gone through.

Travis turned off the engine. "Not bad. Not nearly as bad as I thought it was going to be." He looked at her. "Kim, are you all right?"

She stayed where she was, eyes straight ahead, her hands white as they gripped the handholds. She doubted if her legs were ever going to work again.

Travis got out and went around to her side to open the door. The building was so close that the edge of the door nearly scraped. Nearly. There was about a half inch of clearance. His parking had been precisely perfect.

When he opened the door, Kim's hand stayed on it and her arm was so stiff he couldn't get the door open all the way. Slowly, one by one, he pried her fingers up.

When he finally got the door open, he leaned across her and loosened her other hand, then unbuckled her seat belt. But she was still rigid in the seat.

Bending, he slid one arm behind her back, the other under her knees, and lifted her out of the car. He carried her to the shade of a tree, sat down on an empty wooden spool, and held her on his lap.

"I didn't mean to scare you," he said as he put her head on his shoulder. "I thought—" At the moment he didn't know what he'd been thinking. He'd been around too many women who wanted nothing but thrills. Yet again, he'd screwed up.

Kim was beginning to thaw out. But her first thought was that she didn't want Travis to put her down. She wanted to snuggle on his lap for as long as it took to get him to kiss her.

"Should I take you to your brother?" he asked softly.

She had no idea what he meant until she remembered that Reede was a doctor. "I'm fine," she said.

"You don't seem fine." He pulled her head from his shoulder and looked at her. Her skin was pale and her eyes were wide. She looked like a shock victim—but at the same time there was something else deeper in her eyes.

He leaned back and studied her. "You enjoyed yourself, didn't you?"

"I've never done anything like that before," she said. "It was . . ."

She didn't have to say any more. He could see it all in her face. The ride down the old road had made her feel *alive*. It's how he'd felt that first day when he'd ridden her bicycle.

Smiling, Travis stood her on the ground. "So how do we get inside this place?" He started walking away.

Kim was still a bit dazed, her legs felt weak, and her mind was full of images of what had happened in the car. She could see the tree coming at them, then swerving just before they hit. Twice Travis had taken the car through the air, all four wheels off the ground.

"Is there an alarm system?"

She had to blink to focus on him. "What?"

"Do you know if there's an alarm system on the building?"

"I have no idea." As she walked toward him, she nearly fell once when her legs buckled, but she held her balance.

"I'm going to look around," he said. His eyes were twinkling, as though he knew something she didn't. "Stay here and I'll be back in a few minutes."

"Okay," Kim said, "but if you need help, I'm here."

"I'll keep that in mind." Smiling, Travis went around the side of the building. He'd seen how scared she was during the drive. It was the kind of thing he'd done a hundred times in his stunt work. He had to make the star look as though he could actually *do* things. But Kim hadn't screamed, even though he'd seen that at times she'd been terrified. If at any time he'd felt out of control he would have stopped, but he hadn't. He liked that she'd been brave. Most of all, he liked that she'd trusted him.

Kim went back to the big wooden spool and sat down. "He seems to have learned how to do a lot of things since he rode my bike," she said aloud.

She was sitting there, looking at the old BMW, amazed that it wasn't in flames of protest, when a door in the building opened. She expected to see Mr. Layton, but Travis stepped outside.

"No alarm," he said. "Come inside."

"How'd you get in?" she asked as she went to him.

"He left a window open and I climbed in it. He needs better security."

Kim had only been in the old building once and that had been before the rebuilding had begun. Jecca said her dad had worked the men from New Jersey in shifts 24/7. Whatever he'd done, the transformation was stunning.

They were in a big room with tall ceilings and all around them were boxes. From what was printed on the cartons they appeared to be full of equipment and tools.

"Looks like he kept some trucking companies busy." Travis's frown was deep.

"What's that look for?"

He hesitated.

"We're friends, remember? We share secrets."

He smiled at her. "That's not easy for me to remember, but I'll try. My mother . . . Well, when she ran away from my father, she also took some money from him."

"Six or seven figures?"

"Multiple seven."

"Yeow!" Kim suddenly realized why Travis was frowning. "You think maybe Mr. Layton used your mother's money for . . ." She waved her hand. "To buy all this?"

"What hardware store owner do you know who could afford this much?"

"I don't know," she said, but the truth was that Kim did know quite a bit about opening a business. Her little jewelry shop was a quarter the size of this room, and to get it she'd had to take out a mortgage, borrow from her father, and max out her credit cards. She'd only paid it all off a year ago. She'd celebrated by putting herself back into debt by buying a house that was a bit more than she could afford. At first the bank had said no to the mortgage, but then the bank president had personally called her and said they'd be happy to give her financing. No one ever said, but Kim was sure her father had arranged it.

But Kim said none of this. Jecca was her best friend and this was her father they were talking about.

She looked around the big room and noticed that way up in the top, high above the exposed steel rafters, was an open window. Everything else looked sealed shut. "Is that the window you came through?"

Travis didn't glance up. "Yeah." He was reading the labels on the boxes. Saws, hand tools, power equipment, garden implements. Even at wholesale prices this had cost a lot. Had his mother told this man Layton about the money she had hidden away? She knew Travis had access to her account, so maybe she'd used it as collateral to buy the man's tools.

"Travis?" Kim asked, getting his attention. "That window is at least twenty feet up. How did you get up to it from the outside and down from the inside?"

"Climbed," he said distractedly. "I'm going to look around."

She followed him into a smaller room that held two

large restrooms. Travis went past them but Kim stopped. She knew that Jecca had sent her dad designs that the New Jersey workmen were to follow.

In keeping with the age of Edilean and the fact that the building used to be a factory to make bricks, Jecca had used a color palette of cream and Williamsburg blue. She'd left the bricks exposed wherever she could, and trimmed them in that soft blue that the Colonials had so loved. Kim wasn't sure, but she'd be willing to bet that Lucy Cooper had made the curtains.

Smiling, Kim went back out into the big hall to see that Travis was gone. She found him standing in the next room, which had three offices in it, with windows facing into the hall. He tried the doors, but they were locked.

"I'd like to get into his computer and see his source of income for all this." He looked at Kim as though asking her a question.

"I don't know how to hack into a computer."

"Me neither," he said, sounding as though his education were lax.

"Nice to know there's something you can't do," Kim muttered. So far he'd cleaned her pool, cooked breakfast, driven like something out of an action movie, and scaled a brick wall.

She hurried after him. He was standing in a long, narrow room with windows that opened to the front. He had an expression on his face that she couldn't read. There was nothing in the room, no boxes, no desks, just the walls on three sides, the windows on the other.

She waited, but he just kept staring, saying nothing. "Want to see the room Mr. Layton planned for Jecca to use? She likes to paint and she's quite good at it, so he was going to make her a studio. But Jecca said she'd never get any work done if she was so near her father. She said he'd bully her into working for him because, you see, Jecca knows how to take chain saws apart. She can put them back together too."

Travis was looking at the room as though he were in a trance and she didn't think he'd heard a word she'd said.

"But Jecca would rather raise pink unicorns, so she didn't take her dad up on his offer."

"Where did she get a breeding pair?"

"What?"

"Of pink unicorns?" Travis asked.

"I thought you weren't listening."

"Didn't I tell you that I'm a good listener?"

They exchanged smiles. They had been children and it had only been for two weeks, but they both remembered every minute of that time.

"Do you know what Layton plans to do with this room?" he asked.

"I have no idea. Why?"

Travis went to the windows to look out at the big parking lot. "Where do you buy your outdoor equipment around here?"

"You mean like fishing gear?"

Travis smiled. "I was thinking more of climbing paraphernalia and kayaks. Where do the local guides get their equipment?"

Kim was blinking at him. "Guides?" she said at last.

"Edilean is surrounded by some incredible wilderness. I saw online a place called Stirling Point."

"It's the outdoor make-out point," Kim said, but Travis just looked at her. "The playhouse is the indoor and the—"

"I get it," he said, his face serious. "I saw online that there's hiking, boating, your fishing, and some climbing in the preserve. Where do people buy their gear?"

"I don't know," Kim said yet again in answer to his questions. "Virginia City, Norfolk, maybe Richmond. And Williamsburg must sell that stuff."

"But nothing here in Edilean?"

"No kayak store anywhere."

Travis didn't smile. "Interesting. So where is your friend's unicorn studio?"

Kim opened the connecting door to a big, airy room, this time with the windows along the back, looking out into the woods. Like the other one, the room was empty. It had been restored and the floor rebuilt. All the windows were new, some with the Pella stickers still on them.

"This is great," Travis said softly. "Really great."

Kim went to stand in front of him. "I want to know what's on your mind."

He turned away for a moment. "With every word I hear about Layton, the more concerned I am. You said he's a bully. He—"

"No," Kim said. "I said he bullied Jecca. That's what parents do. They say it's for our own good. My mother bullies me. Doesn't your father use anything he can to make you do what he wants you to?"

"Incessantly," Travis said, "but that's beside the point. I don't know if I'll get my mother to agree to this, but maybe I can rent these two rooms as a sports shop." And get someone to run them, he thought.

Kim's heart instantly jumped into her throat. That would mean he'd *stay* in Edilean. But then she deflated. "Oh," she said. "You'd fake it. You'd get your mother to lend you some money so you could pretend to open a store so you could be around Mr. Layton."

Travis was perplexed by what she'd said, especially about the money, until he thought of the car Penny had bought for him. To tell Kim the truth would mean telling her about his father. He didn't want to do that and see her eyes change.

"More or less," he said.

They heard a car door slam.

"Stay here," Travis said as he went into the narrow room to look out the front windows. He came back to Kim seconds later. "It's a man. He looks like a block of granite with a head on it."

"That's Mr. Layton," Kim said.

"A man that size with my little mother—" Shaking

his head, he took a step forward, but he stopped and looked back at her. "Let's go," he said as he grabbed her hand and they ran out the back door.

"He's not real," Kim said aloud to herself as she wiped down the kitchen counter. "He's not real and he won't stay," she added to make sure she heard herself.

A few hours before, she and Travis had run out the back of what was to become Layton Hardware and into the woods. "He'll see your car," Kim said, out of breath as she leaned against a tree and looked at him.

Travis was so big and so *male*. She still couldn't believe that the boy she'd thought about for so many years had grown into this great, virile being. His shirt clung to his chest and she could see the muscles. What did he do to be built like that? she wondered. Spend six hours a day in a gym?

When he looked at her, she turned away. She didn't want to see that look of his that said she was a little girl.

"Only if he goes out the back," Travis said, smiling at her. "Wait!"

They listened and heard the sound of gravel crunching.

"He's leaving," Travis said. "Shall we return?"

Kim looked about the woods. What she wanted to do was walk with him deep, deep into the forest and—

"Kim?"

"I'm coming," she said and followed him the few feet to the back of the big brick building. Travis held the car door open for her, then got into the driver's side.

"We go out the way we came in, right?" he said.

"But this time I get to drive."

Travis laughed. "Maybe we'll try the paved road."

"Coward!" she said and laughed with him.

He'd driven her home, walked her to the door, unlocked it, but didn't follow her inside. "I need to see my mother," he said. "We have some things we have to talk about."

"Of course," she said as she went inside. She had no doubt that as soon as he returned he'd tell her he was leaving town, nice to have seen her again.

Her cell rang as soon as she closed the door.

"Miss me?" Dave asked.

So much had happened in the last day and a half that she hardly recognized his voice. "Of course I did," she answered. "What about you?"

"I missed you a lot when you didn't answer any of my messages."

Kim pulled her phone from her ear and pushed a button. She had four voice mails. "I'm sorry," she said. "I've been so busy that I didn't check."

"I know. The Johnson wedding, right?"

Oh no! Kim thought. The rings. Please, please let Carla have remembered her request to do them. She started toward the garage door. "Yes, the wedding," she said. She flipped on the light. There on the workbench were two gold rings, their intricate surfaces perfectly polished. Thank you, she mouthed as she left her workroom. "What about you? Busy?"

"If you'd listened to my messages—not that I'm complaining, of course—you would know that I'm swamped. But I'm trying hard to get away this weekend."

She turned off the light and shut the door. "Oh?"

"Kim!" Dave said. "You sound like you forgot. The weekend?"

"Oh, right," she said. She had completely forgotten. But then, the trip hadn't been her idea, but one concocted by her friends and relatives.

"You made the reservations, didn't you?"

She took a few steps to her desk in the corner of the kitchen and looked at the printout. One double room at the Sweet River B&B in Janes Creek, Maryland, for Friday, Saturday, and Sunday nights, this coming weekend. Carla had said she thought Dave was planning to propose to her while they were there. It was true that he'd pretty much invited himself to go with her.

"I've only known him for six months," Kim had said, frowning. "He asked to go with me because he wants some time off from his catering business."

"Uh-huh," Carla said. "You're forgetting that I know his last girlfriend. He *never* took off a weekend for her, and they were together for over two years."

Kim had said she needed to . . . She couldn't think of an excuse, but had just left the room.

"Kim?" Dave asked. "Are you still there?"

"Yes. It's just that a childhood friend of mine has shown up and is staying in my pool house."

"That must be nice for you," Dave said, "but, Kim, no playdates this weekend. I want you all to myself. For our own playdate."

"Okay," she said, and after a few more murmurings, Dave said he had to go, as thirty pounds of shrimp had just been delivered.

She'd put her phone in her pocket and set about cleaning the kitchen—and looking at the clock. It didn't make any sense that she'd be nervous about how long Travis was spending with his mother, but she was.

An hour went by, then two. At the start of the third hour she was sure she'd never see him again. When he tapped on the back glass door, she jumped, then gave him her best smile.

He didn't look to be in the best mood, which was confirmed when he sat down on a stool by the bar and said, "You have any whiskey?"

She poured him a shot of McTarvit single malt, a drink she kept on hand for her male cousins.

He downed it in one gulp.

"You want to talk about it?" she asked gently. When he looked at her, she saw pain in his eyes.

"You ever have a feeling that the thing you dread most in life is coming true?"

She wanted to say that she feared being a fifty-year-old businesswoman with no private life, and so far, that's where she was heading. "Yes," she said. "Is that what you think is happening to you?"

"My mother seems to think so."

She waited for him to elaborate, but he didn't say any more. When they were kids he'd always said as little as possible, and it had been her job to pull him out of himself. "So what are you planning to do tomorrow?"

He looked at her for a moment and smiled. "Not what I'd like to do, but I'm open to alternate suggestions."

"What does that mean? That you can't do what you want to?"

"Nothing," he said. "What are you going to do tomorrow?"

Kim felt the tension in her chest release. She'd been afraid that now that he'd seen his mother he'd say he was leaving. "Work," she said. "What I do every day. You're the one with open plans. Did your mother tell you to leave town?"

"Actually, just the opposite. Is there anything to eat? I burned off a little energy after the mom-talk."

Kim had been so concerned that he was going to leave that she hadn't noticed that his shirt was torn and dirty, and there was a leaf in his hair. Just like when we were kids, she thought. "What in the world did you do?" she asked as she opened the fridge.

"A little climbing. That's a nice cliff you have at Stirling Point."

"How'd you get so dirty going up that trail?"

"Didn't use the trail," he said as he went to the cabinet and withdrew a couple of plates.

She halted with a bowl in her hands. "But that's a sheer face."

Travis gave a half shrug.

Kim didn't smile. "You had no ropes, and you were alone. That was dangerous. Don't do it again," she said sternly.

"For fear of dismemberment?" he said, and something about the word made him grimace. He put potato salad on the plates. "So what did you do while I was out?"

"Tried to form wax into moonlight."

He looked at her in curiosity. "What does that mean?"

"Last night at the wedding I thought the moonlight was so beautiful I wondered if I could translate it into jewelry."

"What does that have to do with wax?" he asked as he began eating.

Kim sat down next to him and took the plate he'd filled for her. It ran through her mind that the food had been cooked by Dave and she really ought to tell Travis about him, but she didn't.

"I make jewelry by construction, welding on a small scale, or the lost wax process."

"Lost wax? Didn't I see that on TV? Some mysterious method that had disappeared over the centuries."

Kim gave a derogatory snort. "Those idiots! It's called 'lost wax' not because the process was lost but because the wax melts and it flows out. The wax is lost in the making."

"You'll have to show me. Maybe you could—"

"Travis!" Kim said, "I want to know what's going on. You said you needed my help and I'm sure it's not to give you a course in jewelry making."

He hesitated. "I have three weeks," he said.

"Three weeks until what?"

"Until I have to face my father with the news that his wife wants a divorce."

"Then what happens?"

"Legal battles," he said. "Dad will fight and I'll fight him. It will be a war."

"But once it's done, will you be free?" she asked.

"Yes," he said. "I don't know what I'll be free to do, but I will no longer have an obligation to either of my parents. Except morally and ethically, and through affection, and . . ."

"But what are your plans for now? For these three weeks?" Kim asked.

"Maybe I'll harness some moonlight so you can put it in wax and lose it."

Kim smiled. "That would be nice. I need some new ideas. I've always been inspired by organic forms and I've pretty much run through the ones I know."

"What about those flowers you used to tie together?"

"They grow from clover, and they're considered weeds."

"I liked them," he said softly and for a moment their eyes locked. But then Travis turned away and picked up the empty plates and put them in the dishwasher.

"If you're going to be here for three weeks we need to tell people who you are."

"People?" he asked. "Who would that be?"

"Travis, this is a small town. I'm sure they are all talking about how I picked up some dark stranger and took him home with me."

"Has your mom called you yet?" he asked, smiling.

"Last I heard she was in New Zealand so the news will take—I hope—another twenty-four hours to reach her. But my brother is here. And so is my cousin Colin."

"The town doctor and the sheriff. You are a well-connected young woman."

"What's our story going to be? Will you tell people Lucy Cooper is your mother?"

"She asked for a week to break the news to Layton that she's married and has a kid."

"If she says it like that he'll be expecting a nine-year-old."

"How old does your mother think *you* are?" Travis asked.

"Five," Kim answered, and they laughed. "What if

we tell the truth but leave out that the lady who sews, Lucy Cooper, is the same as Mrs. Merritt? You visited as a child, we met, you grew up, and have now returned to Edilean for a three-week holiday."

Travis's eyes lit up. "If I can get Mom to postpone telling Layton, I could get to know him before she tells who I am."

"I think we have a plan," Kim said and they exchanged smiles.

Four

Joe Layton unlocked his office and grimaced at the sight of the papers on his desk. Yet again he wondered what the hell he was doing starting over at his age. The old feeling of resentment welled up in him. He'd thought he was going to spend his life in New Jersey running the hardware store his grandfather had started. He'd never thought of it as wildly ambitious or something that anyone would covet. But then his son, Joey, got married, had kids, and his wife had seen Layton Hardware as a gold mine, something that she'd kill to have.

If she hadn't wanted it all for Joe's grandkids he would have fought her with all he had. But Joe's heart wasn't in the battle. In fact he rather liked that the woman was ambitious for her children.

When his daughter, Jecca, decided to marry some man in little Edilean, Virginia, Joe saw it as a way out of the whole mess. At the time, it had seemed simple. He had money in the bank, so he'd use that to open a store in Virginia. His daughter-in-law, Sheila, had screamed that Joe had "no right" to take what he'd earned over the years, that he should "leave" it for them. She spoke as though Joe's death was imminent. Joe had reached his limit of generosity. He knew his daughter-in-law wanted to buy one of those big houses in something called a "gated community."

"Gated?" he'd said with a smirk when he'd first heard the term.

"Yeah!" Sheila had said with her usual belligerence. Unless she was trying to sell someone something, she let people know she was ready to fight. "With a guard out front. For protection."

"From what?" Joe asked in the same tone. "From all the photographers hounding you? They want a picture of Joe Layton's daughter-in-law?"

Whenever Sheila and he got into it, Joey left the room. He refused to be drawn into their arguments. But Joe knew his son wanted to run his own business. Sometimes Joe wondered if his son had married Sheila because he knew she'd stand up to his father. There were even times when Joe thought maybe his son had put his wife up to taking over the store. Heaven knew Sheila didn't have enough brains to figure out how her father-in-law could leave his own business.

One afternoon when Sheila had been on Joe's case about selling some damned curtains in his hardware store, he received a text message from some man he'd never heard of. The man said he was in love with Jecca, wanted to marry her, and how could he win her?

Love was the last thing Joe was thinking of. Between Sheila shouting, Joey skulking off in the next room, and hearing that some guy wanted to marry his daughter, Joe cracked. On impulse—something he never gave in to—he replied to the man by asking if that little town had a hardware store. If Joe's dear, sweet daughter was going to move there, he might as well go too. He was about to push send when he added that he wanted more photos of the pretty woman, Lucy Cooper, who Jecca had sent pictures of and who she'd raved about.

At the time, Joe had only thought how the woman had been the mother Jecca had never had. Joe's wife, the love of his life, had died when Jecca was little more than a baby. After that he'd been too busy with earning a living and raising two kids to try to find another bride. He'd made do with a few dates now and then, and even one sort of serious affair, but all the women came up short. Jecca said he wanted a clone of her mother, not a real person, and Joe knew she was right.

But then, Jecca almost always was right. Not that he would ever tell her that, but that's how he felt.

When he'd heard she was marrying a doctor, he was sure she was making a big mistake. Jecca came from a solidly blue-collar background. How would she deal with a la-di-dah doctor? But Dr. Tris—as people called him—had turned out to be okay. More than okay. He was mad about Jecca and gave up a lot to be with her.

It was through Tristan that Joe was going to be able to open the hardware store in Edilean. Tris pretty much gave him the old building. That it needed a massive renovation was beside the point.

In New Jersey, over the years Joe had helped out a lot of men. When they were out of work, he'd found them jobs. When they needed supplies for a job, he'd let them have credit. When they didn't get paid, Joe held their notes for as long as it took.

They'd repaid him in loyalty, by going to him instead of the big franchises, but even with that, Joe's business was going down. He would have died before he admitted it, but Sheila's idea of opening a design department might have been a good one.

He also would never have admitted that he had less money than he said he did. He didn't lie exactly, just sort of rounded off the numbers.

He and Jecca had had one of their big fights when Joe said he was bringing in construction guys from New Jersey to do the remodeling. He'd said the reason was because he trusted the men. The truth was that Joe collected on a lot of favors. He called men he hadn't talked to in ten years. With few exceptions, they drove down to little Edilean and put in one, two, or three days of work. Some men had been with Joe so long they sent their grandsons—or daughters, an idea Joe had no problem with. His daughter had always worked for him.

For the most part, they worked at their own expense.

Joe paid some of the younger guys, but his old friends refused any payment.

"See that Skil saw?" one man asked. "You sold that to me seventeen years ago this June. It's been repaired by your two kids more times than I can count. I figure I owe you the money I saved by not buying new every time the old one broke."

Joe had acted as the contractor on the job and had overseen the men who came in at all hours of the day or night. Some guys needed no direction, but some of them were so green he had to show them which end of a nail gun to hold.

Joe's expenses had been for materials. The I beams for the roof and the crane to put them in place had nearly cleaned him out.

There were a dozen times when he thought he'd give it up and go home to fight Sheila for what was his. But that meant fighting his son and his grandchildren. What was Joe to do, go back to New Jersey and throw out Sheila's curtain display? Would he try to take the hardware store back to what it was when his kids were little?

It was an absurd idea, but he would have done it, except for one thing: Lucy.

Lucy, he thought as he stared at the papers on the desk. His whole life was coming to revolve around her.

Jecca had met her when she'd rented an apartment in Mrs. Wingate's house. The three women had hit it off so well that every e-mail Jecca sent him had been about those two women. Later Joe found out that Jecca was covering the fact that she'd met a man. She knew her father would ask a lot of questions, so she'd left him out of her correspondence.

Jecca didn't realize that her letters—and photos—of Lucy, and Lucy, and, well, Lucy, had intrigued her father. Lucy Cooper had come to remind Joe of what he'd missed in life. Now that he'd lost his son, and was about to lose his daughter *and* his business, thoughts of Lucy filled the void.

When Joe drove down to Edilean to see the building Dr. Tris was offering, he'd reminded himself that Miss Cooper knew nothing about him. He couldn't greet her as though he knew her from the hundred or so photos he'd seen of her and all that he'd conned Jecca into telling him. He had to be reserved, cool. Play James Bond, he told himself, not be the New Jersey guy who was so old-fashioned he refused to use an electric drill to put in screws.

By the time Joe got to Edilean, Jecca and Tris had had a big fight. She'd run off to New York and Dr. Tris was frantic that he was going to lose her.

Right away Joe saw that everyone was giving the young man lots of sympathy when what he needed was a kick in the pants. Joe gave it to him. He was astonished at the curse words that came out of the man's mouth! And Joe changed his mind about a doctor being too prissy for his Jecca. Over the course of one long night, Joe gave the boy a piece of his mind and lots of advice about Jecca.

It took the boy three days to get over his hangover—Joe was up by nine the next morning—then he started doing what he'd been told he needed to do to get Jecca back.

After Joe got Tristan straightened out, he found Mrs. Wingate's shop in Edilean and asked to rent a room in her house. She was a tall, elegant lady—not his type at all—who looked him up and down and said she didn't have any vacancies.

When he told her he was Jecca's father, she softened. She had some customers then, so he asked if he could go see the house. She hesitated. "I hear you need some repairs," he said. "Maybe I could look at them."

That had made her give in and she had quickly drawn a map. "I'll call Lucy and tell her you're coming," Mrs. Wingate said, again looking him up and down.

He knew that look. Ladies like her didn't want to meet men like him in the dark.

He'd taken his time driving down Aldredge Road to Mrs. Wingate's big old house. He was seriously afraid of meeting Lucy. He had a feeling that he could like her. But what if he'd misjudged what he'd heard about her and she was as snooty as that Mrs. Wingate? She'd looked at him as though he were a tradesman using the wrong entrance. If Lucy looked at him like that too . . .

"I'll go to a motel," he told himself.

The house was big, and as Jecca had said, it was set in a beautiful garden. The house needed a bit of work here and there, but it was in good shape.

He got his old suitcase out of the truck, took a deep breath, and went inside. The house was so girly inside he felt like he was entering a harem—and he sure as hell wasn't the sheik.

He stood at the foot of the stairs a moment and listened. Just as Jecca had said, he could hear a sewing machine running. It was a sweet sound to a man like him whose whole life had been about tools.

He slowly climbed the stairs and when he got to the top a pretty woman with her arms full of what looked like dresses for baby angels ran smack into him. Hard. She would have bounced off his chest and landed on the floor if Joe hadn't caught her arm and pulled her up. He was pleased to see that she had strength in her legs, good reflexes, and she was very flexible. She came up so fast her soft front was pressed against Joe's wide, hard chest.

For a moment time stood still. They looked into each other's eyes and they *knew*. Just plain *knew*.

"I assume you're Joe and I need your help," Lucy said as she stepped away from him. "Harry's acting up and a table leg is wonky and I need help cutting. Put your suitcase there and follow me."

She bent over to pick up the little white dresses, and

he admired her lithe, firm figure. She stopped in the doorway. "Come on. We haven't got all day." She disappeared into the room.

Joe stood there for a moment and it struck him that he and his son might be more alike than he thought. "I *love* bossy women," he said aloud, then followed Lucy into the sewing room.

Five

Kim was in her shop, showing some rings she'd made last summer to a young married couple. They were in town just for the day and couldn't stop talking about how "quaint" Edilean was. The word always made Kim smile. Her cousin's wife, Tess, said they should put up a sign on the road into town saying WE AIN'T QUAINT.

Kim tried to give her attention back to the couple, who she felt sure were going to buy an inexpensive piece.

"Which one do you like best?" the girl asked Kim as she gazed at the tray containing six rings.

She wanted to tell the truth, that she liked them all, since she had designed everything in the shop. "It all depends on what *you* like, but I think—"

There was the whoosh of the door opening, and she heard Carla draw in her breath. That was her "man sound," as Carla was always on the make.

Kim looked up to see Travis standing in the doorway. He had on a forest green shirt and jeans, and with his dark hair and eyes he looked as virile as any man ever had. He seemed to exude masculinity, as though it were an aura around him.

"I am in love," Carla said under her breath as she moved next to Kim. Since Travis had eyes only for Kim, Carla added, "Please tell me he's one of your relatives so he's available to the rest of us."

Kim didn't answer as she gave her attention back to the couple—but the girl was looking at Travis, and her young husband was frowning. Customers lost, Kim thought.

Travis came forward and stopped close to the young woman. When she smiled at him, he smiled back.

"I think we should go," the young man said, but his wife ignored him.

"I see you in aquamarines," Travis said in a voice Kim had never heard him use before. It was soft and sultry, silky.

"Really?" the girl asked, sounding about fourteen.

"With your eyes, what else could you wear?"

The young woman wasn't especially pretty and her eyes were a nondescript brown. On the other hand, the ring Travis was nodding toward was one of the most expensive in the shop.

"I've never thought of wearing aquamarines before." Turning, she batted her eyelashes at her husband. "What do you think, honey?"

Before the young man could answer, Travis leaned

across the counter so his upper torso was in front of the girl. "But if you want something less expensive, those little amber rings would be all right. They don't sparkle in the same way, but the price is easier on the credit card."

The young woman was looking at Travis's neck, at the way his hair curled along his golden skin. She looked as though she were in a hypnotic trance. When she lifted her hand as though she was going to touch his hair, her husband leaned in front of her. Travis stepped back.

"We'll take that ring and the earrings too," the man said, pointing to the aquamarines.

"Good choice," Travis said as he turned and smiled at Kim.

Part of her wanted to say thanks, but the larger part was disgusted by what he'd just done.

"You ready for lunch?" he asked Kim.

She nodded to Carla to write up the sale, then went behind the far counter with Travis following her. "It's ten A.M.," she said, her voice cool. "It isn't time for lunch."

"Are you angry at me?"

"Of course not!" she snapped as she pulled out a tray of bracelets and began to rearrange them.

Travis picked up one and held it up to the light. "Nice."

The bracelet was the smallest but the most intricate, and the stones were the best quality. It was also the most expensive item she carried. She took it from him. "You seem to have learned something about jewelry."

"I've had a lot of experience." He leaned toward her. "I have things to tell you, so let's go walk somewhere and have lunch."

"Travis, I have a business to run. I can't come and go at your whim."

He looked at Carla, who hadn't stopped watching him, and smiled at her. "She looks capable of taking care of the place."

Kim lowered her voice. "Stop flirting with the women in my shop."

"Then come out with me."

"Where were you this morning?"

His face turned serious. "I got up at five, drove into the wilderness, and went for a run. When I got back you'd left for work. It's nice of you to be concerned."

"I'm not," she said as she locked the glass case. He was smiling at her. "All right! So I was worried. With the way you drive you could have run off a mountain and no one would know you were there."

"Sorry," he said, and he did look contrite. "I'm not used to telling anyone where I'm going or when I'll return." He hesitated. "Or anyone caring. Can you go out with me now? Please?"

His dark eyes were pleading, enticing even. She gave in. She went to Carla and asked if she'd look after the store for a while.

Carla bent down behind a counter and motioned

for Kim to come down too. "Who is he? Where did you find him? Is *he* the emergency you had Sunday? Does Dave know about him?"

Kim stood up.

"Does *he* know about *Dave*?" Carla asked from her squatting position.

Kim rolled her eyes, got her purse out of the back, and left the store with Travis.

Before them was the entire town of Edilean, which meant there were two squares, one with a giant oak tree in the center of it.

"Shall we go sit over there?" Travis asked as he nodded toward the benches under the tree. He'd dropped his flirtatious demeanor and was again the Travis she knew.

There wasn't much traffic in the little town as they crossed the road. Politely, he let her sit down before he sat beside her.

"Your shop is nice. Maybe someday when there are no customers, you'll show me around it."

"But would you enjoy it without customers?"

"I promise, no more flirting with them. Although they did buy some nice pieces. I like your things better than what I've seen in jewelry stores in New York."

She knew he was flattering her, but he looked so worried that she wouldn't forgive him, that she did. She smiled at him. "So what did you want to talk to me about?" When he didn't answer right away, she said, "Last night, how bad was it with your mother?"

For a moment he looked ahead and didn't answer, and she got the idea that something was bothering him. "Remember that I said she could go either way, happy or angry?"

"I know that you said women are unpredictable."

"And you promised me *Star Wars* disks."

"*Star Trek,* and no they're not the same. Which way did your mom go?"

"Angry."

Kim looked at him in sympathy, and she could tell that there was more to what had been said than just for Travis to stay out of it. "Was it very bad?"

He was quiet for a moment. "My father bawls me out all the time. He has a vile temper and he uses it to scare people."

"Are you afraid of him?"

"Not in the least." Travis gave a little half smile. "In fact, I like to do things to set him off."

"But if he fired you . . . ?"

Travis laughed. "Think I don't want him to? Which he knows. Anyway, Dad says things to me that should be demoralizing and I laugh at him. But my sweet little mother . . ." He waved his hand.

"I understand," Kim said. "My mother screams at me until her face is red, but I pay no attention to her. But one time when I was in the fourth grade my father said, 'Kim, I'm disappointed in you.' I got so upset my mother made him apologize to me."

Looking at her, Travis shook his head. "Your family

sounds so normal. I can't imagine my mother 'making' my dad do anything. She crumbles in front of him."

Kim had some ideas about how his mother *should* have stood up to her husband when Travis was a boy, but she didn't think now was the time to say so. "If your mother thinks this is none of your business, why did she call and tell you she wanted a divorce?"

"That's exactly what I asked her. Unfortunately, it was after I had made some rather unfortunate remarks about the man she wants to marry."

"You didn't!"

"I'm afraid I did. Between seeing all the equipment he'd bought for that new shop, and the sheer size of him, I jumped to some conclusions. And maybe I told her too much of what I thought."

"I told you Joe Layton was a good guy."

Travis picked up her hand and kissed the back of it. "So you did. I wish I'd listened to you."

Kim was looking at him with wide eyes. He was holding her hand, massaging it actually, as he stared ahead. He didn't seem to be aware of what he was doing. "What exactly did she say?"

"She told me to stay out of it. She said she'd get herself a lawyer and that she'd fight Dad on her own." He took a breath. "And she said I was free to stop working for him because she no longer needed my protection."

"Oh," Kim said as she looked at his profile. He was frowning. "Is that what you're going to do?"

"Certainly not!" he said as he put her hand back on her lap.

In front of them was a mother with two young toddlers, a boy and a girl, probably twins. Kim didn't know the family. The children had balloons on long strings that they were looking at in fascination.

When Travis said nothing more, she looked at him. "What's your plan?"

"I haven't made one yet."

A howl made Kim look at the children. The little boy's balloon had escaped his hold and was floating up into the tree.

Seconds later, Travis stood up and looked up into the tree, as though surveying it. To Kim's astonishment, he grabbed a branch and swung up. Standing on a limb, he looked down at her. "I talked to Mom this morning and told her I wanted to meet this guy, so she's given me a week before she—" He walked out on the branch, then swung up on a higher one. "Before she tells him that I'm here," he said down to her.

By now the little boy had stopped yelling as he watched the man in the tree, and a couple of teenagers were also looking up at him.

Kim was pretty much speechless. She stood up.

"You think you could help me arrange a meeting with Mr. . . ." He glanced at the people near her. He didn't want to say the man's name in public. "With him?" He was now quite high up, on his stomach, and easing out onto a branch that didn't look large enough to hold his weight.

Kim held her breath as she nodded yes to his question.

"And I have to decide about the . . ." He was inching his way out on a very fragile-looking branch, his left arm extended toward the yellow balloon.

Kim put her hand up, her knuckles in her mouth.

"Who the hell is that?" came a voice in her ear.

Turning, she looked at the wide, solid chest of her cousin Colin, Edilean's sheriff.

Kim looked back up at Travis in the tree. She couldn't get any words out.

Colin stood by her and watched as Travis moved forward until he reached the balloon string and grabbed it.

"Vacation." Travis looked back down at Kim. "Good morning, sheriff," he said just before the branch broke.

A girl screamed, and everyone drew in their breaths.

On his way down, Travis grabbed a branch with his right hand while holding onto the balloon with his left. He twisted the string around his fingers, then threw his legs over the branch. He pulled himself up, straddled the limb, stood up, and walked his way back to the core of the tree and went down.

He landed on two feet, walked a few steps to give the balloon back to the little boy, and dusted himself off as he went back to Kim. "What do you think?"

She just stared at him.

Colin said, "He's asking what you think he should do on his vacation in Edilean." He seemed highly amused by what he'd just seen.

"Travis!" Kim said at last.

Colin snorted. "You're in for it." When Kim started to speak again, he interrupted her. "You do that kind of thing often?"

"I used to," Travis said. "I worked in L.A. as a stunt-man for a couple of years."

Colin was looking him up and down. "Still keep in shape?"

"I try to. What do you have in mind?"

"Sometimes tourists get stuck in situations in the preserve and we have to get them out. I'm the closest, so I usually get there first. Sometimes I need help."

Travis smiled as he remembered the way Kim had gushed about this man and her brother being super-heroes in rescuing people. There was no way Travis was going to turn down the opportunity to help out— and maybe to impress Kim. "Do you have your cell phone with you? I'll put my number in it."

Colin handed him his cell, Travis called himself, then put his name by the number. He returned the phone. "Any time, night or day, I'd be glad to help. I've had some experience with ropes and climbing, but I've never rescued anybody. Not for real anyway."

Colin smiled. "Welcome to Edilean." He looked at Kim. "Glad to see you got a *useful* one this time," he murmured, then started toward his office.

"Say hi to Gemma for me," Kim called after him before looking back at Travis.

"I have three weeks' vacation." He still seemed to be waiting for an answer.

"My son wants to say thank you," the mother said, and Travis knelt to the little boy.

"Thank you," the child said, and hugged Travis. The little girl, not to be left out, hugged him too.

The mother smiled at Travis, her eyes lingering on him a bit too long. "Maybe we could have you over for dinner some night."

Travis's dark eyes went to that smoldering look again. "That would be—"

"He's busy," Kim said and her look told the woman to go away.

Still smiling, she took her children and left.

"Can you arrange a meeting?" he asked.

"Travis," Kim said, "what you just did was very scary. You could have been seriously hurt. You could have—"

Bending, he kissed her cheek. "I find that having someone worry about me feels good."

"Does that mean you're going to pull more stunts like that one? It doesn't make sense to risk your life for a balloon."

"At no time was my life in jeopardy and I couldn't care less about the balloon. It was the look in the eyes of that little boy that made it all worth it."

Kim had no reply to that, as he was right.

"So what about a meeting with the man my mother wants to marry?"

"This is Edilean. You don't need an appointment. Mr. Layton's probably at his store right now, so we can just go over there and you can talk to him."

"What excuse will we give him for showing up?"

"To say hello," Kim said, frustrated and somewhat annoyed at his formality—and the way he had flirted with the pretty young mother. "I'll ask how Jecca is or something. Uh-oh."

"What is it?" he asked.

"Here comes my brother. I bet Colin called him. The snitch! Now you'll be grilled within an inch of your life. This won't be easy."

Travis couldn't help smiling at her words. In courtrooms all across the U.S. and in a couple of foreign countries he'd been interrogated by some of the most brilliant lawyers in the world. He had no doubt he could hold his own against Kim's physician brother.

But when Travis saw the man walking toward them, he turned pale. He'd seen Reede Aldredge before, and not under the best of circumstances.

Travis and his mechanic had been in a car race in Morocco. As they came around a corner outside a remote village, they saw a man leading a heavily laden donkey right across their path.

Travis had done well in not hitting the man. He'd

turned his car so hard that it had spun in a circle. It had been difficult to keep it under control and not turn over, but he'd done it.

Unfortunately, in the near crash, the boxes on the donkey had hit the ground. When Travis got his car heading back in the right direction, he saw that there was liquid seeping out of the boxes and the man was shaking his fist at them. His furious face was embedded in Travis's memory.

As they drove away, he'd told his mechanic to call Penny to find out who the man was and to replace whatever had been lost. Days later she'd mentioned that the man was an American doctor and that she'd sent him replacement supplies. And she'd also made a donation to his clinic. She'd not told Travis the doctor's name and he hadn't asked for one.

That man, the doctor who'd yelled obscenities at him in Morocco, was now walking toward him.

"Can I tell him the truth about you?" Kim whispered.

For a moment he thought she meant about the race, but she was talking about their childhood. "Sure," he said, "just don't say that Lucy Cooper is my mother."

"Wouldn't dream of it," she said under her breath as she smiled at her brother.

"Kimberly," Reede said rather sternly. "I hear that you've been causing some commotion this morning."

"Travis rescued a kid's balloon," she said as she

looked up at him, but he had his hand up by his face. "This is—"

"Not *the* Travis," Reede said. "Not the boy you've fantasized about since you were a kid?"

"Reede!" Kim said as she felt her face turning red. "I never did any such thing!"

"It's good to meet you at last," Reede said, extending his hand to shake.

Travis shook it, but he kept his left hand by his eyes.

"I've seen you somewhere," Reede said. "I've done a lot of traveling. You weren't ever a patient of mine, were you?"

"No," Travis said as he turned his head away.

Kim looked from one man to the other. Reede was staring intently as he tried to remember where he'd last seen Travis. And Travis was acting like some trapped animal that desperately wanted to hide in its burrow. "We have to go," she said. "Travis has to go see Mr. Layton about opening a sporting goods store."

"This area needs one," Reede said. "What do you plan to carry?"

"Things for sports," Kim said quickly, wanting to get away from her brother as soon as possible. "Is that one of your nurses waving at you?"

"Yeah," Reede said. "I left two exam rooms and the waiting room full. Let's get together for dinner." He started to walk away but turned back to Travis. "I look forward to hearing about what you've been doing since you were first in Edilean."

As soon as she was alone with Travis she said, "What was that all about?"

"I, uh, I do believe I may have seen your brother somewhere."

When it didn't seem as though he was going to say anything else, she turned and started walking toward her shop.

Travis caught up with her. "What are you doing?"

"If you aren't going to be honest with me I might as well go back to work. I have a new necklace I'm designing right now. I'd planned to use Australian opals in it, but maybe I should get more aquamarines since they go so well with brown eyes."

"All right," he said. "How about if we go somewhere and talk? Maybe you can help me figure out what to do about my mother."

An hour later they were sitting at a picnic table in the preserve. They'd stopped at the grocery and bought sandwiches, salads, and drinks, but it was still too early to eat.

"This is beautiful," Travis said as he looked out over the lake. "You live in a nice place."

"I like it," Kim said. It was so peaceful there that she could barely remember what had made her so angry. Something about Reede. But then lately everything about her brother seemed to make her angry. He didn't want to be a doctor in his little hometown and he complained often—and she was tired of hearing about it.

"I've never actually met your brother before but I nearly killed him," Travis said, then briefly told the story, including that he'd replenished Reede's supplies.

"Reede never mentioned the incident in his letters," Kim said. She could imagine how angry her brother would have been. "Reede thinks everyone should forgo frivolities such as car races and dedicate himself to worthy causes."

Travis was watching her. "Doesn't know how to have fun, does he?" he asked softly.

"Hazards of growing up," she said. "What *have* you done since I met you?"

"Lived by what you taught me," he said, smiling.

Kim didn't smile back. She was noticing that he evaded her questions, skirted around them. Today she sensed that something was bothering him. He'd been quite flippant about what had gone on between him and his mother, but she was beginning to think there was a great deal more to it than he'd told her. "Tell me more about your talk with your mother. What exactly did she say?"

Travis turned away but not before Kim saw his dark brows furrow into a deep frown. It looked like whatever had been said between him and his mother was too unpleasant for him to talk about.

When he looked back at her he was smiling. "She assured me that Joe Layton was a good man and that he loves her. He doesn't know my mother has any money and she doesn't know how he financed the remodeling of that old building."

Kim could tell that he was concealing something from her, and she had an idea that he wasn't going to tell her what it was. All right, she thought, if he could keep secrets, so can I. "When do you want to visit Mr. Layton?"

Travis could tell that Kim had closed down on him and he knew why. The truth was that he'd love to tell her about his talk with his mother, but he couldn't because the worst of it had been about Kim.

Last night he'd met his mother in the garden of Mrs. Wingate's house, and after several minutes of hugging and tears of joy at seeing each other again, Travis had taken on the task of trying to find out about Joe Layton. But from his first word, she had been different from the way he remembered her. She wasn't the quiet, browbeaten little woman he'd grown up with. She thanked Travis for coming to her rescue but she'd made it clear that this was a battle she needed to fight for herself.

Travis had used his best lawyer voice to point out the error of her thinking. He thought he'd made his side clear until she told him he was sounding like his father. That had so completely taken the air out of him that he'd slumped in the chair and stared at her.

In the next second she'd asked him what he was doing with Kim and why hadn't Travis told her the full truth about his father. "Does Kim even know your last name?"

Her words made them settle back into the roles they'd always played, that of mother and son.

"*I just . . . I'd like a woman to care about me, not be dazzled by the Maxwell name,*" Travis said. "*And you know what, Mom? I'd like to know if I can handle being normal. My isolated childhood didn't exactly prepare me for an ordinary adult life.*"

Lucy winced, but Travis kept on. "*And since then the women—*"

"*Please don't elaborate.*"

"*I didn't plan to,*" he said. "*It's just that I've not had the possibility of . . . well, love.*"

"*So what if you do make Kim fall in love with you?*" *Lucy asked.* "*What then?*"

"*What if I fall for her?*" *He was teasing, trying to lighten the mood.*

But Lucy was serious. "*Travis, you have been in love with that girl since you were twelve years old. What I want to know is what happens if she falls for you. Will you look into her eyes, say, 'Wait for me,' then go skiing down some mountain? Will you expect her to be like me and spend every day in fear that I'll receive a call saying you've been paralyzed or dismembered or killed? Will you expect her to share your vagabond life and never settle anywhere?*"

"*I don't know!*" *Travis said in frustration.* "*My life—*"

"*Hasn't been normal,*" *Lucy said.* "*I know that better than anyone.*"

"I went to work for my father to protect—"

"You cannot put that burden onto me," Lucy said loudly. "Travis, you have thrived working for Randall. The excitement, the money, the . . . the power. You've blossomed in it."

Travis fell back against the chair hard. "Are you saying that I'm becoming my father?" he asked softly.

"No, of course not. But I'm afraid . . ."

"Of what?"

"That you could be."

He took his time before speaking. "That's my worry too," he said at last. "Sometimes I see things in myself that I don't like. Whenever I please him I displease myself—and I worry that my displeasure is as strong as his pleasure." He looked at her. "But I'm not sure how to get away from the part of him that's inside me."

Lucy took her son's hand in hers. "Spend time with Kim. Forget about Joe and me. We're fine. He's not after my money and wouldn't be if he knew I had any. He loves me."

"You're sure of that?"

"Absolutely and positively."

"But didn't you once love Dad?"

"I was a girl from a very sheltered upbringing and your father went after me just as he does those companies he buys."

"I'd like to go after Kim like that," he said under his breath.

"Well, don't!" Lucy half shouted. "Don't do it to her!

Don't use the Maxwell charm and money and all you've learned with those awful women you date on Kim. Don't dazzle her. Don't fly her off to Paris to wine and dine her so she's swooning over you. She doesn't deserve treatment like that."

"Whose side are you on?"

"Yours!" she said, then made herself calm down. "Travis, I love you much more than life. I'd die for you, but I want what's real for you. Don't just take this girl to bed and show her what you learned from some ambitious starlet. Find out about her. See if you really do love her. Or is it just gratitude that she showed you how to ride a bicycle? Get to know her now. And let her know you—the real you. Not the slick, smooth lawyer who can outtalk anyone. Let her see that boy who was awed by a little girl who put a string of beads around his neck."

"I'm not sure I know how to do that."

He looked at Kim. She was staring out at the lake, and he didn't know that he'd ever seen anyone as pretty—or more desirable. If she were any other girl he'd be making a pass at her and using anything he could to get her into bed. But then, as his mother had said, he'd leave her. It seemed that all his life he'd had to rush off to somewhere else. If it wasn't to some business meeting for his father, it was to some race or to a climb, or to do some other thing that could possibly, as his mother said, dismember him.

"I guess we should go," Kim said into the silence, startling Travis back into the present.

He didn't move. "I don't mean to be so secretive."

"Then tell me what's bothering you!" she said. "Are you concealing some horrible thing you've done? You couldn't be a wanted criminal, because by now I'm sure Colin has looked you up. If you have a record he knows about it and he would have warned me."

Since neither the sheriff—nor Kim—knew Travis's real last name, nothing would be found, he thought. "No criminal record," he said, and smiled at her. "The truth is that I'm not proud of some of the things I've done in my life."

"Does that mean being a stuntman or running down doctors in Morocco?"

He laughed. "Morocco for sure. But why the hell was your brother leading a donkey across an area that had been marked off for a car race?"

"My guess is that Reede thought everyone should stop for him. His work is important; yours is not."

"I have to agree with him on that. Kim . . . ?"

"Yes?"

"I have some big decisions to make in my life right now."

"About what?"

"What I'm going to do with the rest of it. In three weeks I'm going to stop working for my father."

"What do you do for him now?"

"Put people out of work," Travis said.

Kim looked at him sharply.

"It's not as bad as I'm making it sound. The businesses were going under and all the employees were going to be fired. My father buys the company and fires a mere two-thirds of them." He looked out at the lake. "I'm tired of it and I need some changes. You have any openings in your jewelry store? I think I could sell things."

"By flirting with the customers? No thanks. What do you want my help with?"

He wanted to say, To run away with me, but his mother's words rang in his head. *Get to know her now. And let her know you—the real you.* "To be my friend," he said. "We were friends as children, so maybe we can be again."

"Right," Kim said as she looked back at the lake. Friends. Story of her life, it seemed. Her last two boyfriends had broken off with her because she was more successful than they were. Whenever Kim got a new contract from a company that wanted to sell her jewelry, there would be a fight. She'd calculated that it took just three major arguments to end a relationship. She was sure that the only reason she and Dave had lasted for six whole months was because she hadn't told him that Neiman Marcus wanted a trial run of a display of her jewelry.

"Now you're the one being silent."

"I need a friend too," she said. "In the last couple of years every friend I have has married and most of them are pregnant."

"Why aren't you?" he asked solemnly.

She knew that if she told him the truth it would sound like self-pity and she couldn't bear that. "Because my doctor brother refuses to tell me how a woman *gets* pregnant. I don't think it's from swallowing a watermelon seed, which is what he told me when I was nine. After he said that I refused to eat anything with big seeds in it for two years. My mother threatened to force-feed me. But then I found out that French kissing—which I thought meant kissing in France—made a person pregnant."

Travis was smiling. "And who told you the truth?"

"I've held on to the French idea, since I've never been there and never been pregnant."

"How about if you and I—" He cut himself off as he'd been about to suggest that they fly to Paris for a few days.

"If we what?"

"Eat our sandwiches?"

She knew that yet again he'd held back from telling her something. She handed him a sandwich and began unwrapping hers. It seemed that Travis's idea of friendship was a lot different from hers.

Six

❧

When Joe Layton saw Kim and the young man get out of the car, he knew two things. One, the man was related to Lucy, and two, he was in love with Kim. The first one made him frown and the second one made him smile.

Since Joe had met Lucy he'd tried to get her to tell him about her past, but she would say nothing. If he were a different kind of man he would have enjoyed her attempts to redirect his inquiries. But he didn't like her discomfort, so he was careful not to ask.

But it was easy to see that this young man was connected to Lucy. Her son? he wondered. They had the same eyes, only his were darker. The way his hair curled around his neck was just like hers, and the way he held his hand as he closed the car door was pure Lucy.

So she had a son, he thought. The real question was, Who was the father?

As for the second observation, Joe had felt bad for Kim as all her friends got married and moved on to a different life. She and Jecca had kept in close touch over the years, and Joe had heard how, one by one, all Kim's friends and cousins got married. Even Jecca had left. She'd gone to Edilean to visit Kim but had ended up spending all her time with Dr. Tris.

Now, it was good to see some man in love with Kim. She deserved all the best life had to offer.

Joe cleared his throat and put his shoulders back. It wouldn't do to let his sentimentality show. He opened the front door. "You here for the job?"

"What job?" Kim asked as she kissed Joe's cheek. She'd known him for many years, had spent several nights at his house in New Jersey. One night when she was in college he'd stayed up listening to Kim cry over what some fraternity guy had done to her.

"To help me get this place set up. I had to fire the first one I hired."

Travis was looking hard at the man. He was short and solidly built, and he seemed to be scowling.

"This is my friend Travis"—she hesitated— "Merritt, and I was telling him about your new store. Is that big room you were going to use for Jecca still empty?"

Joe was looking at Travis. His father must be tall, he thought, as the boy was, but his resemblance to Lucy was uncanny. It was a moment before Joe realized that Travis was holding out his hand to shake. Joe took it and kept looking in the boy's eyes. When Travis pulled his hand away, Joe felt the calluses. "You in construction?"

"No," Travis said. "Just a misspent life."

"He was a Hollywood stuntman," Kim said.

"That right? What tricks can you do?"

"Get shot, mostly," Travis said. "I'm the guy in the police uniform who gets killed by the bad guy. I've been killed four times in the same movie. Low budget."

"You'd think that as pretty as you are that you'd be the star of the picture," Joe said.

Travis laughed. "I agree. I even suggested that to a director, so he gave me a screen test. The verdict was that I have no acting talent at all."

"Why would that stop you from being a star?" Joe asked, his face serious.

"Beats me," Travis said. "But anyway, I never liked sitting around in a trailer doing nothing. What's this job you need done?"

"Manager," Joe said. "I need someone to look after the place so I have time to spend with my girls."

"Girls?" Travis asked and his smile disappeared.

"Maybe we could—" Kim began.

"My daughter and my intended," Joe said. "You think you could handle the job? You need to know a lot about tools."

"Travis knows about . . ." Kim began but hesitated. "Balloons," she said at last.

Both men looked at her.

"You the guy that got that kid's balloon out of the tree?"

"Yes," Travis said, "but I didn't think it would be known all over town so fast."

"The sheriff stopped by." Joe nodded toward the doorway to the other side of the building. "You want to see Jecca's studio?"

"Yes, we would," Kim said, and they followed Joe.

"*What do you* think?" Kim asked Travis. They were in a booth in a little restaurant off the road into Williamsburg, eating dinner.

"About what?" he asked as he toyed with his fork.

"Opening a sporting goods store?"

Travis took his time answering. "I liked him."

"Mr. Layton? Of course. He's a nice man. And he was certainly taken with *you*. I couldn't believe he was asking your opinion about his finances."

"Me neither. You don't think he knows . . ."

"That you're Lucy's son? How could he?"

"I've been told that I look like my mother, so maybe he recognized me."

"Since I've never seen your mother, at least not clearly anyway, I wouldn't know." Kim looked at him, at his dark brows like gull wings over his eyes, at his jawline with its dark whiskers just under the skin. She couldn't imagine that anyone as masculine-looking as he was could resemble any female.

What Travis saw in her eyes made him want to reach across the table and drag her to him. She had a pretty mouth that he'd very much like to kiss. When his mother's words rang in his head, he looked away. He didn't know where his life was going and it wasn't fair of him to pull Kim in with him.

Kim had seen the glow in his eyes, had felt the spark between them—but then he'd turned away. For some reason she didn't understand, he wasn't allowing the attraction between them. The normal, sexual pull that men and women felt for each other was being stomped down by him.

So be it, she thought. Friends is what he'd said and friends is what they were going to be. But she couldn't help the anger that rose in her. Was there someone else in his life? Had he decided that a small town girl wasn't good enough for him? Or was it that he just couldn't see her as anything but a child?

Whatever it was, she didn't like it one little bit.

"You mind if I make a phone call?" she asked in the sweetest voice she could muster. It looked like in her case, the old adage about a woman scorned was true.

"No, go ahead. You want some privacy?"

"No, it'll just take a moment. I'm sure he's working."

"He?"

"Dave, my boyfriend."

Travis nearly choked on the bite he'd just taken. "Boyfriend?"

Kim started to speak, but then Dave answered.

"Hey, babe, what's up?" he asked.

Kim held the phone away from her ear so Dave's voice could be heard. "I was wondering if you had any ideas about what to pack for this weekend. Is this B&B formal? Should I take a long dress?"

"I don't know," Dave said. "You found the place, but I can tell you that I'm not taking my tux. I have to wear it too often at work. Hey! Why don't we solve the dilemma by having dinner in bed every night?"

Kim was smiling as she looked at Travis. His eyes were wide, as though he couldn't believe what he was hearing. "I thought breakfast in bed was more usual." Her voice was low, sexy—the same one she'd heard Travis use with women. Women other than her.

"How about if we compromise and do them both in bed?" Dave's voice was low.

"What in the world would we do for lunch?" she asked innocently.

"You're the creative one, so I'll let you figure that out. I gotta go. We're loading the truck for a dinner party. See you Friday at two. And Kim?"

"Yes?"

"Don't pack *anything* to wear at night."

Laughing, she hung up, put her phone away, then took a long sip of her drink.

Travis was staring at her. He hadn't moved a muscle

since she opened her phone. "Boyfriend?" he said at last, his voice close to a whisper.

"Yes. What's wrong? Don't you like your sandwich? We could get something else. You want me to call the waitress?"

"The food is fine. Since when do you have a boyfriend?"

"Dave and I have been together for six months now." She smiled at him. "I think it's serious."

"Serious as in how?"

She gave a one-shouldered shrug. "The usual. Why are you looking at me like that?"

"I'm just surprised is all. I didn't realize there was someone . . . important in your life."

"Please tell me that you didn't assume that since I live in a small town that I was . . . What? Waiting for some big city man to come and rescue me? Not quite."

"Actually," he said, "I thought maybe the wedding going on when I arrived was yours."

If Kim had had any doubts that their relationship was only friendship, it vanished with that statement. He didn't seem bothered that he'd thought she was about to get married. But why should he? They hardly knew each other, and he'd made it clear that in three weeks he was leaving. "So what about you? Anyone special in your life?"

"I don't know . . ." he said. It hadn't occurred to him that Kim had a boyfriend, certainly not one that she called "serious."

"You don't know if there's a woman in your life? If there is and you two need wedding rings, I can design and make them for you. Are you ready to go?"

"Sure," Travis said, but he hadn't recovered from the blow. He didn't know what he'd imagined, but Kim talking of meals in bed with another man hadn't been part of it.

He put money on the table and walked out of the diner behind Kim. A pretty young woman smiled at him, but Travis paid no attention to her.

Kim got behind the wheel of her car. "I have work to do at home," she said, her voice cool.

"Have I made you angry?"

"Of course not. What would I be angry about?" She wanted to yell at him. He flirted with other women but looked at her as though she were his sister—or an eight-year-old girl.

She took a deep breath and when she let it out, she released her anger. It wasn't fair of her to be angry because he wasn't attracted to her. How many times had men come on to her but she'd shot them down? At least once a week some man came into her shop and let her know that he was available. Sometimes his wife would be standing three feet away.

You really can't control sexual attraction, she thought. You either felt it or you didn't. She'd thought she felt it coming from Travis, but it looked like she was wrong. He'd been very clear that he wanted and needed friendship, so that's what she was going to give him.

"How serious are you with this man?"

Think of him as a girlfriend, Kim thought. Don't look at him, don't get pulled in by the smoldering good looks of him. He's a buddy, a friend, and nothing else.

"I think it may be permanent," she said. "Carla giggles every time she mentions this weekend, and one of my best rings is missing from the case. A big sapphire. I can't find the receipt and when I asked her about it she said . . . I don't remember her excuse, but the register receipt isn't there."

"You don't seem worried that this Carla could have stolen it. I guess that means you think this guy is going to give you one of your own rings. As an engagement ring?"

"Maybe," Kim said.

"What was it about a B&B?"

"My cousin Luke's wife, Jocelyn, has been doing the genealogy of the seven founding families of Edilean, but there's a gap in the Aldredge family. A female ancestor of mine went to a place called Janes Creek, Maryland, in the 1890s and came back pregnant. Joce wants to try to find who the father was. But she has two little kids, so she asked me to go up there and see what I could find out."

"And this man is going with you?"

"Yes," Kim said. "Dave owns a catering company and weekends are his busiest time. He's had to pay his employees a lot to cover for him this coming weekend."

"That he's taking off and that a ring and its sales receipt are missing is what makes you think he's going to . . . What? Ask you to marry him?"

Kim could again feel anger rising in her, but she stamped it down. She pulled into her driveway, turned off the engine, and looked at him. "There is also the fact that Dave is mad about me. We spend every day he's off work together. We call each other. We talk about our future together."

"Future? What does that mean?"

"Travis, I really don't like this inquisition. I agreed to help you with your mother and I will, but I'd just as soon keep my private life to myself." She got out and went into the house.

Travis stayed in the car, too stunned to move. Kim was about to accept a marriage proposal from some man who ran a catering company! How could he have ever been so wrong about a person? He'd thought that she was, well, interested in *him*!

He flipped open his phone and punched the button to reach Penny. As soon as she answered he said, "I need to know about a man named Dave, don't know his last name. Lives in a city around Edilean, owns a food catering company. He's registered for this weekend at a B&B in Janes Creek, Maryland. I want to know everything about him, and I mean *everything*."

"Should I cancel the B&B?" Penny asked.

"Yes! No. Book me a connecting room. And fill up

all the other rooms. In fact, fill up all the rooms in the entire town."

"Any choice of guests? Leslie has been calling."

For a moment Travis thought of inviting her. He didn't know whether he was angry at Kim or jealous or . . . well, hurt. Whatever he was feeling, he didn't think Leslie's presence would help.

"She'd probably love Miss Aldredge's jewelry store," Penny said into the silence. When Travis didn't reply, she said, "Life isn't so easy without the Maxwell name, is it?"

Her words came too close to home for Travis's comfort. "Just put some people in the rooms. Your relatives." It occurred to him that he knew nothing about Penny's personal life. "Do you . . . ?"

"Have relatives?" she filled in for him. "Yes I do. Rather a lot of them, actually. My son is your age. I'll e-mail you what I have," she added and for the first time ever, she hung up first.

Travis closed his phone and stared at it for a moment. This was a day for surprises! Kim was about to accept a marriage proposal and his faithful right-hand man, Penny, had a son Travis's age.

At the moment he thought of returning to New York and going back to destroying people's lives. It played less havoc with his emotions.

He got out of Kim's car and wasn't sure what to do. Go inside and talk to her? About what? Ask her to give up her boyfriend in case she and Travis felt something for each other and maybe someday he'd sort out his life and they might possibly get together? Not exactly something any female would accept. Certainly not one like Kim who'd known what she wanted since she was a kid. She was making jewelry at eight and at twenty-six she was still doing it.

"And I haven't decided—" he said aloud, but he didn't want to finish that statement. He saw that Kim had turned the lights on in her garage, which meant that she was working. He didn't like to be disturbed when he was working, so maybe she didn't either. Besides, he didn't know what to say to her.

He walked around the house to get to the guest-house and went to bed.

Seven

Travis had a sleepless night, and when he awoke the next morning, Kim had already gone to work. His car, the old BMW Penny had bought for him, was in the driveway. He wanted to see Kim. But if he did see her, he didn't know what he'd say. His system was still shocked at the news that she had a boyfriend. A "serious" boyfriend.

Without thinking what he was doing, Travis got into his car and started driving. His first impulse was to do something physical. That's what he did when his father demanded too much of him. Climb, run, drive, ski, surf, skate. It didn't matter what he did as long as it left him too tired to think.

But he didn't drive into the preserve, didn't seek out a lake or a cliff. Instead, he found himself pulling into the parking lot of Joe Layton's hardware store.

He sat in the car, looking at the brick front and wondering what the hell he was doing there. When

someone opened the car door, he wasn't surprised to
see Joe.

"You're just in time. I need to check inventory. You
open the boxes, pull the stuff out, and I'll mark it off
on the papers."

"I need to . . ." Travis couldn't think of anyplace he
needed to be. "Sure. But I warn you that I don't know
a saw from a hammer."

"I do, so we'll be fine." Joe held the door open while
Travis got his long body out. "Yesterday you looked
happy. Now you look like the world came crashing
down on you. Kim throw you out?"

Travis wasn't used to revealing his thoughts and
certainly not his feelings to people, and he had no
intention of starting. But maybe unloading boxes of
tools would help him release some energy.

"*So she dumps* it on me that she's got a boyfriend,"
Travis said. It was four hours later and he was covered
in sweat, grime, and those plastic foam packing beans
that someone was going to hell for inventing. Travis
had told Joe the story of how he and Kim had met as
children, and one thing had led to another until he
was telling much more than he'd intended to.

While he talked he had single-handedly unloaded
what seemed to be hundreds of cartons and crates of

tools and supplies. That there were no shelves to put them on didn't seem to bother Joe Layton in the least. But then he just sat in a big leather chair with a clipboard and checked off whatever Travis opened. Joe had let his disgust be known when Travis didn't know a Phillips screwdriver from a flat head.

"My daughter knows—" Joe started again. According to him, his daughter could run the world.

"Yeah, well I know how to hire a mechanic to keep the machines running," Travis had at last snapped. That seemed to release something inside him and in the next minute he was talking about Kim.

"I don't get it," he said as he pulled some electrical tool out of a box. It looked like a plastic wombat.

"Router," Joe said. "Look in there for the bits."

Travis bent over into the box, foam beans sticking in his hair and wiggling their way down into his T-shirt. He couldn't help thinking of the Frankenstein movie. "It's alive! It's alive!"

"What don't you get?" Joe asked.

"I came to this town to see Kim. We were great together as kids. I mean, she was just a little girl and I was close to puberty, but still . . . I helped her with her jewelry. I wonder if she'd have that shop of hers now if I hadn't—"

"Liar!" Joe said loudly.

Travis pulled his head out of the carton. Packing beans stuck out all over him. "I beg your pardon."

"You came here to see your mother about me."

Travis's mouth opened, but no words came out as he stared at Joe.

"Don't look so surprised. You look like my Lucy, talk like her. Did you two think I was so stupid that I wouldn't see the resemblance?"

"I . . . We . . ."

"You want to check me out," Joe said. "It's what a good son would do. Lucy is a prize worth protecting. But I warn you, boy, if you tell her that I know who you are I'll show you what a chain saw can do."

Travis blinked a few times. His mother had made him swear not to tell Joe about her, and now Joe wanted Travis not to tell her that he knew.

"You find those bits yet?" Joe growled.

"No . . ." Travis said softly, still staring.

"Then get busy!" Joe said. "You expect *me* to look for them?"

Travis bent back into the carton, found two more boxes, and pulled them out. When he came up, he looked at Joe in speculation. Where did they go from here? he wondered.

Joe marked off the items Travis held up. "So you came here to see if your mom had gone crazy when she said she wanted to marry some nobody that owned a hardware store."

Since that was pretty much the truth, Travis gave a curt nod.

"And you thought you might as well see Kim, since you were in the same town."

"I saw Kim first," Travis said, feeling defensive as he cut open another carton.

"Only because the wedding was going on and you got sidetracked."

"I told you too much," Travis muttered.

"What was that?" Joe asked.

Travis turned to him. "I told you too much. You know too much. You *see* too much."

Joe chuckled. "That's because I raised two kids on my own. The things I went through with my daughter! Joey was no problem. When he started staying in the bathroom too long I handed him some condoms. I didn't have to tell him anything. But Jecca! She fought me every inch of the way. So who's your dad?"

Travis caught himself before he blurted out the answer. Could he trust this man he barely knew? But there was something about Joe that engendered trust. The expression "salt of the earth" had been created just for him.

"Randall Maxwell," Travis said.

For a second, Joe looked shocked, scared, impressed, horrified. But then he recovered himself. "That explains everything," he said. "So you came here to see if the New Jersey guy was after your mom's money."

"More or less. She's still married to him." Travis looked hard into Joe's eyes. "The divorce is going to be brutal. You think you can handle that?"

"If I get Lucy all to myself in the end, yeah, I can handle that."

Travis didn't try to contain his smile. "I'm a lawyer and—"

"And here I was beginning to actually *like* you."

Travis groaned. "Don't start on me and no lawyer jokes. I've heard them all. How did we go from my problems to yours?"

"It started with you lying to me. You came to see your mother, not Kim. You left that girl alone for all those years, then you came back here for something else, accidently saw the girl you left behind, and now you're whining because she has a boyfriend she might marry. What did you expect? That she would stay a virgin and wait for you? You got any brothers or sisters?"

"No to every question. What is this thing? The egg of some extinct species?"

"Orbital sander. You didn't expect Kim to wait for you?"

"No I didn't, but then I did know—" He bent back into the carton to pull out sandpaper disks.

"Did know what?"

"A bit about her life."

"You've been stalking her?" Joe asked, his voice full of horror.

Travis refused to answer that. It would take too much explaining and he didn't want to have to defend himself. "When are you going to get shelves?"

"They're in those big boxes over there and you're going to put them up."

"No, I'm not," Travis said. "If you need help and can't afford it, I'll hire—"

"With Maxwell's money?"

"I have my own," Travis said, glaring at him. "Where'd you get the money to buy all this?"

"Thirty years of hard work—and a mortgage on my house in New Jersey. Not that it's any of your business. If you're so in love with Kim, why are you here with me now? Why aren't you courting her?"

"Should I be making her do back bends in public?" Travis asked, his eyes narrowed.

Joe grinned. "Heard about that, did you? Lucy can pole dance. I tell you, she can—"

"Don't!" Travis said sternly.

"Understood," Joe said. "The problem seems to be that you don't know how to court a woman."

"You've got to be kidding, old man. I've done things with women you've never even heard of. One time—"

"Not sex, boy! The only sex that matters is if you make the woman you love happy. You can do a threesome with half a dozen gorgeous dames, but if the one you love ain't smiling at you over breakfast, you're a failure in the sex department."

Travis stood still as he thought about that, and it made sense. He bent back to the box but then straightened up again. "Just so you know, a threesome is with three people, not half a dozen." He went back into the carton.

"Make her *need* you," Joe said after a while. "Not want you, but deep down need you. Whether it's to give her a foot rub at the end of the day, or to fix the kitchen sink, find an empty place in her life and fill it."

"Does my mother need you?" Travis asked in curiosity.

"She can hardly thread those sewing machines of hers without me."

Travis smiled at that. Since they'd first visited Edilean his mother had sewn, and she'd never had trouble threading anything.

Joe seemed to understand his smile. "Okay, so Lucy pretends she can't thread the serger or change the needles. But she gave me pointers on filling out the form for the mortgage application. She even told me what to wear and what to say when I went to the bank. She helped me order everything in here, and she and Jecca picked out all the colors of paint and tile. Lucy made the curtains."

"Sounds like you need her more than she needs you."

"That's just it!" Joe said. "She needs me and I need her. We're twisted."

"Intertwined," Travis said.

Joe narrowed his eyes. "You may have been to school more than me, but I got the woman I'm in love with."

"You have a point. What am I supposed to do with these pieces of metal?"

"I'm going to show you how to use a screwdriver."

"My life is at last complete," Travis muttered and picked up a socket wrench.

Eight

"*Hello,*" *Travis said* softly as he opened the door that led to Kim's garage. She was bent over a sturdy workbench, looking through a lighted magnifying glass at something that appeared to be made of gold. "I don't mean to intrude, but I wanted to apologize for yesterday evening."

"It's okay," Kim said without looking up.

"No, it wasn't. I was rude and . . . I guess I just feel protective of you, that's all."

"You and Reede both," Kim said under her breath. Just what she needed, two brothers.

Travis was looking about the large room at all the equipment. There were deep shelves full of boxes, a couple of what looked to be microwaves, a large safe in the corner, a desk with a computer beside a foot-tall stack of fat folders, and three workbenches filled with more tools than Joe had. "This is some workshop," he said. "You need all this to make jewelry?"

"Everything in here. In fact, I need a drafting table, but I don't have the room, and it would get dirty."

Travis thought that what she needed was some natural light. There were three little glass panels in the big garage door and one small window on the far wall. It was night out, but he'd like to see the stars.

Kim glanced up at him and did a double take. "What have you been doing all day?"

"I went to Joe Layton's place and ended up unpacking boxes for him."

"You have . . ." She touched the side of her head.

Reaching up, Travis removed three foam beans from his hair. "Damned things are all over me. Joe made me sweep the floor and flatten boxes before I left." He went to the chair by the desk and dropped down on it. "I wasn't this tired after I climbed Mount Everest."

"What an exciting life you lead." She was using a tiny file on what looked to be a ring held in a padded vise. She had put a black cloth around it to catch the gold shavings.

"So far, the excitement here in Edilean beats everything I've done. Between your brother, who's going to come after me with a shotgun when he remembers where he saw me, your sheriff wanting me to rescue injured tourists, and Joe belittling me because I don't know what an orbital router is, my dad is looking pretty good."

Kim laughed. "Orbital sander. A router is something else."

"*Et tu*, Brute?" Travis said as he put his hand to his heart.

"Just keeping you straight," she said, smiling.

He was looking at the papers and folders on the desk. "Speaking of straight, what is all this?"

Kim groaned. "Money. Accounts. The bane of my life. I used to have a part-time secretary who put it all in the computer for me, but she got married and quit."

"Pregnant yet?" Travis asked. "That seems to be the main occupation of this town. You guys should invest in cable TV."

"You should try not watching TV," Kim retorted. "It's a lot of fun."

"You'll have to show me sometime," he said softly.

Startled, Kim looked at him, but he had pulled the folders onto his lap and was reading the labels.

"Mind if I look inside these? I know some about financial organization."

"If you don't mind seeing how much I make, and how much I spend on everything from groceries to diamonds, go ahead." Kim tried to sound light, but she was actually holding her breath. Never before had she allowed a man other than her father to see her finances. Her success was what had ended her romantic relationships.

But Travis was different. They were *friends*. She nearly choked on the thought.

"Did you say something?" he asked.

"No, nothing."

"Have these receipts been entered into some system?"

"Not for weeks. My accountant is going to scalp me."

"Do you mind?" Travis asked as he nodded at her computer.

Kim shrugged. He could look if he wanted to. She listened as he settled into the chair and started going through the folders. She heard the click of the keys, and now and then looked up, seeing him bent over the papers. She was sure that if anyone knew what she was doing she'd be told she was a fool for letting a man she hadn't seen since she was a child look at her accounting charts, but whatever else she had to say about Travis, she trusted him.

It was nearly two hours since Travis had returned and they were in the kitchen together. He'd gone into her accounting software—but had insisted that she type in her password—and looked at the way her secretary had set it up. He asked if he could consolidate the accounts, and she'd said yes. After that he'd asked some questions about companies and about a few receipts, but for the most part they were quiet.

All in all, it had been very pleasant working with him in the room. As they had when they were children, they just seemed to naturally meld together.

"I can't believe you drove all the way into Williamsburg and got barbeque," Kim said as she pulled the package out of the fridge. As often happened, she hadn't thought aloud about dinner. She'd been surprised, and pleased, when Travis said he'd brought food home.

She'd smiled at his use of the word *home*. It sounded almost as though he lived there too.

"Joe told me about a back road, so it didn't take long," he said, and they looked at each other and laughed. "I went the speed limit and used asphalt." He glanced at the clock. It was late.

"You and Mr. Layton seem to have hit it off well."

Travis took his time answering as he put coleslaw on plates and took them to the table. "He knows who my mother is."

"You're kidding!" Kim said.

"No, he saw the resemblance right away. But he made me swear not to let her know that he'd figured it out."

"And I guess she doesn't want you to tell either."

"Precisely. I have been placed in the middle of my mother and him," Travis said as he looked at her across the table. He'd liked being in her workroom—but he'd always enjoyed the outdoors and he wanted to see it day or night. The converted garage was too closed-in for him. "Joe has no use for that big room at the end of his store. It has windows that look out into the forest. He says Jecca will never use it and I understand why. He greatly admires her ability to reassemble electrical tools and he'd put her to work."

Reaching over, Kim removed a foam pellet clinging to the back of his shirt.

"I feel like I have those things crawling all over me. Could you—?" He held out the back of the neck of his shirt.

Standing, she put her hand on his collar but she didn't touch him. She glanced down his shirt but saw only sun-bronzed skin. And muscles. "Nothing," she said.

"Sure? I itch in places. I should have taken a shower first, but I saw your light on and I wanted to see you." He took her hand in his and kissed her fingertips. "Oops, sorry," he said and released her. "You're soon to be married so you're a 'no touch.'"

Frowning, Kim sat back down. "Hardly that. I haven't been asked, much less said yes."

"So you really like this guy?"

"He's nice," Kim said, but she didn't want to talk about Dave. "What are your plans for tomorrow?"

"According to Joe, I'm to be his slave. Kim, if you want that shop that's supposed to be Jecca's I can get it for you. I'll get Joe to give it to you as a wedding gift. Free rent for at least three months, and very reasonable the rest of the time."

"My garage is fine and why would he give me a gift for his wedding?"

"Not *his* wedding. Yours. To Dave. He's a man and he'll want a place to put his car. Or one of those catering vans. He is going to move in with you, isn't he? I can't imagine that he earns enough to buy a house like this one. But then what you made last year was substantial. Congratulations! You are truly a success."

What he was saying was wonderful. Truly great. But, somehow, it was upsetting her. She hadn't thought of the fact that Dave came with a lot of equipment. He owned five big vans and he had enormous pieces of cookware. He lived in a small apartment and rented a commercial kitchen. But still, he did some cooking at his house. One Sunday afternoon she'd gone to pick him up and had ended up helping him make four gallons of tuna salad. Her clothes had smelled so bad she'd had to soak them before putting them in the washer.

"Dave and I haven't discussed anything like that," Kim said. "The truth is that it's only Carla who's saying that I'm about to receive a marriage proposal, but then she looks at all men as marriage material. She even suggested that the two of you—"

"Me?!" Travis's eyes were wide. "Me and Carla? She is cute. Think she'd go out with me?"

Kim looked at Travis in speculation and suddenly had the feeling that she was being manipulated, but she wasn't sure how. "Are you up to something?"

"Just trying to be your friend is all. I enjoy your company and I want to help out around here so you don't throw me out. Edilean is scary."

Kim couldn't help laughing. "It will be when my brother remembers where he saw you! I couldn't understand why you were standing there with your hand over your face. Did you really come close to killing him?"

"Yes," he said. "I don't know why my heart didn't stop. There I was in Morocco, trying my best to beat Jake Jones's time, Ernie my mechanic was with me, and he had the map out. I went around a corner and there's this guy crossing the street with a donkey so covered in boxes the poor thing was bowlegged."

"That sounds like Reede," Kim said.

Travis got up and pantomimed being behind the wheel of his car. "Before I hit that curve, there were Moroccans on the sides shouting at us in Arabic. I don't know about you, but my Arabic consists of *la* and *shukran—no* and *thanks*. How was I to know they were telling us that a crazy American doctor was meandering across the raceway?"

"You were the only car?"

"Hell no! I was eating Jake's dust every two miles. He'd done something to the fuel injection system but I didn't know what. Every time I got near him, he'd upshift and spew rocks at us. My windshield was a mass of scars."

Travis bent forward, his hands on the wheel. "So there I am, yelling at Ernie—no sound absorption in a race car—about what the hell the Arabs were shouting at us and he's telling me that if I don't slow down the transmission is going to fall out when bam! There's this man."

"With a donkey," Kim said.

"Which froze. The donkey had sense enough to know danger when he saw it."

"But my brother didn't."

"You're right on that! He looked at a car coming at him doing at least a hundred and twenty and—"

"You'd slowed down for the curve," Kim said solemnly.

"Yeah, I did," Travis said and seemed pleased at her understanding. "If your brother had any fear at all, I didn't see it. He just frowned at me like I was an annoyance, then turned back to pull on the donkey's rope."

"When was this?"

"2005."

"Oh heavens!" Kim said. "That wasn't too long after Reede's long-term girlfriend dropped him. He was probably still in that stage of not caring whether he lived or died."

"Like I'd feel if you told me to get out of your life and never come back," Travis said, then quickly went on with his story. "When I yelled, Ernie looked up from his map and screamed like a girl. I turned the wheel as hard as I could, braked until my ankle felt like it was cracking, and we nearly turned over."

Kim was blinking at his statement about how he'd feel if she told him to go away. "I guess . . ." she began.

"Your brother stood there and watched the whole thing. For seconds we looked into each other's eyes; we had a clear view of one another. It was one of those moments when the world seems to stand still. The donkey collapsed from sheer terror, and that's when the boxes it was carrying hit the ground and broke."

"And Reede—"

"By the time I got the car headed back toward him, he was in a rage and shouting at us." Travis put his hand over his heart. "I swear this is true, but I wanted to stop and see about the donkey. I didn't know the contents of the boxes were important. It was Ernie who said, 'Good God! He's an American. Don't stop or he'll have us arrested. Go! Go! Floor it and *go!*' I did."

"Did you win the race?"

"Of course not. The transmission fell out about fifty miles down the road. We were so far from anywhere we had to be helicoptered out."

Kim looked at him as he sat back down. She couldn't help remembering the boy who'd ridden her bicycle. "I agree," she said.

"About what?"

"When my brother remembers where he saw you, he's going to come after you with a shotgun."

"You're no help at all," Travis said, smiling. "I want you to be on *my* side."

"I am. Reede probably knew about the race and wanted to provoke a fight. At that time, he had so much anger inside him about his girlfriend dumping him, he probably wanted to get it out."

Travis sobered. "He came very close to getting himself killed."

She smiled. "Thanks for taking care of my brother. Thank you for not hitting him and thank you for replacing his supplies. If you weren't so good at handling a car, all three of you—and the donkey—could have been killed."

For a moment they looked at each other and again Kim felt drawn to him. It was as if his body called to hers, as though some electrical charge ran from her to him and back again. She could feel the pull, the tingle, the desire that passed between them.

Of its own will, her body took a step toward him. She wanted him to put his arms around her and kiss her. She saw him look at her lips and his eyes grew darker, warmer, hot even.

But in the next second, he turned away and the moment was gone. "It's late," he murmured, "and Joe . . . I'll see you tomorrow." In an instant he had left the house.

Kim sat down on a chair. She felt like a balloon that had its knot untied. Deflated. Worse, she felt defeated.

When Travis got inside the guesthouse, he was shaking. He knew he'd never wanted a woman as much as he did Kim, but the problem was that he cared about her. He didn't want to hurt her, didn't want—

He sat down on the side of the bed and punched Penny's number. "Did I wake you?" he asked.

She hesitated. Never before had Travis been concerned about his secretary's sleeping habits. "No," she said, lying.

"Did you find out anything about the caterer?"

"Just his name, but I sent my son to Edilean to see what he could find out."

"What's your son look like?"

"What does that matter?" Penny asked.

"There's a girl, Carla, who works for Kim, and she's after any half-decent-looking man who comes in the store. She knows something about a missing sapphire ring. I think it's connected to the caterer and I want to find out about it. Can your son handle that?"

"Easily," Penny said and seemed to be amused. "What else have you found out?"

"Not much, just that Kim is doing quite well in her little shop."

"Enough to make this man want it?"

"Yes," Travis said. They knew a lot about what a person would do to own a lucrative business.

"You don't think it's possible that this caterer is actually in love with pretty Kim?"

"He may well be, but let's just say that if he touches her, I'll be needing a pair of dueling pistols."

"Well, well, well," Penny said.

"How's it coming with your relatives in Janes Creek?"

"Everyone is happy for the free weekend. But I need to warn you that even your dad might not be able to afford my uncle Bernie's room service bill."

"That's all right. I'm getting used to dealing with relatives. Mom's new . . ."

"Her what?" Penny asked. She was marveling that they were having a personal conversation that included *her* life.

"The man she's planning to marry. I've been working for him."

"Good dental?" Penny asked, covering her surprise.

Travis scoffed. "No pay, just advice. Lots of advice."

"Good or bad?"

"Depends on the outcome, which I don't know yet. I have to come up with a reason why I should go with Kim to Maryland."

"You're asking her permission to go?" Her surprise turned to shock.

"Yes," Travis said. "I can't talk anymore. Joe wants me at work at seven A.M. tomorrow. I'm attaching steel shelves to brick walls. I can hardly wait."

"I, uh . . ." Penny didn't know what to say so she murmured good night and hung up. "I think I like this Edilean," she said as she got back into bed.

Nine

❦

"*So what's it* like living with him?" Carla asked Kim the next morning. "Great sex, huh? He looks like he'd be fabulous in bed. How's his endurance? Does he—?"

"Carla!" Kim snapped. "Could you please be a bit more professional?"

"Not getting any, are you? Not with an attitude like that. Saving yourself for Dave? But if you change your mind, I know this perfume you could try that might help. It—"

Kim went into her office and shut the door. She hadn't seen Travis this morning, as he'd already gone to work at Joe's new store. He'd left her a funny note on the kitchen counter about how he was looking forward to learning how to drill holes in brick. *They should have turned the bricks on their sides. They already have holes in them,* he'd written, making her smile.

It was nice to start the day with a laugh, but she would have liked to have seen him.

Her cell rang with a number she didn't know.

"Meet me for lunch?" Travis asked. "Please?"

Instantly, her bad mood lifted. "Where?" She refrained from saying, When? How? Should I bring food? How about a few clarity three diamonds?

"How about Delmonico's circa 1899?"

"Love it. I'll get my corset out of storage."

"Can you put it on all by yourself?"

"I may need help," Kim said and felt her heart beating in her throat. She loved this teasing!

"I would like to volunteer to help you, but at the present I am a conjoined twin. Joe has attached himself to me. Can you bear to have lunch with the two of us?"

"I'd be honored," Kim said. "If it's Joe, he wants to go to Al's Diner."

"I've seen that place and I'm not sure it's right. Joe specifically said that he wants al dente pasta and steamed broccoli for lunch. And a tablecloth and—"

"Limoges and Christofle," Kim finished.

"Exactly! See you at the greaseburger at noon?"

"My arteries are looking forward to it," Kim said and went back into the shop with a big smile.

Carla looked up as she was putting a tray of bracelets away. "Whatever made you smile like that isn't half as good as what just happened to *me*."

"Oh?" Kim asked as she glanced at the trays. The bracelet Travis had admired was gone and so was the ring with the big pink diamond. "Good sale?"

"Tremendous! A man was buying for his mother. He had an eye and picked out the best in the store with hardly a glance. And . . ."

"And what?"

"He asked me to go out with him tonight."

"Don't half the men who come in here ask you out?"

"The sleazebags do. And the married losers," Carla said. "The classy ones like him want *you*."

Kim was in such a good mood she was willing to listen to Carla, but the door opened and a very handsome man came in. Not as dark as Travis, and he didn't have that world-weary look that Travis often had, but this man was gorgeous. And the suit he wore must have cost thousands.

He glanced at Kim, gave a quick nod of greeting, then went straight to Carla.

Standing to one side, Kim watched the two of them. They were an incongruous pair. Although Kim had had numerous talks with her about the way she dressed, Carla's blouse was always opened one button too far, her skirt an inch or two too short, and she wore too much makeup. The man looked like he'd just left an exclusive club, while Carla . . . Well, there was a lot of discrepancy between their looks.

"I think I'll take the pearl earrings as well," he said in a smooth, silky voice as he looked at Carla as though he wanted to devour her.

"Sure, Mr. Pendergast," Carla said.

"I told you to call me Russell," he said.

"Will do," Carla said but continued to stand there staring at him.

Kim went to the far counter and got out her best pearl earrings. Since he'd bought two expensive items, she figured they were the earrings he wanted. A curve like a shell, the pearl embraced by it. She put them on the counter, then nudged them along between the two people, who were staring at each other.

The man turned to her, his almost black eyes looking at her with a remarkable intensity, as though he was studying her. If Travis weren't here now, she thought, she'd look back at this man. But she just smiled at him in a professional way.

"You're the designer? Kimberly Aldredge?"

"Yes I am."

"I'm Russell Pendergast. I'm just passing through town and I had no idea there would be a store of such quality here. Your designs are exquisite."

His voice and pronunciation spoke of a very good education. Like Travis, she thought.

Behind him, Carla was glaring, her eyes threatening that if Kim made a play for the man, blood might be shed.

"Where could I get lunch in the area?" he asked.

"I know some places," Carla said from behind him. "I get off at one."

"And what about you, Miss Aldredge? When do you have lunch?"

Kim took a step away from him. As enticing as he was, she wasn't interested. "I'm meeting friends at the local greasy spoon. I wouldn't recommend it to an outsider. Excuse me." She went back into her office.

Interesting, she thought as she picked up her sketchbook and put her mind back on work. Maybe she should make some more designs based on shells. She had to come up with a theme for Neimans, so maybe she'd do something about the sea.

An hour later she left for lunch. Mr. Layton and Travis were already in a booth with their drinks. As soon as he saw her, Travis's dark eyes lit up in a way that made Kim smile. He stood up, kissed her on the cheek, then let her in first.

"Have any idea what you want for lunch?" Travis asked as he nodded toward Joe. "The old man couldn't wait so we ordered."

"Al knows," she said and waved to the big man they could see in the kitchen. It looked like Travis and Mr. Layton were getting to know each other well.

"No kisses for me?" Mr. Layton asked. "You just pass them out to the young bucks now?"

"Sorry," Kim said as she stretched across the table to kiss his cheek. She didn't see Travis as he admired the view of her body. And she didn't see Mr. Layton give him a look that said Travis owed him one.

"What have you two been doing?" she asked.

"Him nothing; me everything," Travis said.

She looked at him. His shirt was dirty and there was

sawdust on his temple. Reaching up, she brushed it away, then was aware of the way Mr. Layton was staring at them.

Kim moved a bit farther down on the seat. "We had an exciting morning."

"Better than cutting pieces of lumber to make sawponies?" Travis asked in sarcasm.

"Saw*horses*," Kim corrected. Mr. Layton's eyes were twinkling. "You're being wicked and I'm going to tell Jecca on you." She looked back at Travis. "A young man came in this morning and bought my three most expensive pieces."

"Did he?" Travis asked.

"He told Carla they were for his mother. He had on a suit that looks like the one you were wearing when I first saw you."

"Before I discovered the joys of T-shirts with trucking logos on them?" Travis asked.

Mr. Layton didn't smile. "What's his name?"

"Russell Pendergast and he asked Carla out on a date tonight."

Travis choked on his drink. "Pendergast?"

"Yes, do you know him?"

"Never met the guy," Travis said and could feel Joe Layton's eyes boring into him. "What's he like?"

"Gorgeous," Kim said. "Smooth. He exudes education and wealth."

"Does he?" Travis asked in curiosity. "And he bought your most expensive pieces for his mother?

Interesting. Where'd he go to school? Maybe I know him."

"I have no idea. But after his date with Carla I'm sure I'll hear everything. I can't really see the two of them together. He—"

"Did he come on to you?" Travis asked, his dark brows in a scowl.

"I don't think that's any of your—" Kim began and could feel her temper rising.

"Ah, good!" Joe said loudly. "Our food is here. If you two'd rather fight than eat, let me know so I can sell tickets."

"There will be no argument," Kim said. "Russell and I are going out Saturday night."

"On Saturday you're going to be in a B&B with your almost fiancé," Travis said grimly.

"That's right," Kim said, smiling at Mr. Layton. "I can't keep all my men straight."

"You ought to take young Travis here with you."

"With me where?" Kim asked.

"Over the weekend," Joe said.

"Take Travis on my weekend with my boyfriend?" Kim asked. Truthfully, she liked the idea but she wasn't going to say so. If Dave did propose, Travis's presence would give her time to think about an answer. And if Dave got too . . . insistent, too whatever, Travis would be there. But she'd eat one of Al's '57 burgers and have an immediate coronary before she told him so.

"Yeah," Joe said as he bit into a pound of meat that

dripped juice—a.k.a. grease—down to his wrists. "Travis here said you were going to do some work. How can you do that if you're fooling around with your boyfriend? Take Travis and he can do all the work."

Travis gave Joe a look that was half thanks, half murder.

"That's not a bad idea," Kim said as she used her fork to move around what was Al's idea of a salad. Lots of fried chicken, not much lettuce. "I'll think about it," she said and didn't dare look at Travis. She had an idea he was smiling much too broadly.

As *the morning* sunlight came through the windows, Travis was sitting in Kim's living room and trying to concentrate on the newspaper, but he couldn't. She'd left for work an hour ago, and since then he'd been waiting for Penny's son to show up.

Yesterday after lunch at Al's with Kim and Joe, Travis had gone to see his mother. As he entered Mrs. Wingate's house, the hum of his mother's sewing machine reached him, and the familiarity of the sound felt good. When he got upstairs, it was easy for him to fall into place with her and begin cutting out a pattern. Sewing was something they'd done together when he was a child. They never talked about it, but it reminded them of their time in Edilean, a time of peace for both of them. Those two weeks had changed both their lives.

Travis had been a bit concerned about what his mother knew about him and Joe, but she soon made him relax. They'd always been close and nearly always in agreement. At first he'd been afraid she'd again lecture him about Kim, but the anger she'd displayed on their first meeting was no longer there.

Instead they easily fell into talking about Joe. Travis told her everything—except that Joe knew Travis was Lucy's son. But all the rest of it, from unpacking to being told sawponies were sawhorses, to having to attach steel shelves to a brick wall, was there.

When Lucy began laughing at Travis's stories, he got her away from the machines—she worked too much—and down to the kitchen. As they'd done when he was growing up, Travis made tea while she made the sandwiches. When they were ready, Lucy led him into the conservatory. For a while he walked around, admiring the orchids that filled the room. When he sat down, Lucy asked him about Kim.

Travis hesitated.

"You can tell me," she said softly. "Are you still in love with her?"

"Yes," he said, then looked at his mother with eyes that showed the depth of his feeling. "More than ever. More than I thought possible."

For a moment tears gathered in Lucy's eyes. She was a mother who hoped her child would find love.

"She's funny and perceptive," Travis said as he picked up a sandwich wedge. When he was little his mother had cut off the crusts and sliced the bread diagonally into four pieces. As he grew up, she'd continued. "And very smart. And you should see the jewelry in her store. It's all beautiful!"

"I have seen it," Lucy said. "Whenever I heard that Kim was out of town, I visited her shop. I like the olive leaves."

"So do I," Travis said. He stood up and fiddled with a long orchid leaf for a moment before turning back. "I feel comfortable with her. I don't feel like I have to impress her. Although I do work at that."

"Joe said you drove down the back road and he couldn't see how you'd done it."

Travis shrugged. "Stunt work. It wasn't difficult."

"And something about a balloon?" Lucy asked.

"I couldn't stand to hear the kid cry, so I climbed up a tree and got it down for him."

"You always have had a soft heart."

"No one in New York would say that," Travis said.

"No, I guess not. You have both your father and me inside you. What are you going to do now?"

Travis sat back down. "Joe fixed it so I'm going to spend the weekend with Kim. I'll be in a connecting room, and she might be with her boyfriend. But still . . . I'll be near her."

"He told me," she said as she smiled at her son. She'd never seen him this way, and it did her heart good.

"Did he? What other of my secrets did that nosy old man blab to you?"

Lucy smiled. Since the two of them had met, all she'd heard from Joe was "Travis." What Travis said, did, his worries, his deep love for Kim, Travis's suggestions about the hardware store. Every word of it, Joe repeated to Lucy.

"You should have seen him with Kim," Joe'd said when he'd called her after their lunch at Al's. "The poor guy can't take his eyes off her."

"What about *her*?" Lucy'd asked. "What does Kim think of my . . . of Travis?" If Joe heard her slip, he didn't seem to register it.

"She acts like she pays no attention to him, that he's just another guy, but if he moves, she sees it. When I suggested that she take young Travis with her to Maryland, her face lit up like a New Year's spotlight."

Lucy looked at her son. "Joe likes you a lot."

"You'd never know it from what he says," Travis said, but he was smiling. "According to Joe Layton, any man who can't use a handsaw properly isn't worth much. I told him I was a lawyer and you know what he said?"

Lucy had heard the story from Joe but she wanted to hear it again from Travis. "I can't imagine."

"He said . . ."

Now, with the newspaper in front of him, Travis couldn't help smiling. Last night had been the way he remembered with his mother, her kindness, her humor, her sweetness. He was glad he hadn't had to endure another session where she bawled him out.

On the other hand, *that* woman might be able to handle Randall Maxwell in a courtroom.

That evening when Travis had returned home—as he'd begun to think of wherever Kim was—she'd been about to throw a couple of frozen dinners into the microwave. When Travis was going through school he'd spent more than one summer crewing on private yachts. One year, to his horror, he was assigned the position of "chef." He didn't know how to boil water.

He put the dinners back in the freezer and looked to see what else was in there as he told Kim the story. "So there I was, not knowing an egg from a watermelon, and I was supposed to spend six weeks cooking three meals a day for the rich old man and his young wife."

Kim crunched on the carrot stick he'd cut for her. "So what did you do?"

"I put on my most helpless look"—he demonstrated—"and asked the wife to help out."

"Did she?"

"Oh yes," Travis said as he put chicken breasts in the microwave to thaw. He was glad his back was to Kim as he thought about that trip. He didn't want her to see his face.

But she'd understood. "What else did she teach you?"

Travis started laughing. "A little bit here and there." Moonlight, stars, the old man snoring below. He'd been nineteen years old and innocent. Not so innocent when they got back to the U.S.

He and Kim had a dinner that he'd never wanted to end. She told him more about her jewelry and what she hoped to do. "I have a big commission coming up and I need some new inspiration."

"This trip to Maryland will be good for you."

"That was my idea when I let Joce talk me into going."

"You didn't originally plan to go with this guy, did you?"

"Dave? No, I didn't."

"He invited himself?" Travis asked.

"More or less," Kim said, "but I do think he has something important to say to me. Between him and Carla I've been given enough hints."

A lot of things came into Travis's mind that he wanted to say, but he thought he'd better keep his opinions to himself. Penny's son, Russell, was on a date with Carla and the plan was for him to meet Travis in the morning and report on what he found out.

But it was now midmorning and Russell still hadn't shown up. At that thought, Travis had to smile. The small town mind-set was getting to him. In New York he often didn't get up until this time. But then he'd usually been out late the night before. Clients loved to be entertained and shown New York nightlife.

When the doorbell rang, Travis put down the paper and went to the door in a few long strides. He was curious to see this man Kim had described as "gorgeous," and he wanted to meet the son of the woman who his father had described as his "most trusted employee." She'd worked for Randall Maxwell since she was young, and when Travis had been coerced into working for him, Randall had released Penny to Travis to "take care of him."

Travis opened the door to find himself staring into the angriest eyes he'd ever looked into. Considering all the things his father had had him do, that was a lot.

The two men were almost exactly the same height, appeared to be the same age, and they were both handsome. But Travis's face showed a lifetime of struggle, a life of loneliness. Every time he'd faced death in his extreme sports was in his eyes, and the war between his parents showed on him.

Russell's eyes were angry. He'd grown up in the shadow of the powerful Maxwell family, and he'd come to hate the name because whatever that family wanted came first. This week he hadn't been surprised when his mother asked him to help Travis Maxwell. It was a name he'd known before his own. He hadn't even been shocked to be told that Travis had never heard of Russell, didn't know he existed. The anger he'd felt was on his face, in the way he stood, as though he'd just love for Travis to say something that would allow him to fight.

"You're Penny's son," Travis said as they stood at the

door. "I didn't know she . . ." He trailed off at the look in the man's angry eyes. "Please come in," he said formally, then stepped back as Russell entered the house and went into Kim's blue and white living room.

"A bit of a downsize for you, isn't it?"

Behind him, Travis let out his breath. The Maxwell name! Being in Edilean and especially being around Joe, had nearly made him forget the preconceived ideas people had about him. All his life he'd heard, "He's Randall Maxwell's son so he is—" Fill in the blank.

It seemed that Penny's son had already decided that Travis was a clone of his father.

Travis's face went from the friendly one he'd adopted in the last week to the one he wore in New York. No one could get to him, so no one could hurt him.

Russell took the big chair and Travis saw it for what it was: establishing that he was in charge.

Travis sat on the couch. "What did you find out?" he asked, his voice cool.

"David Borman wants control of Kimberly Aldredge's business."

Travis grimaced. "I was afraid of that. Damn! I was hoping—" He looked back at Russell and thought, the hell with it! This was Penny's son, and this was about Kim. It had nothing to do with the Maxwell name. "You want some coffee? Tea? A shot of tequila?"

Russell stared at Travis as though he were trying to

figure him out—and whether or not to take him up on his offer. "Coffee would be fine."

Travis started toward the kitchen but Russell didn't follow. "I need to make it. You want to come in here and talk while I do?"

The ordinariness of the invitation seemed to take some of the anger out of Russell's eyes as he got up and went to the kitchen. He sat down on a stool and watched Travis get a bag of beans out of the refrigerator and pour some into an electric grinder.

"I guess I was hoping," Travis said loudly over the noise, "that I was going to have to fight him over Kim. A duel, I guess." He lifted his hand off the top of the machine and the noise stopped. "It's going to hurt Kim to find this out."

Russell's eyes were wide as he watched Travis put the grounds into a filter and drop it into a machine. He didn't seem to be able to grasp the concept that a Maxwell could do something so mundane as make coffee. Where were the servants? The butler? "He's the third one."

"Third one what?"

"He's the third man who was more concerned with her success than with her."

"What does that mean?"

"According to Carla . . ." Russell paused as he ran his hand over the back of his neck.

"Was the date bad?" Travis asked.

"She's an aggressive young woman."

Travis snorted. "Seemed to be. Keep you out late?"

"Till three," Russell said. "I barely escaped with . . ."

"Your honor intact?" Travis gave a half smile.

"Exactly," Russell said.

"Have you had breakfast? I make a mean omelet."

"No. That is . . ." Russell was still staring at Travis as though he couldn't believe what he was seeing.

"It's the best I can do for Penny's son after all she's put up with from *me*."

"All right," Russell said slowly.

Travis began getting things out of the fridge. "Tell me everything from the beginning."

"Do you mean Carla's complete sex history that she delighted in telling me in detail, or what I could dredge out of her about Miss Aldredge?"

Travis laughed. "No Carla, but lots of Kim."

"It seems that small town men can't handle a woman who earns more than they do."

Travis would have liked to think that he could deal with that, but he'd always had the opposite problem. "So they dumped her?"

"Yes," Russell said as he watched Travis pour him a cup of freshly brewed coffee and set it on the counter along with containers of milk and sugar. He wasn't surprised that the coffee was excellent. "St. Helena?"

"It is," Travis said. "I get it here in Edilean at the local grocery. Can you believe that?" He was pleasantly surprised that Russell had recognized the taste of the rare and expensive coffee. "I take it that this Dave is different from the others."

"Carla and Borman's ex-girlfriend are friends, and Carla told the girl all about Kim, even about the men who'd walked away from her. Carla has no understanding of the word *discretion.*"

"Or *loyalty,*" Travis said. "Onions, peppers, and tomatoes all right with you?"

"Yes," Russell said. "As far as I can piece together, the girlfriend told Borman and he made a plan."

"Let me guess. He dropped the girlfriend and went after Kim."

Russell reached into the inside pocket of his coat and pulled out several pieces of paper folded together into a thick stack. "These are the financials of Borman's company for the last two years."

Travis let the vegetables sizzle while he went through the first pages, but then he had to stop to add the eggs to the skillet and put bread in the toaster. "Would you . . . ?" he asked Russell.

He took the papers and started to go through them, but then paused to remove his suit jacket and drape it over a dining chair. He loosened his tie. "The bottom line is that David Borman isn't a good cook, he spends too much, and he's lazy."

Travis slid the omelet onto a plate, put it before Russell, and got a knife and fork out of a drawer. "So he dropped his girlfriend and went after Kim—or rather, her business."

"It gets worse," Russell said as he took a bite. "Not bad."

"Worse isn't bad?"

"No. Borman gets worse; the omelet isn't bad."

"Oh," Travis said as he watched Russell eat. He could see things about him that reminded him of Penny. He'd spent a lot of late nights with her and they'd shared many meals. Now he wondered why he'd never asked her about her personal life. But then, he would have thought that if he had, Penny probably wouldn't have answered.

Russell looked up at him as though expecting something from Travis.

"The ring," Travis said. "What about the ring?"

"Borman took Carla out to dinner, told her a sob story about how he was in love with Kim. He got Carla to 'lend' him a ring to give to her when he proposed this weekend."

"Then Carla told the whole town that's what Borman was going to do." Travis handed Russell the toast and got out the butter. "That's why Borman invited himself to go with her to Maryland."

"Carla didn't seem to see anything wrong in the fact that you and Miss Aldredge are living together just before she's to get a marriage proposal from Borman. Carla's exact words were, 'I think you should take things when they're offered.'"

"I'm staying in the guesthouse," Travis said absently as he thought about what he'd just heard.

"The whole town thinks you and Kim are . . ."

"It's just gossip," Travis said, then looked back to see

Russell staring at him, his eyes disbelieving. Travis felt anger rising in him. "It looks like you believed them."

Russell looked back down at his food. "It's not for me to judge."

"And a Maxwell takes whatever he wants, is that it?" If Travis had been hoping for an argument, he didn't get it.

Calmly, Russell finished his coffee. "In my experience, yes."

The truth of that made Travis's anger calm down. He refilled Russell's cup. "Maybe so," Travis said. "Taking what he wants is a creed of my father's."

"But not yours?" Russell asked.

Travis wasn't fooled by the man's nonchalant tone. He was asking a very serious question. "No, it's not what I believe in at all."

Russell ate his toast and for a moment he didn't reply. "How do you plan to get the ring back?"

"I'm a lawyer, remember? I'll threaten him with grand larceny and prison."

Russell used the napkin Travis had given him to wipe his mouth. "And what will you tell Miss Aldredge? That her boyfriend only wanted her for her successful little shop?"

Travis grimaced. "That will kill her ego."

"And this weekend you'll have a depressed, crying female on your hands."

Travis looked at Russell and they exchanged a male

understanding between them. An unhappy woman wasn't a good companion.

Russell stood, picked up his coat and prepared to leave, but then he turned back to look at Travis. There was no humor in his eyes. "If you leave your father's firm, what will happen to my mother? Will she be thrown out with the rubbish?"

Travis was used to being attacked, used to barely suppressed rage from people who'd had encounters with his father. But this man was different. His resentment was for Travis. "It's all happened so quickly that I haven't had time to think about it. I guess I assumed she'd go back to working for my father."

"No," Russell said. His expression said that he wasn't going to elaborate on that statement, but it was final.

"Tell me what she wants and I'll see that she gets it."

"It must feel like being an emperor to have such power," Russell said.

Travis understood the man's hostility toward him. He knew the late hours, weekends, and holidays that Penny had worked for his father. And Travis hadn't been much better. He'd never thought twice of calling her on Sunday afternoons—and Penny had never complained, never even commented. Her son must have spent most of his life without his mother. He must hate the Maxwell name. And it looked like he especially hated Travis, the Maxwell son who was the same age as he was. But then, did he think Travis grew up with loving parents who doted on him?

"What do you do? For a living, I mean?" Travis asked.

The friendliness that had started between them was gone. Russell's face was hard, unforgiving. "I don't need anything from you or your father, so there's no need to pretend interest. I'll get back to you about my mother and I expect you to keep your word."

The hostility in his voice and eyes made Travis's hair stand on end. To lighten the mood, he said, "Within reason, of course. I can't give her the Taj Mahal. It isn't for sale."

Russell didn't smile. "If it were, your father would have bought it and fired the caretakers. Are we finished here?"

"Yes, I think so."

As soon as Russell was out of the house, Travis called Penny. She seemed to be expecting the call because she answered before the first ring finished. The first thing he needed taken care of was business. He wanted to know where David Borman was right now. As Travis expected, Penny said she'd find out and text an answer.

That was Travis's cue to hang up, but he didn't. "I met your son," he said tentatively. "He, uh . . ."

Penny knew what he was trying to say. A few weeks ago, she wouldn't have dared comment, but lately Travis seemed to be jumping off the fast track to becoming a second Randall Maxwell. "Hates everything with the Maxwell name on it," she finished for him.

"Exactly. Is it curable?"

"Probably not."

Travis took a breath. "I promised him that when I leave the Maxwell firm I'd see that you got whatever you wanted. To make sure I get it right, why don't you tell me what it is you want?"

"Happiness for my son. Grandkids," Penny said quickly.

"You sound like my mother."

"From you, that is high praise indeed," she said. "But let me think about this. From what Russ says about Edilean, I may want to retire there."

"Not a bad idea. You see the jewelry he bought for you?"

Penny chuckled. "I did. Quite, quite beautiful! Your young Kim is very talented."

"She is," Travis said, smiling.

They exchanged good-byes and hung up. She texted him the address of where Borman was working before he got the kitchen cleaned up.

"I'm going to kill him," he muttered and started for the door.

Ten

But Travis didn't make it to the door. His male instinct was to find the man and tear him apart. He could almost feel his fists in his face. But then what? Do as he'd told Russell and threaten the man with prosecution? With prison time? Would Travis use the Maxwell name to intimidate the man?

And what would be the repercussions? A man like Borman who had no morals—or he wouldn't have planned to marry for money—wouldn't skulk away quietly. He'd go to Kim and . . . Travis didn't want to think what damage the man could cause.

For a moment Travis stood there and tried to cool his temper enough that he could think clearly about what needed to be done. He had to become more calm and figure out how to solve this in a way that would guarantee that Kim wouldn't be hurt.

Travis realized that this meeting could be the most important of his life. The last thing he should do was go in there with guns blazing, so to speak. Travis had dealt with men like Borman before, ones who thought that whatever they did to obtain what they wanted was permissible. If it took marrying a woman to get her business, then that was all right with them.

Travis had also learned that men who lost in a big way tended to retaliate in a like manner. If he threatened the man and forced him to get out of Kim's life, Borman could contact Kim, and maybe he could turn it all against Travis.

No, it was better to get rid of the man in a way that made him believe that he had won, even that he'd put one over on someone. That way, he wouldn't feel a need for revenge, wouldn't want to get back at Kim, wouldn't want to hurt her.

Travis called Penny again, and she picked up immediately.

"Rethinking the dueling pistols?" she asked.

"Yes," he said.

"I thought you might," she said and seemed to be proud of him. "The Maxwell in you always keeps a cool head."

Travis wasn't sure he was pleased by her words. "I want you to set up a meeting between Borman and me for today. I need for it to be held somewhere impressive. Maybe a library. Big desk. Rich surroundings. All the grandeur you can find. Talk to him, tell him I want to buy his catering business, that I'm in awe of what he's done with it. Flatter him."

"I'm not sure I'm that good of a liar."

"If you worked for my father, you can lie."

"More than you know," she said, sounding amused.

"I'll need a contract saying he turns everything over to me, equipment, employees, all of it. Leave the price blank. I'm planning to give him a ridiculous amount of money to buy that dying business of his. Then I want you to tell him—in confidence—that you happen to know that I'm afraid of the competition from him so he has to leave the state. Today. Before nightfall. He can't even take time to move out of his apartment."

"What name do you want to use on the contract?"

Travis frowned. "If Maxwell is on there, he'll come back to get more."

"How about if it's signed by Russell Pendergast? I can run the money through his account."

"Perfect," Travis said.

"Want Borman to call Kim to say good-bye?"

"No! But I'll take care of that. Let me know when it's all set up. Think you can do all this in just a few hours?"

Penny didn't bother to answer his question. "How about four P.M.? That'll get you home in time to have dinner with Kim."

"Penny, I love you!" he said.

She took a while to respond and he thought maybe he'd overstepped himself. "I'm going to have a Realtor send me some information about living in Edilean. I think it must be a magic place."

"Dad will be glad to buy you a house."

For some reason, Penny found that statement downright funny. She was laughing as she hung up.

At a quarter to four, Travis drove onto the palatial estate of a man who'd benefitted greatly from his association with Randall Maxwell. It was an hour outside of Williamsburg and Travis had had three calls with Penny on the drive down. The idea was for him to be familiar with everything in the room where he was to meet Borman so it looked like the place belonged to Travis.

"The contract will be on the desk," Penny said, "and both Russell and I have already talked to Borman. He's primed to sell, and he thinks you're so afraid of the competition of his company that you'll pay anything to get him out of your way."

"Which I will," Travis said. "Just not for the reason he thinks. What's it worth?"

"Russ said no more than a hundred grand, if that. He has too much equipment and not enough commissions. Last week he used a cheap fish in place of crab for a job. He told an employee that no one would be able to tell the difference, but the bride's mother did. The father refused to pay him."

"Good to know," Travis said. "Wish me luck on this."

"I do, and you may not believe this, but so does Russ. Whatever you did this morning has softened his edges more than I've been able to do in his lifetime."

Travis smiled. "For all that a couple of times he

looked at me as though he wanted to burn me at a stake, I liked him. He reminds me of you."

"Does he?" Penny asked, sounding pleased. "I'll see you tomorrow in Janes Creek."

"I'm looking forward to it," Travis said and hung up. If this came off all right, tomorrow night he'd be in a cozy little B&B in a room with a connecting door that led to Kim.

A few minutes later he pulled into the huge circular drive of the Westwood estate and turned his key over to the young man who was waiting for it. If this place was like his father's, when Travis left, his car would have been vacuumed, washed, and waxed.

A uniformed butler opened the door before Travis got up the stairs. "Mr. Pendergast is waiting for you in the south parlor," he said as he led Travis to a large, pretty room with walnut paneling and a blue and cream rug. The furniture was meant to look as though it had been there for years. Old money. But Travis's discerning eye saw that it was all new.

"This is more your style," Russell said as he walked toward Travis.

"Cut it out or I'll tell your mother on you."

Russell caught himself before he smiled. "I was told to tell you that Borman will take two hundred grand, two fifty tops. But that's way too much. Those vans of his aren't worth much, and he owes some back wages."

Travis nodded. "Where is he?"

"In the library. Got here twenty minutes early."

"Eager to get rid of everything, isn't he? Has he been told the terms?"

"To get out of town fast. To help him along, I used Mom's AmEx to buy him a plane ticket to Costa Rica. You'll get the bill."

"I bet you enjoyed doing that," Travis said.

"Very much."

Shaking his head, Travis looked at his watch. He had on his best suit and a black tie with a gold stripe. He still had three minutes before four. "Your mom wants to retire to Edilean."

"So she told me."

"What about you? Where do you live?"

Russell didn't answer the question. "I think it's time you went in. Should I carry the papers for you?"

"I believe I can manage." As Travis went to the doors leading into the library he remembered that Penny had told him the contract would be on the desk. But Russell had been here to hand it to him—which meant that he'd shown up without his mother's knowledge. Interesting. "You ever do any climbing? Skiing? Sailing?"

"Yes," Russell said, then nodded toward the door. It looked like he wasn't going to reveal any more about himself. "You might like to know," Russell said, "that I got Borman down to one seventy-five."

Travis blinked a few times. He wasn't used to anyone else doing his negotiating for him, but in this case, he was grateful. "Thank you," he said. "I appreciate—"

Russell cut him off. "It's four."

Travis took a breath and opened the door. David Borman was sitting in a leather chair so big that it made him look small and insignificant—and Travis was sure that Russell had put that chair there on purpose. It was difficult not to smile. In spite of Russell's hostility and his refusal to answer questions, Travis was beginning to like the guy.

As Travis looked at the man sitting in the big chair, his first thought was: Kim could do better. Borman wasn't tall, was slightly built, and was so blond he was almost invisible. It wasn't easy for Travis to reconcile what he knew of this man to what he saw. He certainly didn't look treacherous.

"You're Westwood, the owner of this place?" the man asked. His wide eyes showed how in awe of it he was—which was what Travis had wanted.

Travis didn't answer, just looked at him with what he'd heard people call "the Maxwell glare."

Borman sat back against the chair, his nervousness obvious.

Travis sat down and took his time looking over the contract. It was very simple. He was buying Borman Catering et al. He would get the name, the equipment, and even keep the employees.

The document had been signed by Russell Pendergast. Travis took more time looking at the signature than he did at the contract. It was bold, sure of itself—and it reminded him of something but he couldn't think what.

When he looked up, Borman was chewing on his thumbnail and there was sweat on his upper lip.

"Mr. Borman," Travis said as he folded his hands on top of the contract. "I have just been informed of a situation that may cause insurmountable problems."

Borman drew in his breath and muttered, "What is it?"

"It has come to my attention that there's something about a missing ring. I don't want any problems with law enforcement."

Borman gave a sigh of relief and lifted to one side to remove his wallet from his hip pocket. "That has nothing to do with my business. It's personal." He withdrew a small square of paper from his wallet and leaned forward to put it on the desk. "I must say that you have been doing your homework. So where do I sign?"

"This is a pawn ticket," Travis said and knew what it meant. The employee that Kim trusted had given this man a ring, and Borman had pawned it. But Travis had long ago learned that he couldn't jump to conclusions, that he shouldn't base his assessments of a situation on hearsay. When it came down to it, he only had Russell's word about what this man had been up to.

As much as Travis wanted to get rid of the man, get him out of his sight, at the same time he wanted evidence directly from the source. He leaned back in his chair and pointedly looked at the ticket on the big desk. "Mr. Borman, I run a legitimate business. I don't sign contracts if pawnshops and the police are involved."

"Police? I don't know what you're talking about. I owe a little money, for supplies and that sort of thing, but I've done nothing illegal."

"From what I heard, this ring is worth several thousand dollars. I don't want to retrieve it from the pawnshop then find out that it's been stolen."

Borman leaned back in the leather chair, glanced at the unsigned contract on the desk, then back at Travis. He looked thoroughly annoyed. "It's nothing," he said. "It's about a woman, that's all. Get the ring out of hock and return it to her. No one will press charges."

Travis's face was stern, the one he wore when he was working for his father. "Perhaps you should tell me exactly what this is about. Or maybe I should cancel this." He picked up the contract and acted as though he was about to tear it in half.

"No!" Borman shouted, then calmed. "It's just women stuff, that's all." When Travis didn't relent, he said, "There was a woman, a cute little redhead. She has a jewelry store near here. It's little, nothing special. The problem was that she's a woman. You know what I mean?"

"I'm not sure I understand." Travis put the contract down and gave Borman his full attention.

"The problem was that she worked on a small scale when she should have been thinking big. I tried to talk to her about it, for her own good. But she wouldn't listen to me. I wanted to take her store national, make it into a chain. I was going to call it The Family Jewels. Get it?"

"I get it," Travis said. Under the desk his hands were in fists.

"But she just laughed at me. Not that I told her I was serious about the name, as she can be a real prude. She's the kind of girl that goes to church every Sunday. Anyway, she wouldn't even consider going national, so I decided that the best thing would be to marry her, then I'd be able to help her out. I was really thinking of her. Know what I mean?"

"Yes, I do." Travis took a breath. "Did she know why you wanted to marry her?"

"Hell no! She's a clever little thing, so I had to be careful. I was very nice to her, sweetest person imaginable. Treated her with the respect of a choirboy. Even in the sack I was good. Nothing creative, if you know what I mean."

Travis had to work to keep from diving across the desk and going for the man's throat. "What about the ring? Where did it fit into all this?"

Dave shrugged, and his expression said that he was pleased by Travis's interest. "If I was going to ask her to marry me I had to give her a ring, didn't I? But why should I go buy one when she has a store full of them? They were just sitting there in her shop, about fifty of them, and they were free—or would be once we got married." He leaned forward, as though he was about to reveal a confidence to Travis. "She has a safe inside her garage that's full of . . . I can't imagine what's in there. She lives in a world of gold and jewels. An Aladdin's cave of diamonds and pearls. She likes pearls. One time she even tried to lecture me on the different kinds of them. Like I care, right?"

"Did you see inside the safe?"

"Naw," Dave said with a grimace. "I tried to get her to show me but she wouldn't. I even tried to get her to give me the combination, but she refused."

In his entire life, Travis had never felt such anger, such *hatred* for anyone before. "You understand the terms of the contract, don't you?"

"Of course I do." He looked at Travis as though they were men who shared a secret. "You don't want any competition. You're like me. We're both businessmen and we understand each other. Too bad the women don't get that."

Travis didn't dare respond as he didn't trust himself not to say what he was actually feeling. He gave Borman a fake smile, as though he thought the man was a genius, then filled in the outrageous price Russell had negotiated for him. Travis would have paid more. He pretended to sign it in the place where Russell's name already was.

Eagerly, Dave leaped up, signed the bottom without reading it, and Travis handed him his copy.

"Planning to call her to say good-bye?" Travis asked even while his hands were itching to hit the man.

"Don't have time," Dave said as he turned toward

the door. "I have important things to do, including getting my old girlfriend back. Now there's a girl who knows what to do to make a man happy in bed. If you get my meaning."

"Yes I do," Travis said, then stood there and watched David Borman leave the room. He felt like he needed a shower with a disinfectant.

Travis didn't know how long he stood there before Russell came in through the side door.

"Did he take it?"

Travis hesitated. "The money? Of course."

"What's this?" When Travis didn't immediately turn around, Russell stood quietly and waited.

Finally, Travis looked at what Russell was holding. "That's a pawn ticket."

"I can see that. What's it for? Oh! The ring." Russell looked at the address on the ticket. "Wonder what his plan was going to be for this weekend when he asked Miss Aldredge to marry him but didn't have a ring to give her?"

"My guess is that he'd say he knew nothing about a missing ring."

"His word against Carla's, and she was the one who stole it from the shop."

"That's what I think," Travis said as he reached out to take the ticket. "I'll go by there and get it."

"Do you have any cash on you?" Russell asked.

"A few hundred, but I have cards."

"A pawnshop that takes credit cards? Besides, you can't use yours." Russell raised an eyebrow.

Travis knew nothing about pawnshops and what kind of payment they took.

"I'll get the ring out of hock and you can go with me. Besides, your car has two flat tires."

"My car—?" Travis began but stopped. He had a feeling that Russell was lying about Travis's car being incapacitated, but he didn't mind. Right now he felt like he needed some company, needed something to take the stench of Dave Borman from him. "Fine," Travis said, "but I drive."

Russell gave a noise like a snort.

Two hours later they had the ring and were almost back to Edilean. Russell was driving. For the most part it had been a quiet ride, and Travis wasn't feeling that hostility from Russell that he'd first seen.

"What does Miss Aldredge think your last name is?" Russell asked.

"She hasn't asked and I haven't told her."

"Good, solid foundation between you two," Russell mumbled.

"Your life is better?" Travis snapped.

"Certainly not as complicated," Russell said calmly.

Travis looked out the window. "Yes, I think it's time to tell her."

"Are you going to tell her why Borman won't show up in Janes Creek? About the little play you put on in the library? How about that you're now the owner of Borman Catering?"

"What are you? A federal court judge? You want all the facts?"

"Just curious how the great Maxwell son conducts his life."

Travis started to reply to that, but they'd reached Kim's house and there was a strange car in the drive. "You don't think that's Borman's, do you?"

"I wouldn't think so," Russell said, "but I wouldn't put it past him."

"Park around the corner and I'm going to go in through the back door." Minutes later, Travis was heading toward Kim's house, Russell close behind him. "Where are you going?"

"Mom said to help you in any way I can. If it's Bor man, you might need backup."

Travis knew that if it came to a confrontation, he wouldn't need help with Borman. On the other hand, Travis didn't know how Kim was going to react to what he had to tell her. And how much should he tell her? If he was going to tell her the truth about himself, maybe he should tell her about Borman and the ring as well. Or maybe he'd postpone the part about setting Borman up and buying his company and—

"I can see the yellow stripe down your back through your clothes," Russell said.

"I wish Penny had spent more time with you and taught you some manners."

"She tried, but she was too busy working for your family to do much for me."

"If you ever want to compare childhoods, I'm ready," Travis said.

"At least you had—" Russell began but they both stopped talking when they heard a man's voice raised in anger.

Travis hurried to the back door. As usual, it was unlocked. He slipped inside, Russell right behind him.

As soon as Travis heard his name, he knew he should leave, but he couldn't make himself move. He could feel Russell beside him, and he was as transfixed, and as immobile, as Travis was.

"Kim! Are you crazy?" Dr. Reede Aldredge was shouting at his sister. "You don't even know who that man is."

"That's a stupid thing to say. I've known him since I was eight years old. He's Travis . . ." She wasn't sure if his last name was Cooper or Merritt or something else.

"He is John Travis Maxwell and his father is Randall Maxwell."

"So? I've heard the name but . . ."

"You ought to read something besides jewelry magazines. Look on the *Forbes* Web site. Randall Maxwell is one of the richest men in the world. And his son Travis is his right-hand man. Maxwell specializes in taking over other people's companies. When some guy is down and out, Maxwell steps in and buys the place for a song, then he sends in his crew to clean it up. He fires people by the thousands, puts them out of work. And you know who makes all this possible? His brilliant son, Travis the lawyer—the guy living in your guesthouse."

Kim set her jaw. "There are extenuating circumstances that you know nothing about."

"So tell me."

"I can't. I promised Travis—"

"Are you insinuating that *I* wouldn't keep a confidence? Do you have any idea how many lies and secrets and intrigues I know about in this town? I want to know why Travis Maxwell is here in Edilean. If he's planning to buy some business for his father, I think we should tell people."

"It's not like that," Kim said. "Travis only works for his father so he can protect his mother."

"That makes no sense. Is that the crap he's been feeding you?"

Kim's hands made into fists. "His mother is Lucy Cooper, the woman who's been hiding from me for four years. She was afraid I'd recognize her from when I was a kid."

Reede took a breath to calm himself. He could see that he was making his sister angry, and an angry Kim didn't listen to anyone. "Maybe that's so," Reede said. "Maybe this guy Maxwell came here because of his mother. But what does that have to do with *you*?"

"Nothing, I guess," Kim said. "Except that I'm helping him. We're making plans about what to do. We're—"

"You think you're helping him to make plans?" There was contempt in Reede's voice. "Kim, I don't want to burst your bubble, but Travis Maxwell is a notorious playboy. And now he's using you."

"For what?"

"For what all men want!" he said in exasperation. "He's already manipulated you into giving him the guesthouse you promised to *me*."

Kim looked at her brother in surprise for a moment, then couldn't help laughing. "You're talking about sex, aren't you? You think Travis conned me into lending him the little guesthouse that you don't want just so he can have sex with me."

Reede glared at her in silence.

"You know what, Reede, I have never been so flattered in my life. That a man would go to so much trouble to get me into bed is the best thing I've heard this century. Men today don't make any effort to get a woman. If they ask you on a date, they tell you when and where to meet them. That's so if you don't pass their every test for beauty and for making less money than they do, they can walk out and leave you. They don't even have to drive you home because you have your own car."

"Not all men are like that," Reede said. "And they're not the point. This man you're playing around with isn't like Paul the Caterer. Maxwell is—"

"Dave!" Kim said. "His name is Dave and I've been going out with him for six whole months and I've withstood the most boring sex imaginable. Someone should tell David Borman that there is more than one position."

"I'd prefer not to hear—"

"Not to hear that your baby sister isn't a virgin?"

"I never thought—" Reede began, then threw up his hands. "I knew you wouldn't listen to me. You never do. Kim, you're my sister and I don't want to see you hurt. Whatever reason Maxwell is here for, when he's done, he'll leave you." He looked away for a moment. "Kim, I know what it's like to have your heart ripped out. I don't want to see that happen to you."

Kim saw the pain in his eyes. When Reede was in high school and through most of college, he'd been in love with a hometown girl. He never looked at anyone else. Then suddenly, she dumped him, said she was marrying someone else. It had taken Reede years to get over the pain. "I know," she said softly. "I understand why you're so upset, but Reede, I know what I'm doing. I know that Travis is a long way from being someone from Edilean. He's not here to get married, move into some three/two house, and have kids."

"But that's what *you* want," Reede said. "I know it is. When Jecca and Tris got married you cried through the whole ceremony."

"Yes," Kim said gently. "It *is* what I want. With all my soul. Do you think I bought this big house because of the damned garage? I . . ." She had to hold back tears as she said what she knew to be true; it was going to hurt to say it out loud. "Sometimes I think I bought it as bait, to lure some nice guy here, to make it easy for him to move in, to—"

Reede put his arms around her, held her head to his chest, and stroked her hair. "Don't say such things. Any man would be honored to have you. You're smart and funny and caring and—"

"So where is he?" Kim said as she hugged her brother. "Where is this man who is going to see my good qualities and overlook my bad ones? I've spent six whole months with Dave the Caterer and I've never complained about how boring he is." She pulled away from him and wiped her eyes. "At least Travis made an effort."

"Yeah, but for what?" Reede asked as he handed Kim a tissue.

She blew her nose loudly. "I hope it's because he wants wild, all-night sex with me."

"Kim!" Reede said, sounding like a Victorian father.

"Look, I know Travis is going to leave. Once he fully believes that Joe Layton is a great guy who is mad about Lucy, Travis will leave as abruptly as he arrived. It'll be like when we were kids and one day he just wasn't there. No note, nothing. And he came back just as abruptly, with no warning. I know that he appears and disappears according to his own whims, without regard to other people."

"I agree," Reede said. "He'll go back to his dad's empire and . . . Someday, Kim, Travis Maxwell will be just like his father. You don't want to be part of that, do you?"

"No," Kim said, then looked at her brother over the tissue. "But right now while he's here, I'll take all the passionate sex I can get. Days of it. Weeks if I can get it. Months would be divine."

"That's—" Reede said sternly, then shook his head. "It's difficult for me to think of my little sister doing—" He couldn't seem to find words to express his feelings. Instead, he looked at his watch. "I have to go. I'm already late. I want you to promise me that you'll do an Internet search on Travis Maxwell and see what you're up against. He's been dating some model named Leslie who is a truly beautiful woman."

"Not like me, huh?"

Reede groaned as he knew he'd said that wrong. "That's not what I meant and you know it. I just don't want you to be hurt. Is that bad of me?"

"Of course not. You better go now. Your patients need you."

"I'll talk to you later," he said, then kissed her on the cheek.

"I'll walk you out," she said and followed him outside.

Even after the door closed, Travis stood where he was, unable to move, just stood there, staring at the doorway into the living room. He hadn't liked what he'd heard about himself.

"We'd better leave," Russell said softly. "It wouldn't be good for her to know that you heard that."

Travis's mind seemed to race forward and to stand still at the same time. He couldn't figure out what to do. Go to her? Run away? Stay and defend himself? Reassure her that he wasn't what she'd been told?

Russell put his hand on Travis's arm and turned him toward the back door.

"Ironic, isn't it?" Travis said. "I want love and *she* wants sex."

Russell gave a bit of a laugh then pushed Travis to take a step toward the door. But they were too late.

"Stop right there," Kim said from behind them.

Eleven

❦

Russell dropped his hand from Travis's arm and stepped away.

"When were you going to tell me?" Kim asked, her eyes on Travis. If she thought about what she'd just said to her brother and that Travis had heard every word of it, she knew she'd die of embarrassment.

Travis took his time turning around, and when he did, he wished he'd made it outside without seeing her. He'd never seen any woman with such anger in her eyes. That's the second person who has hated me, he thought. Russell this morning and now Kim looking at him like he was the devil's spawn. "I came in here to tell you about me."

"How convenient," Kim said. "But why didn't you tell me before? You told me about your mother hiding from your father, about her wanting to marry Joe Layton, but you didn't happen to mention that you're a lawyer and your name is Maxwell. Did you think I'd turn greedy and go after your family's wealth?"

"Of course not," Travis said. He didn't know where to begin. "I just thought . . . I mean . . ."

"Excuse me, but I'm a bit peckish," Russell said. "Do you mind if I . . . ?" He gestured toward the refrigerator.

"Help yourself," Kim said, still looking at Travis.

"Kim, honey," Travis said. When Kim's eyes looked like they were about to emit fire, he backtracked. "I didn't mean—"

"He was afraid you'd hate him because of the Maxwell reputation," Russell said from behind the refrigerator door.

"Yes," Travis said. "The Maxwell name brings out the bad in a lot of people."

"Does in me," Russell said. "Is there any mustard? Ah, here it is."

Kim turned to look at him. "You're the man in the shop. The one who was after Carla."

"Russell Pendergast," he said, smiling. "I'd shake your hand but . . ." He had his arms full of deli meat and bread. "Anyone else want a sandwich?"

"No!" Travis and Kim said in unison.

"He's my secretary's son," Travis said. "I only met him this morning. I didn't even know he existed until a couple of days ago when Penny said her son would help me. From the way she said it, she could have been talking about a six-year-old. But then she is his mother. You and I talked about how parents do that. Remember, Kim?"

She was still glaring at him. "What did your secretary's son help you with that involved *my* shop and *my* employee?"

Travis drew in his breath. It looked like his attempt to distract her hadn't worked.

Russell didn't help matters by chuckling.

"You want to leave us alone?" Travis said to him, frowning.

"Actually, no," Russell said. "No Broadway show has ever been this good, but I'll leave if Miss Aldredge wants me to."

"I never want to be alone with this man ever again. And please call me Kim."

"Gladly," he said as he gave her a look of appreciation.

"Russell!" Travis snapped. "So help me if you——"

"If he what?!" Kim said loudly. "Travis, I am waiting for an answer."

Never in his life had Travis ever found himself in a situation that he couldn't talk his way out of. But too much rested on this now for him to think coherently. "I . . ." He hesitated, not sure what to say, then he reached into his trousers pocket and withdrew the big sapphire ring that Borman had stolen.

"I got this back for you," he said, his voice hopeful.

Kim didn't take it, so he set it on the kitchen countertop. "I see. The missing ring." She took a moment to think. "If you have the ring, that means that whatever you two have been up to involves my boyfriend, Dave. You must have met him."

Travis's face grew serious. "Yes we did and, Kim, you don't know him. He's not what you think he is. The truth is that he's after—"

"He wants to take my jewelry business national and name it The Family Jewels. I treated it as the joke it was. Not the national part, but the name."

Both men were so shocked at her words that Russell stopped eating and Travis stared at her.

Kim turned away. There was so much anger in her that she could hardly breathe. Her friend Gemma was a boxer. Right now, if Kim had the know-how, she'd hit Travis so hard his head would roll across the floor.

She looked back at him. "Why did you assume that I didn't know what Dave was after? Did he seem subtle to you? Secretive?"

"No," Travis said. "But if you knew the truth, why would you consider marrying him?"

Kim was almost sure that if Dave had asked her she would have said no. Before Travis had shown up she might have said yes, but she blamed that on her friend Jecca's recent wedding. Of course, when she came to her senses, she wouldn't have gone through with it. But she was damned well not going to tell Travis that! "Is there a man on earth who *doesn't* have his own agenda for marriage? At least Dave was *honest* with me. He let me know that he was very interested in my business, and he had some good ideas."

"But . . ." Travis said.

"But what? I should wait for a man like *you*? Compared to the amount of lying and manipulation *you* have done, Dave is up for sainthood."

She wanted to get this back on track. This was about him, Travis, and what he had done, not David Borman. That was none of Travis's business. "I want to see if I get your story straight. You're a Maxwell, son of one of the richest men in the world." When Travis just stood there, she looked at Russell and he nodded in verification.

"You came to Edilean when you were twelve, spent two weeks with me, then left without so much as a note."

"Kim," Travis said, "come on, I was twelve. I did what my mother told me to."

"You could write," Russell said, his mouth full.

Travis glared at him.

"Do you know that for eighteen years I searched for you? I used to sneak into my brother's room to use his unblocked Internet service to try to find you."

"But you couldn't find him because you didn't know his correct last name," Russell said. "Mind if I get a beer?"

"Please do," Kim said. "Eighteen years and nothing. I was forgotten by you."

"That's not really true. I always knew where—" Travis said, then shut his mouth.

Kim looked at Russell in question.

"Mom said that you were never out of his radar. She said he used to—"

"I saw your shows," Travis said quickly before Russell could say any more.

Kim's eyes widened. "You! It was *you*. Jecca saw you there. She used to call you the TDH Stranger. She even drew your portrait, but I had no idea who you were."

"TDH?" Travis asked.

"Tall, dark, and handsome," Russell said. "This beer is good. I've never had it before." He looked at Travis. "Want one?"

"Only if it doesn't have hemlock in it," Travis muttered as Russell, smiling, got a beer out, opened it, and handed it to him.

Travis drank half of it in one gulp, then dropped down onto a stool. He looked back at Kim as though to say he was ready to receive more of her verbal lashes. "I thought I was watching over you," he said.

"Ah, right, how noble. 'Watching over me.' 'Looking out for me.' Is that right?"

"I thought so," Travis said and drank more beer.

Russell started making a sandwich for Travis. Neither of them had eaten since breakfast.

"So now," Kim said, "you returned to Edilean not for me—oh no, not for *me*—but because your mother called you."

"Actually," Russell said as he cut the bread, "she called my mother and told her."

"Even better," Kim said. "Lucy Merritt or Cooper or Maxwell called . . . What *is* her name?" she asked Russell.

"Cooper and Merritt are made up. Her name is Lucy Jane Travis Maxwell of the Boston Travises. She got the name and education but none of the family's old money. My mother is Barbara Pendergast of no money and no name. Just hard work."

"Thank you," Kim said. She looked back at Travis as he bit into the sandwich Russell had made for him. He looked like a man walking up the gallows steps. "Whatever the name, the point is that you didn't come back for me, but for your mother."

Travis got up to get two more beers.

"Because of Jecca's wedding you happened to see me and . . . one thing led to another."

Russell looked at Travis in question.

"She means inviting me to stay in her guesthouse," Travis said.

Russell nodded and looked back at Kim as though to say the floor was hers.

"You moved into my guesthouse and talked to me so much about friendship that I was beginning to think you were gay. And you—"

Russell gave a snort of laughter.

"I never meant—" Travis began.

"How's Leslie?" Kim asked, letting every millimeter of her anger show.

Travis looked down at his sandwich.

She picked up the ring and looked at Russell. "When I said I had a boyfriend, he almost had a grand mal seizure of old-fashioned jealousy."

"I did not," Travis said as he started to defend himself. But every word Kim was saying was true. "I was shocked, that's all," he mumbled.

"Shocked that I had a boyfriend?" Kim said. "You are . . ." Her eyes widened in disbelief. "You've watched me—stalked me—enough that you knew when I had a boyfriend or not." It was a statement, not a question.

Travis wouldn't have answered that if someone had set his feet on fire. That his mother had listened to Edilean gossip and told him about Kim on nearly every call was beside the point. It suddenly went through his mind to wonder if it was a coincidence that she called just when Kim was getting serious about some guy. And she called when there was going to be a wedding next door to her where Kim was a bridesmaid. His mother had called Penny—who she'd always disliked—and it was his secretary who got him to go to Edilean ASAP. Had it been up to Travis, he might have postponed going to Edilean, but Penny set everything up. Right now it seemed as though the two women had worked together to get Travis to Edilean at a time when he was sure to see Kim again. But that couldn't be true. Surely, all of it was coincidence.

Kim's hands were in fists and she had to turn away for a moment to catch her breath. "You thought . . ." she said softly. "You thought that since you're a big city lawyer and you were born into great wealth, that you know more about life than I do."

"Kim, I never thought that," Travis said as he put down his sandwich. "It wasn't like that at all."

"You assumed that I was a naive, simple, small town girl who was so desperate to get married that I couldn't see the truth about some guy I was dating regularly."

"Kim, you're not being fair," Travis said as he came off the stool. "Borman was a real bastard. He conned Carla into giving him that ring, saying he was going to give it to you when he asked you to marry him. But then he pawned it. I—we—think that he was going to say he knew nothing about the ring and let Carla take the blame."

Kim didn't allow the shock of that information to show on her face. "How did *you* get it?"

Travis sat back down and looked at his plate.

"He bought Borman Catering," Russell said.

Travis looked at him with murder in his eyes.

"You did what?" Kim asked in disbelief.

"He paid a hundred and seventy-five grand for the company," Russell said. He'd finished his sandwich and was working on the second beer. "He was going to pay more, but I got Borman down to that. It's still too much."

"Much too much," Kim said. "Those vans of his are worn-out and Dave's lost commissions because he doesn't deliver what he promises."

"I thought it was too much too," Russell said, "but we were up against a deadline."

Travis looked at Russell in disgust for ratting on him. "Kim, I think we're losing sight of the main issue here. Borman was going to ask you to marry him and I was afraid you'd say yes."

"And when he proposed, he'd give me my ring back!" Kim said loudly. She threw up her hands. "Men! I've had all of you I can take this week. Today I had to threaten Carla with firing her because of what she'd done."

"You should fire her," Travis said seriously. "What she did was a prosecutable offense."

"She was conned by a *man*! It's a hazard of being female. And for your information, in Edilean we don't discard someone for making a single mistake."

"As I did," Travis said softly as he looked at her with eyes begging for forgiveness.

"*You* have made a thousand mistakes. And stop looking at me like that! You already showed me that face, remember? You used it to get the pretty young wife of the old man to teach you how to cook—along with other things."

Russell laughed. "She's got *you* figured out."

"Kim, I never meant—"

"I know!" she said loudly. "I'm sure that from your view you came swooping in on your white horse and rescued me. But I didn't *need* rescuing. I didn't need someone to make me look like a fool, to make me feel that I'm an idiot who can't run my own life. What I need is—" She couldn't take any more. "Out! Both of you get out of my house and out of my life. I never want to see either of you again."

Both of the men got up and started for the door. When Travis passed her she said, "Did you ever think that it's not the Maxwell name that brings out the bad in people? That it's *you*?"

Travis had no answer for her.

Kim slammed the door behind them, locked it, then leaned back against it. "For your information, John Travis Maxwell, *I* want love too."

Two minutes later she was calling the person she wanted to talk to about all this. He answered on the first ring and said he'd meet her right away. Twenty minutes later she was pulling into Joe Layton's parking lot.

Twelve

Joe Layton's solution to every problem was the same: food and work. After he'd spent thirty minutes listening to Kim's nearly incoherent words that she uttered in between copious tears, and feeding her, he put her to work. As he had her help him put the supplies Travis had unpacked on the shelves that he'd installed, Joe couldn't help musing on the fact that their turbulent love life was giving him a lot of free labor.

"I don't get it," she said as she picked up boxes of electric drills and put them on the shelves. "Why would he make so much effort to get a man away from me if all he plans to do is leave me and go back to . . . to wherever he lives?"

"New York," Joe said. "Lives on the top floor of some big building."

"He told you that?"

"No, but I found out."

"That means you've known Travis's last name and

you looked him up on the Internet," Kim said with a sigh. "Reede said I'd find out everything there, but he couldn't wait to send me info. But who wants to find out about someone on the Web? But then, why does everything Travis tells me have to be a lie? Or an evasion? What's happened in his life that makes him think even the most ordinary things have to be kept secret?"

"I don't know," Joe said. They were questions that were bothering him too. He'd given Lucy every opportunity to tell him about her son, but she hadn't. Three times she'd almost said "my son" but each time she'd caught herself. Joe was trying hard not to get angry about it, but it wasn't easy. "Are you in love with young Travis?" he blurted out.

Kim paused for a moment in putting a box on the shelf. "How can I be? I thought I knew the boy Travis, but the adult . . . I don't know who he is. He seems to think he has a right to oversee my life. He takes away from me but gives nothing in return." She knew that wasn't true, but her anger wasn't allowing her to reason.

The red light on Joe's cell phone came on again. He had it on silent so Kim couldn't hear it, but Joe knew that Travis had called him eight times since she'd arrived. He also knew he was going to have to deal with the young man or he'd show up at the door. And with the mood Kim was in now, she might throw an anvil at him.

"Didn't I hear that you were supposed to do something special this weekend?" Joe asked.

Kim groaned. As angry as she was, it didn't dampen her artist's eye as she arranged the small machines on the shelves. She put them up with all the finesse that she used to display her jewelry. "Jocelyn—she's married to my cousin—wants me to go to some little town in Maryland to see if I can find out about some great-great-grandaunt of mine. Joce is doing genealogy charts, and this woman in Maryland had a kid but there's no father listed. This is back in 1890-something. I don't know how I'm supposed to do this. But anyway, Dave wanted to go with me and we were going to make it a minivacation. He was going to . . ." She waved her hand. If she continued talking, she'd start crying again. "I think I'd better cancel my reservation."

She couldn't help thinking about what might have been. What *would* she have done if Dave had asked her to marry him? She'd told Travis she'd known all about the man, but she hadn't. Hearing that he'd pawned the ring he'd slick-talked Carla into "giving" him had made Kim feel sick. She'd not seen anything in Dave that made her think he was capable of such thievery. He'd always been so very nice—boring, but pleasant and likeable. His talks about her going national with her jewelry had always been presented in the most respectful way, saying that it was her decision, and he was only tossing out ideas. And she really had thought the name he'd suggested was just a crude joke.

She'd only heard about Dave's company's failure the day before Jecca's wedding, the day before Travis reappeared in her life. She'd seen that two of his vans were on their last legs, but he'd laughed and said he had too much work to do to order new ones. She'd had no reason to disbelieve him.

But the day before the wedding, when everything was chaos and there were so many people around, Kim had overheard a woman saying she was glad Jecca hadn't used that "dreadful" Borman Catering. Kim had tried to get him for the wedding, but he'd been booked solid. Kim had asked the woman why she didn't like Borman Catering and she'd been told the story of the switched ingredients. And she'd heard that people were canceling their future orders with him. At the time, Kim had been so busy helping Jecca that she hadn't thought about what that meant. When Kim looked back on it, she realized that she hadn't wanted to see that Dave's business was going under. And she didn't want to think about that in connection to how often he asked for the combination to her safe.

Was Dave yet another man in her life who couldn't see past her success?

Kim arranged a hand drill in its case as artistically as she could manage, then started putting up the boxes of bits.

When Joe excused himself to make a call, Kim continued to work—and to think.

Okay, so maybe it was true that she didn't know as much about Dave as she'd told Travis she did, but did that give him the right to . . . to . . . take over?

She thought of Travis buying Borman Catering. Why? But she knew the answer. He paid all that money just to send Dave away. On the drive to Joe's she'd called a client who lived in Dave's building and was told that he'd left with six suitcases and had told the landlord he wasn't coming back.

"The landlord was furious," the woman said. "Dave left so much junk behind and the landlord has to take care of it. But then some man called and said he'd come get everything. The whole building is talking about it. What do you know?"

"Nothing," Kim said and politely hung up.

She'd told Travis she hated the way he'd swooped in and taken over, but there was a part of her that was grateful that he'd saved her from Dave. Kim now wondered if she would have agreed to marry him. Had Jecca's wedding, her happiness, made Kim so envious that she would have said yes just to . . . ? She didn't want to think about what could have happened.

Earlier, as Kim had pulled into Joe's parking lot, her cell buzzed. It was an e-mail from her brother and there was an attachment. Kim hesitated before opening it because she knew what it was going to be. But she also knew she needed to see the truth. She pushed the button and the first thing she saw was a photo of some drop-dead gorgeous woman named Leslie. The caption read WEDDING BELLS FOR A MAXWELL? The article told how the beautiful model had been going steady with the megarich son of Randall Maxwell for months now. *"Travis—über rich, über beautiful—never dates anyone for longer than six weeks. But he and the luscious Leslie have been together for nearly a year now. Can we look forward to a wedding like the world has never before seen?"*

Kim couldn't stand to read the rest of the documents her brother had sent. That one was quite enough.

When she got out of the car, Joe was standing in the doorway, and he opened his arms to her. If her dad had been home she would have gone to him, but Jecca's father was nearly as good.

She'd cried hard for a while, then Joe had ordered in pizza and huge colas and enough cinnamon sticks to fatten half of Edilean. Kim had cried and eaten, then cried some more.

"I don't understand why he lied to me," she said.

"Borman or young Travis?" Joe asked.

"Travis," Kim said. "Dave is . . . He's a real person, so of course he lies."

Joe raised his eyebrows but he didn't comment on that statement. In dealing with his children of opposite sexes he'd learned a hard fact. If Joey came to him with a problem, he was asking for help to find a solution. But if Jecca had a problem, she just wanted Joe to listen. No advice. Whereas Joe had been free in telling Travis what he thought, Joe didn't dare offer Kim so much as a suggestion.

"He lied to me about everything. From day one, I

was completely honest with him, but he told me nothing but lies."

Joe had to refrain from rolling his eyes. That's pretty much exactly what Travis had said about Kim. He'd said she'd concealed the fact that she had a boyfriend and had glossed over a story about a missing ring. But Joe made no comment. His cell light went on again and the ID said it was Travis. At the ninth unanswered call, Joe excused himself and went outside.

Minutes later, he was back—and Kim was still ranting.

Joe wanted to help her but he didn't know how. He'd talked to Travis and he was miserable. He said he just wanted to make sure Kim was all right. "She was so angry I was afraid for her to drive."

"I guess that means you followed her," Joe said. Travis's silence was answer enough. "What have you done about this weekend?"

"Weekend?" Travis asked, sounding as though he hadn't thought about it. "You mean Janes Creek?"

"Don't dance around me, boy! What have you *done*?"

Cautiously, Travis told him of renting every room in the two inns in the little town.

Joe gave a low whistle. "Did your dad teach you to take over everybody's life?"

"I think it's more that I was born with it in me than that I learned it," Travis said gloomily.

Joe almost laughed but didn't. "I'll get Kim to go to

that town, but you have to take it from there. Think you can manage that?"

"But Kim said she never wants to see me again," Travis said, his voice full of his despair.

Joe snorted in exasperation. "And that's going to stop you? Haven't you ever had a woman tell you to get lost?" To him it was a rhetorical question requiring no answer. Of course women had said that to Travis, to all men.

"No. Not actually," Travis said. "Never."

"What a world you live in!" Joe muttered, then said louder, "That's because Kim sees *you* and not the Maxwell name. Try being yourself with her."

"But . . ." Travis said, then trailed off. "Will you see that she gets home all right?"

"Of course," Joe said and hung up. He took a deep breath, spent a few minutes looking at the stars and wishing he was snuggled up with Lucy, then went back into the shop. He was going to have to say the sentences that women so loved to hear. Every male chromosome in him fought against it, but he *had* to say them.

"Kimberly," he said when he got inside, "I think you need to do something good for yourself. Take care of *you*. You should treat yourself to a weekend away. Get your nails done, buy yourself some new shoes."

Joe stood there looking at Kim and wondering if she'd fall for it. Jecca would know he was up to something, but would Kim?

Instantly, some of the misery began to drain from Kim's face. "I think you're right," she said. "I'm not going to cancel my reservation. I'm going to Janes Creek and spend the whole weekend thinking about my jewelry and my ancestors. No men anywhere."

She went to Joe and kissed his cheek. "I understand why Jecca loves you so much." She was smiling even though her eyes were still red. "Thanks for everything."

She left by the front door and Joe sat down heavily in his big chair. When did he become the man who solved other people's love problems? He couldn't even solve his own.

In the next moment he picked up his phone and punched the button to reach Lucy.

"Where are you?" she asked. "I just got out of the tub and I have on my—"

"Lucy," he said firmly before he lost his nerve, "I think it's time you and I talked about your son. And your husband."

She hesitated. "All right," she said softly. "I'll be waiting for you."

Joe let out his breath, and the tension left his big body. "What were you saying about what you have on?"

Kim did her best to sleep that night, but too much was going around in her head. Her dreams were of

Travis and in each one, he left. Just walked away as he'd done so many years before.

She got up at two, started to get some milk, but then poured herself a shot of single malt. She tried to watch a movie but couldn't keep her mind on it. She told herself it was absurd to compare something a twelve-year-old boy did while hiding with his mother from an abusive father to the man he was now. And when it came down to it, Travis had the right to not tell anyone his last name. She'd never been around anyone who had to deal with paparazzi, so who was she to judge?

But no matter what her thoughts, or how rational she was, she still felt betrayed.

When she'd come back from Mr. Layton's she'd seen that Travis had moved out of the guesthouse. He'd locked the door and left the key on her kitchen countertop.

She looked at the key but didn't touch it. To touch it would make his leaving seem real.

She took a shower, washed her hair, and told herself that everything was for the better. Travis had found out what a snake Dave was; Kim had found out that Travis . . . She wasn't sure what she'd discovered about him. Finding out that he was the son of some rich, powerful man hadn't surprised her in the least.

At 4:00 A.M. she went back to bed and slept until eight. She felt better when she woke up and knew that the last thing she wanted to do was go to work.

For one thing, she couldn't bear to see Carla. It was going to take a while before she could trust the woman again. Yesterday morning, Carla had confessed to what she'd done. In defending herself, she'd said that Dave had been so very persuasive as he talked about how much he loved Kim. And Carla had fallen for it. She'd taken the ring out of the display case and given it to him because he'd said he was going to present it to Kim on their weekend together. He'd elaborated on how there would be candlelight and he would be on one knee. Carla's sense of romance had overwhelmed her.

It was Carla's date with Russell Pendergast Wednesday night that had made her rethink what she'd done. He'd leaned across the table and looked at her with his beautiful dark eyes and coaxed the truth out of her. Afterward, he'd been clear that he didn't think what she'd done was in the least romantic. In fact, he'd said that if she didn't want to go to prison, she *had* to tell Kim the truth.

It had taken all her courage but Carla had told Kim the next morning.

At the time, Kim had been angry but it's what she'd thought had happened—and why she hadn't pursued the matter. At no time did Kim think Dave was scheming to steal the ring. Like Carla, she believed the man's hints of marriage and a future together. Her problem had been how she was going to answer Dave's proposal. Travis had shown strong signs of jealousy about Dave, so maybe Travis had plans for the two of them.

Kim hadn't allowed herself to think of that. She'd reminded herself that Travis was as elusive as a nightingale, that he didn't stay anywhere too long.

All that day she'd been nervous, and she'd kept wondering where Travis was and what he was doing. When there was no call from him at lunchtime, she wanted to go home early. Maybe Travis was doing laps in the pool. But customers kept her late, and as soon as she pulled into her driveway, Reede parked beside her. When she saw his face, she knew what was coming. He'd at last remembered where he'd seen Travis— on a racecourse when Travis had nearly hit Reede and his donkey.

As she walked to her front door, Kim thought about how she was going to defend Travis. She would point out that Reede had been in the way, that he shouldn't have been standing in the roadway. Kim was totally on Travis's side.

What she hadn't expected was that Reede couldn't care less about what had happened in Morocco. In fact, he admitted that the whole thing had been his fault. "That doesn't matter," Reede said, then proceeded to tell her the truth about Travis.

It didn't matter to Kim whether Travis was rich or poor, but it did concern her that he'd not told her such fundamental information about himself.

Why? Did he think she couldn't handle it? Did he

think she was so provincial that she'd be overcome to find out he'd spent his life in a different circle than she had? Did he think the truth about himself would change what was between them?

She had no answers to her questions.

The scene with Reede had been bad enough, but then to walk into her kitchen and see Travis and Carla's date standing there was almost more than she could bear. She could tell by Travis's face, white with shock—and she had to admit some pain from what he'd heard—that if she didn't get angry she would have died of embarrassment. She would just plain curl up into a ball and disappear.

Somehow she'd managed to keep cool enough to tell Travis what she thought of him. But when she began to remember how she'd told her brother that she wanted to spend days in bed with Travis, her anger was taken over by the embarrassment. She knew that if those two men stayed, she'd dissolve into tears in front of them, so she told them to leave. But she couldn't bear to be alone, so she went to see Mr. Layton.

Now the morning light was coming through her kitchen window and she was doing her best to be cheerful about her coming weekend. Alone. She tried to think of those old axioms about bowls of cherries and lemonade, but she couldn't seem to remember them. She'd already called Carla and told her she was to take care of the shop Friday and Saturday. There was another girl who could help, but Kim wouldn't be there. Carla hadn't argued or asked for overtime.

Kim packed quickly and was on the road by 10:00 A.M. It was a four-hour drive to Janes Creek, and she used the time to try to think about her next series of jewelry designs. She needed something different, something a person didn't see every day.

She also needed to think about the task Joce had given her to do. Everything she was to research was based on a few sentences that Colin's wife, Gemma, had found in a letter written around the turn of the century.

"Please tell me you're not trying to find more relatives," Kim said to Joce and Gemma the day they'd asked her to take on the project. They looked at her as though to say yes, that is exactly what they wanted, and why didn't she understand?

Kim had to remind herself that neither of the women had grown up in Edilean surrounded by what seemed to be thousands of relatives. Joce and Gemma had come from small families where they didn't know their aunts and uncles, much less their fourth and fifth cousins. Between this lack and their shared love of history, the two women were fiendish at finding out everything about everyone—and as far back as they could go.

"Why me?" Kim had asked when she'd been invited to Joce's house for lunch. She lived in the big old Edilean Manor, the place Kim had so hated as a child. Joce had done a lot with it, and it was beautiful now, but Kim wouldn't have taken the house if it were given to her. She much preferred her one-story newer house with its big windows, and floors that didn't creak with age.

In answer to her question, Gemma had put her hand on her growing belly and Joce had glanced at all the toys around them. She had toddler twins.

Kim grimaced. "If I get pregnant in the next two weeks can I get out of this?"

"No!" Joce and Gemma said in unison.

Joce had done everything. She'd made the reservation at the B&B in Janes Creek and she'd prepared a portfolio with papers that told all that they knew about Clarissa Aldredge, the ancestor she was to search for information about.

Gemma had written a veritable treatise of where Kim should look for the information they sought. Kim glanced at it, saw "cemeteries" at the top, and closed the folder. She didn't understand why those two women liked doing this.

Kim had been almost grateful when Dave invited himself along. He didn't seem interested in looking for dead ancestors, but at least he'd be someone to share meals with.

When Carla started giggling and talking about the weekend and saying that she had put a ring in the safe before closing time, it didn't take much for Kim to figure out what was going on. Just the weekend before, Dave had admired the ring and made a joke about it exactly fitting Kim. His eyes had said the rest of it.

But that had all changed. Just a few days ago Travis . . . Maxwell—she wasn't used to the name— had shown up and turned Kim's life upside down.

"But that's over now," she said as she pulled into the Sweet River B&B. It was 2:00 P.M. and the parking lot was full of cars bearing plates from the Northeast. She hadn't seen the town but had assumed it was about the size of Edilean. Maybe they were having some local event and that's why they were so full.

She got her bag out of the back, put the portfolio under her arm, and went inside. It was an old house that had been converted into some semblance of a hotel. She could hear voices in the back but saw no one. She thought she should get her camera out and photograph the interior for Joce and Gemma, as she figured they'd like the place. There were carvings everywhere, where the ceiling joined the walls, on the stair posts, and on an enormous cabinet against the wall. She was sure there were people who would love the house, but to her it was dark and gloomy.

"Just like me," she said aloud, then turned at a sound.

"You must be Miss Aldredge," a young woman said. She was blonde and thin and pretty, and was looking at Kim as though she'd been waiting for her.

"Yes, I'm Kim. I'm early, but is my room ready?"

"Of course," she said. "I mean it is now, but . . ."

"But what?"

"Nothing."

Kim got out her credit card but the girl wouldn't take it.

"Everything has been taken care of," she said. "Meals, extras, it's all been paid for in advance."

Luke, Kim thought. Her rich writer-cousin, Joce's husband, was footing the bill. "All right," Kim said and did her best to smile but she couldn't quite make it.

"You're on the top floor," the girl said, then picked up Kim's bag and went up the stairs.

The room was lovely. Large and airy and done in peach and green florals, with striped curtains at the tall windows. Had Kim been in a better mood, she would have been more appreciative.

Kim started to tip the girl but she refused and minutes later Kim was alone.

She flopped down in a chair. Now what? she wondered. Unpack then go look at cemeteries?

"What a fun life I lead," she muttered.

She knew she was indulging in self-pity. Every self-help book said she needed to look at the positive, not the negative. But at the moment all she could think was that she had lost *two* men in *one* day.

Jewelry! she thought. Think about jewelry. But then she remembered the necklace she'd made for Travis so long ago. He'd said he still had it.

That thought made her realize that she'd never see

him again. Why was it that when you asked a man to do something like stop driving so fast that he paid no attention to you? You could tell him a hundred times and he'd still "forget." But tell him one time to go away and never come back and he obeyed absolutely. No second chances. No reminders needed.

Kim told herself to get a grip. The two men she'd lost weren't worth all this angst. Dave was . . . She didn't know how to describe him. In fact, she could hardly remember him. In less than a week, Travis had taken over her mind.

"But not my body," she said as she heaved herself up out of the chair. What she needed to do was to "bury herself in work," that phrase she read so often in books.

That was easy to do when you worked in an office. The other people, the noise, would distract a person. But Kim's job was creating. She did it alone, just her and a piece of clay or wax, or paper and pen. There were no other people to help put her mind on something other than what she'd lost. No boss telling her he wanted the report done *now* so she was forced to think of something else.

Kim looked at the wall in front of her and saw three big white doors. She assumed one was a closet and one led to a bathroom, but what was the other one?

"Lady or the tiger?" she murmured as she reached for the middle door and turned the knob.

It was a door into an adjoining room that was just

as big and beautiful as her room. Standing there, at the end of a four-poster bed, was Travis. He had on a pair of sweatpants that hung down low on his hips, his beautiful upper body nude. Muscles played under his golden skin, richly tanned and glowing with warmth.

Kim stood there, frozen in place, staring at him. In some deep recess inside her she still had a mind, could still think rationally. If Travis was here it meant he had again manipulated her and her life to suit himself.

But those thoughts were at the bottom of a very deep well. Right now all Kim could do was *feel*. Every molecule in her body was alive, vibrating, pulsating with her want, her *need* of this man.

Travis didn't say a word, just turned toward her and opened his arms.

Kim ran to him, her arms going around his neck, her mouth on his. His kiss was hungry, as ravenous as she was for him. His lips were on hers, hard, searching, first on her mouth, then her cheeks, her neck.

Kim put her head back and let his hands and lips take what they wanted.

Her clothes came off. She didn't know how. She didn't feel buttons being undone, heard no fabric tearing. One minute she was dressed and the next she wasn't.

She laughed as Travis picked her up and flung her on the end of the bed. Covers and pillows billowed out around her and she laughed again. This wasn't polite, respectful sex but pure, raw passion.

Travis stood over her, looking down at her nude

form for a moment, then he gave a grin that was so devilish, so wicked, that Kim fell back on the bed and opened her arms to him.

He picked her up with one arm around her shoulders, the other entwined in her hair, and pulled her head back to give him access to her face.

When he put his mouth on hers it was with all the passion he felt.

His sweatpants fell to the floor and she wasn't surprised to feel that he had nothing on under them. Her hands went down his back over the hills and valleys of his muscles. She curved out over the firm set of his buttocks, then down his thighs. His mouth was on hers, his kiss deepening, becoming more urgent with every second.

Kim's hands went to his thighs, then up to put them on the male center of him. He was rampant with desire for her, his maleness strong, hard, big. She felt her body melting with wanting him to take her. She felt like she'd been waiting for him for most of her life.

When Travis began kissing her neck, she leaned back, meaning to lie on the bed, to open herself to him.

But Travis didn't let her lie back. As though she weighed nothing at all, he picked her up with one arm, his other one pulling her legs around his waist.

With perfect aim he set her down on his manhood. He slid in easily.

"A perfect fit," she murmured.

"Did you ever doubt that we would be?" he said into her neck.

He held her to him and she loved that her full weight was on him, that she was touching only him. His hands, his big, strong hands, were clasped onto her bottom and raised and lowered her.

Kim let her head go back, let him move her slowly, deeply, the long strokes filling her as no man ever had before.

When she thought she was about to explode, he fell with her onto the bed. He pulled her up toward the headboard, never breaking the contact between them, as his strokes became more urgent, faster.

Kim wanted to scream. She'd never before felt this intensity, this sensation that her mind, her body, her very soul was being touched by this man.

When she came, she wrapped her legs around his waist so tight she thought she might cut him in half. But Travis was feeling his own climax and his shudders went through both of them.

He collapsed onto the bed beside her and pulled her close into his arms. Kim put her thigh over his, feeling the dampness of him. His body felt so strange but at the same time so familiar. He was the boy she knew so well, and the man she didn't know at all.

"What do you want to know about me?" he asked softly, his fingers in her hair, his palm against her cheek.

"What did you—?" she began, but cut herself off.

Did she really want to lie in his arms and talk about his father? Did she want to hear more about his isolated childhood? Or should she be one of those girls who demanded that a man tell her about his past sexual exploits? In other words, did she want to lie beside him and ask about the beautiful Leslie?

"Kim," he said, "I'll tell you anything you want to know. I'll confess how I rented out this whole place because I couldn't bear to think of you here with another man. How I got Borman to tell me what he was up to. How I—"

Kim leaned over and kissed him, her breasts touching his chest. "Do you know anything about research?"

"I know everything about it," he said solemnly. "When I want to know about something I call Penny and tell her to do it. She can research anything."

"Oh!" Kim said, rolling off him and putting the back of her hand to her forehead. "How do I deal with someone so spoiled?"

Travis turned on his side toward her and ran his hands over her breasts. "Penny is a necessity. She frees me so I can spend all my time masterminding my dad's evil operations." Bending, he put his mouth on the pink tip of her breast. "You are as pretty as wild roses in the morning. Pink and white against the mahogany of your hair. I've never seen anyone more beautiful than you."

What he said, the way he said it, took her breath away. But at the same time there were images of another woman in her head. "That's not what my brother says about you and . . . and the others." Her tone was light but she was serious.

"Your brother? You mean the guy who stands in the middle of a racecourse holding a terrified donkey?"

The image made her laugh—and it made her brother sound too dumb to know anything.

Travis began to nuzzle her neck. She could feel his whiskers on her skin; she could smell the maleness of him. Closing her eyes, she let her senses take over.

"I love to hear you laugh," he whispered as his lips traveled down her shoulder. "When we were children I knew I'd never seen anyone as happy as you." His mouth went across her collarbone as his hand came up to her breasts. He lifted his head to look at her. "Your love of life, what I learned from you, has sustained me through the years."

She started to ask him why he hadn't contacted her when she was in college, but Travis's mouth descended on hers and she forgot her question.

His hands explored her body, running over her legs, between them. When he touched the soft center of her, she gasped. Gently, he caressed her and she closed her eyes, giving herself over to the sensation of him, to the pleasure of his touch.

Slowly, he moved on top of her. The weight of him felt wonderful, reminding her of his maleness.

He entered her slowly, filling her, and his strokes were long and deep. He took his time as he watched her, smiling as he saw the pleasure on her face.

It was minutes before Kim's eyes opened and she looked at him in surprise. She could feel the waves in her beginning to rise higher and higher. She'd never felt this way before, never . . . "Travis," she whispered.

"I'm here, baby," he said, then held her as he flipped onto his back, with her straddling him. His hands were on her hips.

Kim grabbed his shoulders, her fingertips biting into him as she rose and lowered on him, their bodies coming together with the force of a tidal wave.

When she felt herself building until she couldn't take any more, he pushed her down to the bed, her thighs around his hips, and came into her with a force to match hers.

He fell against her, weak, sated—and loving. His arms held her to him as though he was afraid she'd disappear.

For a moment she thought he'd fallen asleep but when she moved her foot, he loosened his arm.

"Am I hurting you?"

"Far from it," she said.

Travis moved his upper body half off her, put his head on his hand, and looked at her. "So what do you want to do?"

"Ask you questions about your past girlfriends," she said with a straight face.

She was rewarded with a split second's look of terror before he smiled.

"You're going to punish me, aren't you?"

"Yes," she said as she reached up to touch his hair. Since the first night he'd appeared in the moonlight at Jecca's wedding, she'd wanted to touch him. "I'm going to make you regret lying to me."

"I didn't really lie."

"Isn't there a law about evading being as bad as flat-out lying?"

"What would I know about the law?" he said, his eyes twinkling. Turning, he put his hands behind his head and looked up at the canopy. When Kim started to move away he pulled her back. Her head exactly fit in the curve of his shoulder. Her hand ran over the light hair on his chest.

"Did you look around this place?" he asked.

She was so distracted by his skin that she didn't at first know what he meant. She lifted on one arm and looked at his chest. "What are all these scars from?" There were three on his ribs, one across the side of his stomach.

"Stunt work," he said and didn't seem to be interested in saying any more. "This town."

"What about it?"

He rolled over to look down at her. "Have you seen this little town?"

She lifted a bit for him to kiss her and he did. "No," she said at last.

He lay back down beside her.

When he said nothing else, she looked at him. "Was that a hint about something?"

"Didn't you come here for a reason? Other than to marry some lowlife loser, that is."

"I wouldn't have—" She wasn't going to let him bait her into an argument. "Good thing you bought him out for me, isn't it? Are you going to learn to cook so you can run your new catering company?"

"I'm going to make Russell a gift of the whole business."

"For having only recently met, you two are certainly chummy," Kim said.

"Seeing me miserable seems to delight him."

"Why were you unhappy?" she asked before she remembered.

Travis looked at her.

She narrowed her eyes at him. "If you try to make me feel sorry for you I'll start asking you why you came to my art shows but didn't make yourself known."

For a moment Travis looked affronted, but then he gave a one-sided grin. "Sounds like we're even. You think there's any food in this room?"

"If not, you can buy the hotel and use your own catering company. Set up a Maxwell Industries right here in Janes Creek."

Travis shook his head. "You and my father are going to get along well. In fact, he might be a little afraid of you."

"Funny!" Kim said, but she was pleased by his words because he was saying that he was going to introduce her to his father. Maybe even his mother. Again.

When Travis rolled off the bed and stood up, Kim put her hands behind her head and watched him. She had pulled the bedspread over her and it was nice— erotic even—to be covered but to see him in the nude.

All those sports he did had given him a truly beautiful body, with muscles rippling under his skin. There were scars here and there, but they only added to the very male beauty of him.

"Do I pass?" Travis asked, his voice husky as he looked down at her.

"Yes," she said as she smiled up at him.

Smiling back, he pulled on his discarded sweatpants. He walked around, looking at things, then went into her room. He returned with the big portfolio Gemma had made for her.

"What's this?"

"The real reason I'm here."

"Mind if I . . . ?"

"Sure, look all you want. I haven't read any of it."

As Kim watched Travis stretch out beside her and begin to read the paper, she thought how little she knew about him. On the other hand, maybe she knew everything about him. The man who had scars from doing dangerous stunts was the same boy who learned to ride a bike and an hour later was doing wheelies. The boy who sat in a tree and read about Alice and the Mad Hatter was this man who was giving his full attention to some historical documents.

"Did you really not read these?" Travis asked as he

put the papers on his stomach and drew her to him.

"I saw the word *cemeteries* and closed the file. What did I miss?"

"Let's see . . . You want the facts presented as a fairy tale or as in a courtroom?"

She was tempted by the courtroom idea. She'd like to see him talking to a jury. But then, he'd probably use his good looks to charm the jurors—and she wouldn't like to see that. "Fairy tale," she said.

"All right." He was smiling. "Once upon a time, way back in 1893, a young woman from Edilean, Virginia, by the name of Clarissa Aldredge, wanted to spend the summer in Janes Creek, Maryland."

"Why?" Kim asked. "Why did she leave Edilean?" She knew her tone told something deeper than her words.

Travis kissed her forehead. "I can't imagine why she'd leave a town where everyone knows everything about everyone else."

"Except people's mothers," Kim muttered.

"Are you going to listen or throw barbs at me?"

"Let me think on that," she said. At Travis's look she told him to continue.

"Where was I? Miss Clarissa Aldredge went to Janes Creek, Maryland, in the summer of 1893. No one knows why she went there but it's my guess that she had friends in the little town and she wanted to spend the summer with them. Okay?"

Kim nodded.

"Whatever the reason she left, all that's known for sure is that when she returned to Edilean in September of that year, she was pregnant. She wouldn't tell anyone about the father, so the townspeople—who are given to a bit of gossip now and then—assumed that he was married. Clarissa never corrected anyone no matter what they said. The big problem was that after Clarissa returned, she was different. Melancholic. Depressed."

"I would think so," Kim said. "Unmarried and pregnant in 1893? It's a wonder she wasn't stoned."

"I think that happened in a much earlier time period. Anyway, it seems that poor Clarissa died a few hours after her son was born."

"Oh!" Kim said. "Joce and Gemma didn't tell me that part."

"Probably didn't want to upset you. On her deathbed Clarissa said to her brother Patrick, 'Name him Tristan and pray that he'll be a doctor like his father.'" Travis put the papers down and looked at Kim. "Aren't the Aldredge doctors today still named Tristan?"

"That name is saved for the ones who inherit Aldredge House." Her voice showed that her mind wasn't completely on what he was telling her.

"Not your branch?"

"No, which is why my brother is named Reede."

"So I remember," Travis said as he slid down in the bed beside her. "What's wrong?"

She couldn't tell him what was in her mind, that

she and Clarissa had a lot in common. Everything was temporary between her and Travis. He'd come to Edilean to help his mother and soon he'd be involved in a big divorce case. He'd go back to being a lawyer, back to his glamorous life in New York. Kim and boring little Edilean would be just a memory. Years from now, would he smile when he thought of her? She tried to put those images out of her mind. They were together *now* and that's what mattered. She gave her attention back to him. "I'm fine," she said. "Go on with the story."

"It seems to me that if Clarissa admitted the father was a doctor and his name was Tristan, wouldn't that make it easy for your friends to find him through an online site?"

"Actually, they did," Kim said. "They told me that they found a Dr. Tristan Janes—"

"Like the town name."

"Yes." She gave a sigh. "He died in 1893."

"I see," Travis said as he began to piece the story together. "Clarissa comes to Janes Creek to visit, falls for the local doctor, they tumble in the hay, but before they can get married she's pregnant and he dies. She returns to Edilean, has the baby, then . . ."

"Joins him," Kim said.

"Let's hope that's the way it works." He paused. "If your friends know all this, why did they send you here?"

"Joce and Gemma are newcomers."

Travis waited for her to explain that odd statement.

"They weren't born in Edilean. They want me to see if this Dr. Tristan was married and if so, did he have any other children."

"Cousins," Travis said. "Is this about finding more relatives?"

"'Fraid so," Kim said. "If I do find any young descendants, Joce will probably adopt them and Gemma will want to research the whole family."

"And will you decorate them?"

Kim groaned. "If I come up with some new ideas, yes. Since I met you, I haven't had even one new design for jewelry come to me. In fact I can hardly remember what I do for a living."

Travis's eyes were serious. "Kim, if you wanted to—"

She wasn't certain what he was about to say, but she thought maybe he was going to speak of his ability to pay for things. She didn't want to hear it. She changed the subject. "So when do we talk to the natives and ask who's old enough to remember 1893?"

"If Dr. Tristan died here, we should look for a grave marker and photograph it. Maybe there's something on it, and maybe someone is buried near him. If he had a wife, she'd be there."

"Maybe we'll be lucky and her name was Leslie." Kim hadn't meant to say that—or anything like it. She wanted to be cool and sophisticated. Instead, she was sounding like someone from . . . well, from a small

Southern town. "I'd better get dressed," she said and started to get off the bed.

But Travis caught her arm. "I think I should tell you the truth."

She kept her back to him, the sheet covering her front. She felt as though her words had bared a lot more to him than just her body. "Your life is your own. I'm just in it for the . . ." She wanted to say "sex" but couldn't do it. With her other boyfriends she'd always managed to keep it light between them. One of them had said she made jokes about everything. But this was Travis. The day after he'd returned to town she'd sent an e-mail to her friend Jecca saying the man she'd been in love with since she was eight years old had come back to town. Lover or not, she couldn't make a joke about him and his beautiful girlfriend.

When she didn't turn to look at him, Travis dropped his hold on her. "It took me so long to get back to you because I had to find out about myself," he said softly. "I was a rich man's son and I needed to know if I could support myself. I didn't want to be one of those trust fund guys who lives off his father. What kind of a man would I be if that's all I had to offer you?" When Kim didn't move, he took a breath. "After I passed the New York bar, Dad offered me a high-powered, highly paid job, but I turned him down. He was furious! He shut off my trust fund, so I was on my own. He said I'd not make it and the truth was that I was afraid he was right."

Kim turned to look at him.

"I wanted to get as far away from him as possible, so I bummed a ride with someone"—Travis gave a half grin—"on a private jet to L.A. I stayed with a college buddy while I looked for work. I was so angry that when I heard of an opening for stunt work, it appealed to me. I got the job because I'm the same size as Ben Affleck. I was shot twice for that man."

He smiled at her. "I succeeded and I proved that I was able to support myself. But I'd made it in the physical world by performing stunts. I was good at it, but I could see that my body wouldn't last, so I quit. And besides, it was no life for . . . for you."

"Me?" She blinked at him.

"Of course for you. I told you that my life has always been about you."

"But . . ." She'd thought he was saying one of those things that all men do. She hadn't taken it literally. "So what did you do?"

"My plan was to join a law firm. I was hired by a nice, conservative place in northern California. I thought I would work there for a year or so, then I'd return to Edilean to see you again. I wanted to know if there could be anything . . . adult between us. And if I had a year or two of legal work under my belt, maybe I could get work in or around Edilean."

Kim caught her breath, but said nothing.

"Everything was right on schedule until my mother stole millions out of one of my dad's accounts. He came to me in a rage and said he was going to kill her."

Kim gasped.

"He didn't mean it literally, but I knew he'd make her so unhappy she'd wish she were dead. I knew exactly where she'd gone: the town where she and I had been the happiest."

"Edilean."

"Right. And knowing that, I knew my hope of seeing you again anytime soon was gone. I knew my dad. He'd have me followed and when he did, he'd find my mother."

"So you went to work for him."

"Yes."

"You didn't plan to stay with him forever, did you?"

"I didn't think that far ahead. It seemed that one moment I was on my way to obtaining my lifelong dream—since I was twelve, anyway—and the next I was working eighty hour weeks for my father. I didn't have time to sleep, much less *think*."

"But you had time to see shows of my jewelry," Kim couldn't help saying, and there was anger in her voice. "If I meant so much to you, why didn't you say something to me? 'Hi, Kim. Remember me?' It could have been anything. I didn't know your last name and I searched for you for years. I—"

Reaching out, Travis pulled her into his arms and stroked her hair. "How could I come to you? You were doing so well. You were a rising star in the jewelry world. I had an Internet alert on you and it seemed that every day you achieved something new. While I . . . I was still my father's puppet. I needed to prove myself as a man."

"And in bed?" she said and more venom than she meant came out.

"Yes," he said. "I had to prove myself there too. It's one thing to have a girl teach you how to ride a bicycle but quite another for her to teach you what to do in bed. 'Now *where* do I put this big thing?'" he said in a falsetto voice.

Kim couldn't help laughing, then she pulled back and looked at him. "Did you break me up with any men besides Dave?"

"No, but I kept a close eye on them."

"What does that mean?"

Travis shrugged.

"What did you do?" she demanded.

"A few background checks, that's all. Nothing invasive. When I saw that they were much less successful than you, I relaxed. You would scare the hell out of them."

"Thanks a lot," she said. "You make me sound like I wield a sword and ride bareback."

"I like the image." His eyes were laughing.

"You!" she began. "You've put me through hell for years. I missed you and I couldn't find you and—" She broke off when he kissed her.

"I want to make it up to you." He kissed her nose. "I want to spend years and years making it right between us."

For all that she liked what he was doing, she drew back to look at him. "What does that mean? Exactly."

"I love you and I want to marry you. If you'll have me, that is."

Kim suddenly lost the power of speech. "But . . ."

"But what?"

"We hardly know each other. You've been back for a week and before that—"

He kissed her again. "How about this? You take as long as you want to get to know me, and every day I'll ask you to marry me. When you feel that you know me well enough, say yes and we'll go find a preacher. How's that?" Turning, he put his feet on the floor. "I'm starving. What about you? Penny has an uncle who eats so much she said I wouldn't be able to afford his bill. I'd like to see that, what about you?"

"I, uh . . ." Kim's head was still reeling from what he'd just said to her. "Where will you live?" she managed to get out. Travis was on his way to the bathroom.

"With you if you'll have me. I like your house, but I think you should move your workroom to Joe's place. You want to take a shower with me? That way your garage will be free. I believe in taking care of automobiles. Are there any good mechanics in town?"

As he disappeared behind the bathroom door, Kim sat there, staring. The sheet fell away but she didn't notice.

Travis looked around the door. "If you keep sitting there like that, I'll have to come back and make love to you again and I really am hungry. Have mercy on me, will you?"

He moved out of view but Kim still sat there. She wasn't at all sure of what she'd heard or what she was feeling. This weekend she'd expected a man she'd known for months to ask her to marry him. Instead, she'd just received a proposal from . . . From Travis, she thought and smiled. She envisioned him on the bicycle as he flew down the hill of dirt. His face and clothes were filthy, his teeth were coated in grime—but she'd never seen anyone happier. That boy had just asked her to marry him!

She heard the shower water. She took a few more seconds to blink, then she went running. "I like where my workroom is," she said. "I don't have to get in a car to get there, so I can work late at night. You can't—" She didn't say any more because Travis's long arm swept out and encircled her waist. The shower curtain was trapped between them.

"I'll drive you," he said before he kissed her again. "I'm good at driving."

"Yeah, if you like roller coasters without brakes."

"And you do," he said as he kissed her again.

Thirteen

Kim was sitting outside the B&B waiting for Travis. Just as they were at last dressed—the shower had taken a very long time—his cell phone rang. "On this number it's either Penny or my mother or you," he said as he dug the phone out of his trouser's pocket. "Penny," he said as he answered the call.

Minutes later he told Kim that "an incompetent moron named Forester" was having a meltdown and needed some help. "Sorry," Travis said, "but this will take some time. He'll destroy the entire deal if I don't walk him through it. Do you mind?"

"Of course not," Kim said. "I'll wait for you outside." As she left the room, she picked up her sketchbook. Maybe she'd have an idea or two for her designs. She doubted that she would, since all she could think about was what Travis had said to her. Had he really planned his entire life around her? Was that possible? But then, a part of Kim wondered if she'd done the same thing. Not consciously, as Travis seemed to have done, but unconsciously. Since she was a child and began sneaking into her brother's room where there was an Internet connection that wasn't ruled by her mother's iron parental controls, Kim had been searching for him. Her quest to find Travis had fluctuated with how her personal life was going. After a breakup with a boyfriend she had cried, eaten ice cream, and spent whole days on the Internet.

Now she realized that she'd probably seen photos of the rich Travis Maxwell, but she hadn't given them a second glance. She'd long ago figured out that Travis and his mother had been running from an abusive father. No one ever thought of super rich young men as having been anything but pampered and spoiled. She'd kept her searches off the society pages.

As for what Travis said about their getting married, more than anything in the world, Kim wanted to throw her arms around his neck and say yes. But she couldn't do that. There were too many problems yet to solve. Travis was still too connected to his other life, to his bastard of a father. How could they be happy until all that was settled? And his mother was going to need a great deal of help. As much as they all loved Joe, he was a small town man; he'd never be a match for Travis's notorious father. Randall Maxwell was known all over the world as a man who held his own against any-one—on a global scale. How could Joe, the owner of a small hardware store, cope with that? Travis would have to step in and take care of it all. How long did it take to divorce a superwealthy man who didn't want to part with a dime? Years? How could she and Travis have a life when he was constantly wrapped up in that mess?

It seemed that the obstacles around them were insurmountable. Not that she'd give him up. Not ever. But it was a question of time before they'd have their own lives, their own home, their own . . . children.

When she stepped outside into the cool evening air, she took a breath. She reminded herself that no matter what the obstructions, they'd have each other and there was light at the end of the tunnel. The thought that she did have a future where she wasn't alone—as she'd started to fear—made her smile, and as she did, her mind began to clear. And as she had since she was a child, she began to think about jewelry. In the fading light the leaves on a nearby maple tree looked like moonstones. Or maybe cut quartz. Of course the ones in the shadows were pure garnets. She hadn't used garnets in a long time so maybe now was the time to start again.

There was a little seating area set back under the trees, and she sat down on a pretty wooden bench and began to draw what she saw in her mind. The stones, even the curve of the leaves reminded her of a woman's neck. She could make the gold flow along the skin, then angle up over a collarbone. If she did it right, the necklace could be really sensual. Of course each one would have to be fitted to the wearer, but that would be nice to do. She hated those necklaces that were a stiff, round circle. No one had a perfectly round neck and she thought the jewelry stood out awkwardly.

She was so busy with her thoughts and her drawing that she didn't see or hear anyone until a man almost tripped over her feet.

"I'm sorry," he said. "I didn't mean to disturb you."

Kim looked up to see a short, stout, sixtyish man standing to her right and holding a broom. He had on an old pair of jeans and a plaid shirt that looked as though it had been washed hundreds of times. He was smiling at her in a way that reminded her of people at home.

"Please go back to what you were doing." He nodded toward her sketch pad in a way that made her think he was curious.

"I like the way the light plays on those maple leaves," she said.

"They are beautiful, aren't they?" He put his hands on the top of the broom handle and stared at the leaves. "Are you one of the people staying here?"

"I am."

"I don't mean to be nosy, but is it a family reunion? We don't usually have this many guests here."

Kim suppressed a laugh as she thought of the truth of why so many people were there. Travis had planned to oversee her and Dave. Only Dave had been sent away. "No," she said. "It's just my . . ." She wasn't sure what to call Travis. Her fiancé? But then he hadn't officially asked her to marry him, not with a ring (what Kim told the young men who wandered into her store was necessary for a proposal), and she certainly hadn't accepted.

"Your young man?" he asked.

It was an old-fashioned term that seemed to fit the situation. "Yes, my young man invited some people."

They were silent for a moment, then the man glanced at her sketchbook. "I'll let you get back to what you were doing, but if you need any help with anything, let me know. Just ask for Red. That's what my hair used to be." He started to walk away.

"We have that in common. Actually," Kim said, "maybe you can help us find someone."

Halting, he looked back at her. There was something about him that she liked. He had a sweet smile. "I have trouble keeping all the newcomers straight, but if the person is over forty I can probably help."

She smiled at his use of "newcomers." It was the same term they used in Edilean. "How about if the person died in 1893?"

"Then I probably went to school with him."

Kim laughed. "Dr. Tristan Janes. I assume the town was named after his family?"

"Yes it was," the man said as he motioned toward one of the empty chairs across from her. He was asking her permission to sit there.

"Please," she said.

As he took a seat, he said, "Will your young man mind that you're having a tête-à-tête with another man?"

"I'm sure he'll be wild with jealousy, but I'll be able to calm his beastly spirit."

Red chuckled. "Spoken like a woman in love."

Kim couldn't help blushing. "What about Dr. Janes?"

"There used to be a library here, but when the mill closed the town pretty much died with it. They moved all the books and papers to the state capital. If they hadn't done that you could go to the library and read it all. I'm a poor second best. Anyway," he said, "a Mr. Gustav Janes started the town back in 1857 when he opened a mill that ground the flour for everyone in a fifty-mile radius. His only child, Tristan, became a doctor. I read that ol' Gustav, who couldn't read or write, was deeply proud of his son."

"As he should be," Kim said. "Tristan died young, didn't he?"

"He did. He was rescuing some miners and the walls collapsed on him. It took them a week to find his body. He was well loved and hundreds of people attended his funeral."

"And I'm sure that number included an ancestor of mine," Kim said. "It seems that she was carrying his child, who was my—let me get this straight—my great-granduncle."

"I think that makes you an honorary native of Janes Creek."

"Not a newcomer?"

"Far from it." In the distance they heard voices coming toward them, and Red stood up. "I think your young man is returning and I should go."

"The question everyone in my hometown wants to know is whether or not Dr. Janes was married."

"Oh no. I read that he was the town catch, a beautiful young man, but he never married. I'm sure that if he'd lived he would have married your ancestor. Especially if she was half as pretty as you are."

"Thank you," Kim said as Red started to walk away. "Oh!" she called out. "Do you know where he's buried?"

"All the Janes family are at the Old Mill. If you go out there, be careful. The place is falling down. Take companions with you. Big, strong ones."

"All right, I will," she said as he disappeared around a corner and out of sight.

To the left, on the other side of the dense hedge, came Travis, frowning as he spoke on his cell phone. But when he saw Kim he smiled and said, "Forester, just *do* it!" and hung up.

He held out his arm to Kim. "Ready for dinner?"

"Yes," she said as they walked toward the main building.

Concealed in the bushes and watching them was the older man, Red. He was smiling.

"Sir?" said a man in a suit.

"What is it?" Red snapped.

"You have a call from Hong Kong and Mr. Forester needs—"

Red frowned. "My son took care of Forester. I need you to send someone to the state capital. I want to know everything about the Dr. Tristan Janes who died in 1893."

"In the morning I'll—"

Red gave the man a sharp look.

"I'll call the governor."

"You do that," Red said as he walked away from the hotel.

The man picked up the broom and followed Randall Maxwell to the waiting car.

The sound of the shower running woke Kim, and as memories came to her, she stretched luxuriously. Last night had been wonderful. At dinner a table had been set up for them on a little glassed-in porch, and Travis had chosen the meal ahead of time. They'd had three different wines with their six-course dinner. Outside, the stars sparkled and the moonlight flowed over the soft glow from the candles. By the dessert course they were feeding each other—and it was all Kim could do not to jump on Travis and rip his clothes off.

"Shall we retire to our rooms?" he asked before dessert was finished.

"If you're ready," Kim said in her most demure voice.

"I have been . . . ready for the last hour." He sounded like a man in pain.

Kim gave a very unadult giggle.

They managed to bid their server—the same young woman who'd checked Kim in—good night and didn't so much as touch each other on the long trip up the stairs. Travis opened the door and let Kim go in ahead of him. He closed the chain lock, and turned to look at her.

There were no words needed. She made a leap and was in his arms. Clothes flew across the room and puddled on the floor. By the time they'd covered the few steps to the bed they were naked. They came together with all the passion they felt. And five minutes after their mutual climax, they began again, this time exploring each other's bodies and finding what the other liked.

"What about this?" Travis whispered, his hand between her legs.

"Yes, very much." Part of her still wished that they'd been together from the start of their adulthood. It would have been nice to learn about one another together. On the other hand, Travis knew some truly lovely things about a woman's body. He knew just what to do to take her to new heights of ecstasy, and keep her there.

As for Kim, she'd learned a thing or two also, and when she lowered her mouth onto the center of him, she was pleased by his gasp. Twenty minutes later she moved back up to his neck.

"Where did you learn to do that?" he asked, his eyes full of wonder.

"Late night TV," she said without cracking a smile.

Travis let her know he wasn't sure whether to believe her or not, but he liked thinking she'd learned from TV and not from another man.

"You make me crazy, you know that?" he said as he rolled her to her back and began kissing her.

They hadn't gone to sleep until 3:00 A.M. They'd fallen across each other, naked, sweaty, and as limp as rag dolls. At some point Travis had awakened. He moved Kim from lying crosswise on the bed, positioned her head on his shoulder, pulled the covers over them, and immediately went back to sleep.

It was morning now, and as Kim listened to the shower running, she kept smiling as she remembered last night.

Travis entered the room wearing a towel and drying his hair with another one. "You continue looking at me like that and I'll need another shower." He gave her a hot little look. "In an hour or so, that is."

Smiling, Kim stretched. "I had a good time last night."

"Yeah?" he said as he sat down on the bed beside her and stroked her hair back from her face. "I did too. How about if today we—"

"Oh!" she said and sat up straighter. "I forgot to tell you that I know where Tristan Janes is buried."

"That isn't what I was going to suggest we do, but we did come here for that purpose."

"Right. To find more of my relatives." Bending, he kissed her earlobe. "Maybe we could just call people named Janes and ask what they know."

Travis got up and headed for the bathroom. "I already checked the local phone book and I asked Penny. There are no Janeses left."

"When did you talk to her?" Kim asked.

"This morning while you were asleep," he called from across the room.

Kim glanced at the clock. It was a little after nine and she didn't think she'd ever slept so late in her life. When they were kids she and Travis had been outside before six. "Are you still a morning person?"

He put his head around the doorway, his cheeks covered in shaving foam. "I'm usually at the office by seven. What about you?"

"In my garage workshop at six."

"Of course I'm having breakfast by five," he said.

"Four-thirty for me."

"I'm in the gym at four."

"I don't bother to sleep at all," she said and they laughed together at their one-upmanship.

He came out of the bathroom, freshly shaved and nude. At Kim's look he paused in starting to dress, but then he turned away. "I don't know about you, but I'm starving."

As she started to get out of bed, she realized she too was naked and hesitated. Travis had his back to her but he was watching her in the mirror. It's not as though he hasn't seen me nude before, she thought as she threw back the cover and walked across the room with all the bravado she could muster. She paused at the bathroom door and looked back at him. He was buttoning his shirt—and he was smiling broadly.

She showered and washed her hair, copiously applying conditioner to make it as silky as she could. When she got out, she dried off, put on the hotel robe hanging from a hook on the door, and began to blow-dry her hair. Travis came in, fully dressed, and took the dryer from her. She was glad to see that he was a bit awkward with the big hand dryer—which meant he hadn't done such a domestic task before. As Kim bent her head forward and felt his hands on the back of her neck and in her hair, she didn't think she'd ever felt anything so sensual. There was something so very intimate, so private, about what he was doing that she thought it might possibly be sexier than sex. What a funny thought! Sexier than sex.

"What's that laugh for?" he asked as he turned the dryer off.

"Nothing, just silliness." Turning, she put her arms around his neck and kissed him. "Thanks," she said. "I enjoyed that."

"Me too." He ran his hands down the back of her body, and gave a pat to her rear end. "Get dressed so I can get some food! You wore me out last night." He left the bathroom.

"You?" she asked as she began putting on her

makeup. "You spent most of the time on your back. I was the one doing all the work."

Travis looked around the doorjamb. "So what channels of TV do you watch when you stay up all night? I think we should watch them together."

"Go away," she said, laughing, "and let me get ready."

He went back into the bedroom and put on his watch. "So tell me how you found out where Janes is buried."

With a curler clasped to her lashes, she told him about meeting the caretaker, Red, and the highlights of what he'd told her. Minutes later, she was finished and went to the bedroom to get dressed. Travis sat down in a chair to watch the show.

"So who's here that we can take with us?" she concluded as she started to fasten her bracelet, but then held out her arm to Travis.

"The man said we should take someone big and strong with us? Is that in case a rock falls on one of us and the other can't pull it off?"

"I don't know why he said that. You think Russell is here?"

"Probably. And since I'm footing the bill, I'm sure he's eating truffles and Beluga."

"Sounds good to me," Kim said. "After we go see this Old Mill, maybe we can walk through town."

"And see if there are any jewelry stores to check out?"

"Exactly," Kim said, pleased that he knew that about her.

He smiled as he opened the door into the hallway, and they started down the stairs. "I think I'd enjoy that. Maybe we could find a ring that you'd like."

"I don't copy other people's work," she said stiffly. They were outside the main dining room, which Kim hadn't seen.

"I was thinking more of something you'd like to wear for the rest of your life."

"I—" She wanted to say more but was cut off by a chorus of good mornings. The dining room had eight tables, and all of them were occupied by people she'd never seen before. But they all seemed to know them, as they said hello to Travis and "Miss Aldredge." "You'll have to introduce me."

Travis nodded to a table for four. "That's Penny and you know her kid. I've never seen the rest of them."

"Your room fillers," she said, amused. When Travis went after something he didn't hold back; he covered all the bases. Am *I* what he wants next? she couldn't help wondering.

Penny—Mrs. Pendergast—looked at Kim and nodded toward the two empty chairs at their table. She was a handsome woman, younger-looking than Kim had expected. Her face was unlined, and she'd kept her slim figure, which she showed off in black linen trousers and a white shirt. Peeping out from under her hair, which fell softly to her collar, were the pearl earrings that Russell had bought in Kim's shop.

"Your choice," Travis said.

Kim didn't hesitate as she walked to the table and took a seat. Her eyes were on Mrs. Pendergast. "I've heard nothing but good about you," she said. "Travis doesn't seem able to conduct his life without you."

"He gets in trouble; Mom gets him out," Russell said.

Penny gave her son a look to stop it, but he just smiled.

"And I have heard about you for years," Penny said.

"Really?" Kim asked, surprised. "I had no idea that Travis had ever spoken of me to anyone."

"Did you show her the plaque?"

"Not yet," Travis said as he gave his order to the server. There was an antique sideboard against the wall that was covered with silver chafing dishes, but it looked like he wanted the meal served to him.

Penny leaned toward Kim. "If you want something from the buffet, you'd better get it now before my uncle Bernie eats it all." She nodded toward a corner table where a tall, skinny man was digging into three piled-high plates.

Kim excused herself and went to get scrambled eggs, sausages, and whole wheat toast. When she turned back toward the table, she paused to look at the three of them. Travis and Mrs. Pendergast had their heads together, talking quietly. Actually, she was talking while Travis nodded solemnly, a slight frown on his brow.

The familiarity between them didn't surprise her, but what did was seeing Travis and Russell next to each other. When Kim had last seen Russell she'd been too upset to comprehend much of anything, but now she saw the similarities between the two men. They were the same height, had the same dark hair and eyes, and when they reached for their coffee cups, their hands moved in exactly the same way. Having lived in Edilean all her life, if there was one thing Kim knew about it was relatives. It was easy to see that Travis and Russell were closely related.

With her eyes wide, Kim looked up to see Penny staring at her. Kim raised her brows, as though to ask if Travis knew. Penny gave one sideways movement of her head to say no, and her eyes were pleading. They said, Please don't tell him. Not yet.

Kim didn't like to keep secrets from Travis, but there was more here than she knew about. She gave a curt nod to Penny, then sat down.

Travis and Penny went on talking about what the "moron" in New York was doing about some deal. While it was interesting to see another side of him, Kim was more fascinated by the similarities between him and Russell. She watched Travis's hand gestures, the way he held a fork. When Russell spoke to his mother, she listened to his voice. It was very like Travis's deep resonance.

After a few moments of unabashedly staring, Kim

felt Russ's eyes on her, and she looked at him. He was smiling at her as though they shared a secret—and it looked as though they did. A very *big* secret.

When Kim looked at Russell, he raised his glass of OJ slightly, as though in salute to her. She couldn't help giving a little laugh. Unless she missed her guess, Travis had a half brother.

"Sorry," Travis said as he leaned away from Penny and looked at Kim. "We're ignoring you."

"No one is ignoring me," she said. "In fact I'm being well entertained." She turned to Penny. "Didn't you use to work for Travis's father?"

"For many years." Penny's eyes were alight, as though she was wondering what Kim was going to say next. Announce what she'd just figured out?

But Kim wasn't even tempted to tell. Hearing that he had a brother was going to change Travis's world, and *she* was not the one to tell him. That news needed to come from Russell and Penny—and a lot of explaining was going to have to be done.

"Maybe Russell could go with us today," Kim said.

"Go where?" He was looking at Kim as though he expected her to tell what she'd just discovered.

"To some derelict old building," Travis said. "Last night while I was working, the love of my life was flirting with another man, and he told her where to go today. He said that she'd need the help of someone big and strong. Kim seems to think that's *you*." His tone was light and teasing.

His words "the love of my life" made Penny and Russell look hard at Kim. Penny glanced at Kim's left hand, obviously noting that there was no ring.

Kim knew there was more going on in the silence than in the words being spoken. "In case all of you forgot, I'm here to find my ancestor."

"And his possible descendants," Travis said.

"It seems that there's a grave site near an old mill, so Travis and I are going to go see it." She looked directly at Russell. "I think you should go with us. If this place is a ruin it'll be quiet there. A person can think. Or talk."

Russell gave a little smile. "I'm about talked out," he said and looked at his mother. "What about you? Finished with your New York business?"

"Completely," she said.

"Penny is going to retire," Travis said to Kim, "and she's thinking of moving to Edilean. Any good houses there for sale?"

"Old or new?" Kim asked.

"Old, small, on at least an acre. I like to garden. But I don't want it to be too far out of town."

"I know a place. It used to be an overseer's house. It would need some renovation." Kim turned to Russell. "And what about you? Where do *you* live?"

"Not in Edilean," he said as he put his napkin on the table and stood up. "When do you want to go to this falling down old building? Anyone bring a camera? Notebook and pen?"

Travis stood up to stand beside Russell. They were exactly the same build and wore the same expressions of challenge on their handsome faces.

Kim glanced at Penny. Why didn't Travis see the resemblance? Again Penny looked at Kim with that expression of pleading. Please don't tell, she seemed to be saying.

Kim hadn't made herself a success by being intimidated by anyone, no matter who she worked for. "Tomorrow," she said softly, and Penny nodded. She had twenty-four hours to tell Travis the truth and if she didn't, Kim would tell him.

Travis was waiting for her by the door. "Russ rented a Jeep and he went to get directions." He lowered his voice. "Kim, if you'd rather that you and I spend time alone together, I can turn this whole thing over to Penny. She'll find out about Dr. Janes."

"No," Kim said. "I think you should—" She'd almost said "get to know your brother" but she didn't. She wondered how he was going to react when he found out that his beloved assistant had had an affair with his father. Travis already had enough issues with his father and he didn't need any more.

"Think I should what?"

"Nothing. Here's Russ. Shall we go?"

Travis wanted to drive, but Russell wouldn't let him. "My car, my hands on the wheel," he said.

Kim rode in front with Russ. Travis was in back with the handwritten directions.

"Looks like you failed penmanship," Travis said. "I can't read this."

"Maybe you should have gone to better schools to improve your comprehension," Russ shot back. "Oh wait. I went to the same ones you did."

"Did you pass any of the classes?" Travis mumbled.

Kim looked out the window to hide her smile. They sounded like her and Reede.

The Old Mill was beautiful. It was wide and low, U-shaped, with the middle part one story, flanked by two-story sections. The building had a low stone wall along the front, which made a courtyard in the center of the U.

For a few moments the three of them stood, looking at the wonderful old building. Part of it had no roof and doves flew out when they walked up. But the two-story section on the left had new tiles on the roof. The little stone wall looked to be falling down, but in places the rocks had been replaced.

"Someone's been working on it," Travis said.

"*That* is perfect," Kim said. She was pointing inside the courtyard to the right. There, behind another low stone wall was a perfect little garden—except that it looked like something out of an eighteenth-century book about gardening. It had gravel paths laid out in the shape of a double circle with an X through it. Inside the eight quarters were wild, weedy-looking plants of different colors, heights, and textures. They had all been carefully, meticulously tended.

"Unless I miss my guess, those are medicinal herbs," Kim said, grinning, "and that means there's still a Tristan here."

Travis and Russ looked at each other, then back at Kim.

"What does that mean?" Russ asked.

"The Tristans are doctors so . . ." Kim said.

"Medicinal herbs," Travis finished for her.

"All the Tristans have the greenest thumbs imaginable. When we were kids we made Tris plant things for us. If he planted them they grew for sure. When the rest of us put anything in the ground, half the time it didn't grow."

"So maybe a descendant owns this place," Russ said.

A tile came rattling down from the roof, hit the ground, and broke.

"One who can't afford to restore it," Travis said, looking at Kim. "I think you are going to find some relatives here."

She looked at Russ. "Finding new relatives—ones you didn't know you had—can be very rewarding, don't you think?"

"It can also be terrifying," he said softly. "Traumatic."

"Possibly. But then I always find truth to be better than deep secrets."

"Depends on the truth," Russ said. His eyes were laughing, as though he were greatly enjoying the exchange.

Travis had walked away to the center of the building and pushed open a door. "Are you two going to spend the day in some cryptic, philosophical exchange or are we going to look around?"

"I vote that you scale this wall and walk along the ridgepole. Show us what you learned in Hollywood," Russ said.

"Only if you show us that you know how to do anything at all," Travis shot back as he went through the doorway.

Russ went to the door, and turned back to Kim. "Are you coming?"

"I . . ." There was something about the herb garden that she liked. Maybe it was the shape of it, or the light on the yellow-green leaves of one of the plants, but she was glad she had her sketch pad with her.

Travis came back to the door, and went to Kim. "Why don't you stay here and draw? The kid and I will find the cemetery and record everything." He kissed the top of her head.

She was grateful to him for understanding. When a spurt of creativity hit, it needed all her attention. To put it off might allow it to disappear. And too, unlike her history-loving cousins, Kim couldn't abide cemeteries. "Thank you," she said.

"Don't leave here, don't talk to strangers, and—"

"And don't eat any of those plants," Russ said.

"I'll try to behave myself," Kim said as she shooed

them away. She really did want to put those shapes down on paper.

Travis kissed her again, this time on the cheek, then went to the door.

"I thought you were a ladies' man," Kim heard Russell say, "but you don't even know where to kiss the girl."

"I could show you a lot about . . ." She heard Travis say as their voices faded into the distance.

Kim sat down on a flat stone near the plants she most admired. They were tall, with seed-filled heads that looked as delicate as rays of sunshine. She pulled out her phone, snapped a photo of one of them, and sent it to her cousin Tristan. WHAT IS THIS? she wrote.

Kim started sketching, translating the shapes into jewelry. The chain would be made of long, thin tendrils, like the leaves of the plant. She drew a curved shape with tiny spirals inside it that would clasp one edge of the chain. She'd put a pearl at the center of each one. The earrings had a thin leaf that would curve up a woman's ear.

Her phone buzzed; it was Tristan. ANGELICA, he wrote. WHERE DID YOU SEE THAT?

Standing, she stepped back to get a full view of the garden. When she couldn't get a good photo that showed the design of it, she climbed on the surrounding wall, snapped, and sent it to Tris.

When she started to get down, the loose rocks slid

under her feet, which flew out from under her. She would have fallen but a strong arm caught her.

It was Red from the B&B.

"Are you all right?" he asked as he helped her down.

"Fine, but thanks."

"I told you this place was dangerous," he said, his tone sounding severe. "Last year a woman nearly broke her leg here."

Kim sat down in the shade on an old doorsill.

"Don't lean back," he said. "That door doesn't look to be securely on its hinges."

She wiped dirt off her trousers and flicked sand out of her hair. "Are you the town watchdog?"

"More or less," he said. "I was on the way to the garage but made a detour by here. Looks like my worry paid off. You didn't come here alone, did you?"

"No. I have two big strong men with me."

He laughed. "Your young man and . . . ?"

"His—" She hesitated. "His friend."

"But not yours?" Bending, Red picked up her sketchbook. "May I?"

She gestured that it was all right for him to look at what she'd drawn.

"These are pretty," he said as he brushed off some dirt. "Do you make these into jewelry?"

"Yes. I have a shop in Edilean. That's in—"

"Virginia!" he said. "I used to go fishing there. Nice little town. I like the old houses. I don't remember a jewelry store, but I do remember a place that sold baby clothes." Red sat down on the low wall. "Why would I remember that?"

"Because they are extraordinary," Kim said. "The shop is called Yesterday and it's owned by a lovely woman, Mrs. Olivia Wingate."

"Does she make the clothes?"

"No. Lucy makes most of them."

"Lucy Wingate?"

"No. She's . . ." Kim trailed off. Everything about Lucy was too much of a secret to talk about. "Do you know who owns this place?" She gestured at the Old Mill.

"I'm not sure," he said. "I've seen a young woman here, but I don't know who she is."

"She's under forty?"

He smiled at her good memory. "Yes, she is. I'm sure you could find the property records in the county courthouse."

"Today? Saturday?"

"Oh. Right," he said. "But then, you don't want to waste your time with your young man in a dusty old courthouse, do you?"

"No," Kim said, "I don't, especially since we don't have much time together before he—" She waved her hand.

Red looked concerned. "You sound like he's ill. Oh, my dear, please say that isn't so."

"No, no," Kim said. "He just . . ."

"He's in the military? Facing combat?"

"No," Kim said. "He has some personal business he has to take care of, so he has to leave."

Red sighed in relief. "That doesn't sound so bad."

Kim snorted. "It has to do with his father and from what I've heard . . ." Again, she waved her hand. "That's . . ."

"I understand. It's private, but there's a reason that I'm known around town as everyone's grandfather. I'm a good listener."

Kim smiled. "That's what Travis says he is."

"And is he?"

"Yes, very good."

"Does he have other good qualities?"

"Of course. Lots of them."

"Then perhaps . . ." He trailed off.

"Perhaps what?"

"Sometimes children can't see their parents clearly. They remember that their mother wouldn't let them eat what they liked. What they don't remember is that they wanted to eat paint flaking off an old wall."

From what she'd heard, Travis's father hadn't been around enough to know what his son was eating. Was he having an affair with Mrs. Pendergast all those years? But she couldn't say any of that to anyone, especially not to a stranger.

Red stood up. "I believe I hear your young men returning, so I better go."

Kim got up. "Stay and meet them."

"Maybe this evening," he said as he began to walk

quickly. "I just remembered that I have a hundred pounds of ice in the back of the truck."

"It's probably melted by now," she called after him as she watched him hurry out of sight.

"Were you talking to someone?" Travis asked as he came back into the courtyard, Russ behind him.

"The caretaker from the B&B stopped by. He—" She broke off as her phone buzzed. It was from Tristan.

GORGEOUS GARDEN. I WANT TO MEET WHOEVER MADE IT. I SEE COMFREY. IS IT POSSIBLY BOCKING 14? I NEED SOME TO MAKE COMPOST TEA.

She gave the phone to Travis, he read it, and handed it to Russ. All three of them looked at the herb garden. To a person who knew nothing about herbs, the plants looked very much alike. How could he pick out one from a cell phone photo?

"Told you," Kim said. "There's a Tristan here. So what did you guys find out?"

Travis spoke first. "Dr. Tristan Janes, born 1861, died 1893, aged thirty-two years." He turned to Russell. "What did it say on the stone about him?"

"'A Well-Loved Man,'" Russ answered. "Not a bad thing to have people say about you. Sorry, but there was no evidence of a wife or kids."

"His father was named—"

"Gustav," Kim supplied.

"Right," Travis said. "No doubt that was told to you by the mysterious man named Red."

"What's mysterious about him?"

"Just that he disappears whenever we show up," Travis said.

"He's probably heard you're a Maxwell and he runs away," Russ said. "Smart man."

Kim squinted her eyes at Russell. He was as much a Maxwell as Travis was.

Russ gave a one-sided grin. He understood Kim's meaning perfectly. "So what do we do now?"

"*We* don't do anything," Travis said. "*You* are going to walk around town and ask questions until you find the owner of this old place. Kim and I are going to look at jewelry."

"Oh?" Russ asked, an eyebrow raised.

"For designs," Kim said quickly.

Travis pulled her arm through his. "Keys," he said to Russell, his hand extended.

"I need to—"

"Keys!" Travis said in a voice meant to be obeyed.

Russ laughed. "Big—Maxwell commands." He tossed Travis the car keys.

Kim was sure Russ had been about to say that "big brother commands."

With a grin, Russ winked at Kim.

He's enjoying this, she thought. And he's going to delight in dropping this brotherly bombshell on Travis.

When they were in the car, Kim asked Travis what he and Russ had talked about when they were alone.

"Nothing much, why?"

"Did you two keep arguing the whole time you were there?"

"Naw," he said, smiling. "That's all done for your benefit. He was actually good help. There are only six headstones in the little cemetery, and I took photos while Russ wrote down names and dates. I guess your friends will want all the data."

"I'm sure they will," Kim said.

"So what did you do, other than meet a man in secret?"

She ignored his comment as she opened her sketchbook. They had reached the center of the little town and Travis expertly parallel parked the car, turned off the engine, and took the book to look at Kim's designs.

"So this slides around a woman's neck?" he asked.

"Yes, and the earrings go up."

"Not down? Not grazing her shoulders?"

"I'm not much on chandelier earrings."

"Me neither. They get in a man's way." He leaned across the seat and kissed her earlobe. She had on small gold earrings with stones of citrine just off center.

She smiled at him, glad he'd really looked at her drawings. Most people just glanced at them and said how pretty they were, but they couldn't actually visualize her designs.

"Want to wander through every store or go directly to the one and only jewelry shop in town?"

She looked at him in disbelief. "Don't tell me you're

a man who likes going shopping with women? Going in and out of stores and looking at every little thing in the shop?"

"Well, I . . ." He looked out the windshield.

"Oh, I see. You're just being polite. You added the jewelry bit on the end to entice me there."

"I'm glad you're not a judge in a courtroom or I'd never be able to put anything over on you. I tell you what, today is yours. I'll go in and out of every one of these insufferably cute little stores, but in the future . . ."

"I'm on my own? You'll get a beer while I wander?"

"Pretty much," he said, and they smiled at each other. That they were speaking as though their future together was set in place, a given, a done deal, was pleasing to both of them.

They got out of the car and stood on the sidewalk, holding hands. So normal, Kim thought. So . . . so satisfyingly, deeply *normal*.

"Where to first?" Travis asked.

"There." Kim pointed to a used bookstore across the street. Its windows were covered in years of dirt and the few books she could see had curled, faded covers.

"Local history, right?" Travis asked. When Kim nodded, he raised her hand and kissed it. "Jewelry store last? To be savored?"

"Exactly," she said.

In the bookstore Kim was glad to see that Travis didn't mind going through boxes that had twenty years of dust coating them and digging for out-of-print books and local pamphlets. He found a cookbook put together in the twenties by the women of a local church.

They looked through it, saw there was no contributor named Janes, so Kim said it was no use to them. But Travis said a person never knew when relatives were going to turn up. Kim started to ask what he meant by that but he'd walked away.

He talked with the shop owner while Kim went through the shelves of books on the history of jewelry. She chose a big one on Peter Carl Fabergé.

They left the store with a box full of books, and Travis put them in the Jeep he'd commandeered from Russell.

"Do you think he walked?"

"Who?" Travis asked.

"Russell. You left him there at the Old Mill without transportation. Do you think he walked to . . . to wherever he went?"

"Probably called Penny and she picked him up," Travis said.

"So how long has she worked for you?" They were crossing the street again.

"Since I started at my dad's."

"And your father let her go so she could work for *you*?"

"Why all these questions?"

"I'm just trying to find out about your life, that's all."

He paused in front of a little shop that had some very pretty clothes in the window. "When my dad rooked me into working for him, Penny said she was going to help me. Dad didn't want to let her go, but she threatened to quit if he didn't, and since she knows more about the business than he does, he couldn't allow that."

"Why was she so adamant about working for you?"

"Felt sorry for me, I guess. I'd just come from Hollywood and my way of handling things was physical. I had trouble even remembering my law training."

"But Mrs. Pendergast took you under her wing and mothered you?"

Travis snorted. "She kicked me fifty times a day. Made me think. Made me put my anger at my father aside enough so that I could do the job. That first year was hell. Do you like that?"

"That your first year was bad?"

"No. I mean that shirt. Those pants. I think you'd look good in them."

"And trying them on would stop me from interrogating you, wouldn't it?"

"I never want to go against you in a courtroom." His hand was on her back as he urged her toward the doorway.

They spent two hours going from one store to another. For all that Travis had said he didn't like such things, he was a dream to shop with. He sat down and waited while Kim tried on clothes, and he gave his opinion on each one.

But for all that he seemed to give his full attention to her, twice he was on his phone, and each time he erased a frown when he saw her. She asked what was going on.

"Closing up business. You ready for lunch?"

As Kim turned away, she was reminded of all that was still facing them, especially the court case for the divorce. "Sure," she said as Travis opened the door for her.

But as soon as they were outside, his phone rang again. "Damn!" he muttered as he looked at it. "It's Penny. I . . ." He looked at Kim in question.

"Take it," she said. "I'll meet you at the diner." But she saw a flash of movement in the window of an antiques shop across the road. It was Mrs. Pendergast's arm, and she was waving at Kim, a phone to her ear.

Kim looked at Travis's back, then at Mrs. Pendergast. She was motioning for Kim to come to the store. They *did* need to talk.

"Thirty minutes, the diner," Kim said to Travis, and he nodded as he frowned at the call, and Kim hurried across the road.

Joe Layton took a couple of deep breaths as he picked up the phone receiver in his office. He was a believer in land lines. Their connections were better, less likely to fade out, and since the call he was about to make would change his—and Lucy's—life, he wanted to hear every word.

It had been simple to get the number of the headquarters of Maxwell Industries, but getting the man himself on the phone wasn't going to be easy. Joe thought maybe he'd tell whoever answered the phone that it was a matter of life and death. That way he'd keep the truth between him and Maxwell. But the snooty woman who was at the end of the line of a long succession of secretaries brought out the truth in Joe.

"You can't just call and expect to speak directly to Mr. Maxwell." Her tone was patronizing, but at the same time amused. It was obvious that she saw herself as Big City while Joe was Country Bumpkin.

Joe was fed up with all of them. "Tell him I'm the man who wants to marry his wife."

The secretary was silent for a moment, then her tone changed to brisk efficiency. "I'll see if he's available."

It was only moments before Randall Maxwell was on the line. "So you're Joe Layton."

"Looks like nobody's kept a secret from you," Joe said.

"Not if I want to know what's going on, they can't. So what's Lucy up to now?"

"I want to settle this thing between you and me."

"By 'thing' do you mean a divorce?" Randall asked.

"Yes, that's exactly what I mean."

"Layton, you weren't born yesterday," Randall snapped in a voice that often intimidated people. "There's more involved in this than just a few grand."

Joe wasn't intimidated in the least. "Keep your money," Joe growled. "Keep every goddamn cent of it."

"That's an interesting concept. What about the money she stole from me?"

"You mean the money you so conveniently left for her to find?"

Randall chuckled. "Lucy always did like clever men."

Joe didn't answer. When Lucy told him about "accidently" seeing her husband's laptop with his online banking account left wide open, Joe knew Maxwell had meant for her to see it. Lucy said there was five million in the account and she took three and a half. Joe admired her restraint. She spoke of how unusual it had been for Randall to leave his laptop where she could see it. "He must have been under a lot of stress." There was guilt in her voice, showing that she felt bad for what she'd done. The idea that half of what Randall Maxwell owned was hers didn't seem to have entered her mind.

If Maxwell had purposefully left the account open, he'd done it for a reason. If Lucy were a different kind of woman Joe would have thought that Maxwell suspected her of seeing other men and that he wanted to know where she went when she had money. But as Joe heard more of Lucy's story, he thought it was possible that Maxwell was giving his wife freedom.

Maybe Maxwell thought he'd failed with his son, so he no longer needed to use Lucy to hold Travis to him. If Joe knew anything in life it was the pleasure/pain you got from your family. He loved his son with all his heart, but there were times when the boy's wife made Joe want to disown him.

"So how's Travis?" Randall asked into the silence.

There was a soft undertone in his voice that told Joe a lot. Maxwell loved his son very much. "He's a good kid," Joe said. "You raised him right."

It was Randall's turn for a moment of silence. "Lucy can keep the money and I'll give her a divorce—and I'll be fair with her."

Joe drew in his breath. "If by that you mean you'll give her more millions, *don't*! Save it for Travis—and your other kid that I've been seeing around town. Seems his mother is your former secretary. Must have been convenient for you."

Randall laughed. "Layton, you ever want a job with me, you got it."

"No thanks," Joe said, but he was grinning as he hung up.

Fourteen

"So *what questions* do you have for me?" Penny asked Kim.

They were sitting at a rusty old table outside the back of the antiques store. There was a tall wooden fence on three sides, and leaning against it were dozens of old metal advertising signs. The Mobil Pegasus was directly behind Penny's perfectly coiffed head.

The first thing Kim was aware of was that Mrs. Pendergast had put herself in the position of power. Her chair's back was facing the fence, a solid barrier, while Kim's back was to the door and windows of the store, a more vulnerable position. But more important than that, Penny's words had cast Kim as the one who was to ask the questions and maybe she'd receive answers.

Kim wasn't falling for it. First, she moved her chair so that she was no longer backed against the openness of the store, then she looked at Penny. "I want you to tell me everything."

Penny gave a bit of a smile in acknowledgment of what Kim had done, and shrugged.

"Late night, champagne to celebrate a deal, handsome boss, fight with my boyfriend. It all went together to make it happen."

"And afterward?" Kim asked.

Penny took her time in replying, and Kim doubted that she'd ever told the story before. Mrs. Pendergast didn't seem to be the type to share intimate details of her life with anyone.

"That wasn't so easy. I didn't realize I was pregnant until I was four months along. By that time the boyfriend was gone and besides, Randall was . . ."

"Married."

"Yes. Married to a woman who couldn't care less about him or his business, his dreams, or about anything else to do with him." There was a hint of bitterness in her voice.

"So that makes it all right to jump into bed with him?" Kim asked. She was on Lucy's side.

"When you get older you're going to learn that there are always two sides to everything. Lucy married Randall Maxwell because her family pressured her into it. They were an old family, great lineage, but not a cent to their names. Randall supported her parents until their deaths, and he still pays the bills of Lucy's two lazy brothers."

Kim looked down at the table for a moment. "Why did he keep Travis so isolated?"

"Randall had a hard childhood. He was very poor and he's a bit dyslexic. He was bullied in school."

"So he gave his son tutors and privacy?"

"That's it," Penny said.

Kim was silent as she waited for Penny to continue. It was obvious that the older woman didn't want to go on—or maybe she did. Penny had been the one who set up the meeting, so maybe she was hoping Kim would help smooth the way between Travis and Russell.

"Randall thought he was doing well by his son when he had him homeschooled," Penny began. She looked down at her hands. "I know you're friends with Lucy, but . . ."

"I can take the truth, whatever it is."

"I think that at the beginning Randall believed he was in love with Lucy, but the truth was, he was in love with the idea of a family. He had visions of the two of them conquering the world together. He'd make the money, buy her a magnificent house, and she'd be the hostess who was renowned for her dinner parties. It would be like something out of a magazine."

"From what I've seen of Lucy's life now, that wouldn't be for her. She likes to sew and stay with a few close friends."

"Exactly," Penny said. "And Randall likes to *work*. And besides, he hates dinner parties. He loved the thought of them, but couldn't bear the boredom when he was there."

Kim was beginning to see the whole picture. Two extremely mismatched people married to each other. Lucy bullied by her relatives, almost sold by them, to a man who had a chip on his shoulder and something to prove to the world.

It looked like Travis had been caught in the middle.

"What about you? Where do you come in?" Kim asked.

"I . . ." Penny hesitated. "I'm more like Randall than Lucy. I also grew up poor and was desperate to get out of it. I met Randall at a party. I liked him because he was talking business instead of hitting on the girls. I stood to one side and unabashedly eavesdropped. He was so intent on the deal he was trying to make that I didn't think he even saw me. But when the other young men got bored and left, Randall turned to me and said, 'Did you get all that?' I said, 'Most of it,' and told him the numbers. He looked at me for a moment, then asked for my phone number and I gave it to him."

"I guess he called you."

"Yes," Penny said, smiling, "and it was all business. It's always been business between us."

"Except once."

Penny smiled broadly. "And that gave me Russell."

"Was Mr. Maxwell married when you met him?"

"No," Penny said. "He hadn't even met Lucy back then, but he knew what he wanted and he went after it."

"If you two were so alike, why didn't he . . . ?"

"Look at me as a prospective mate?" Penny laughed.

"You'd have to know Randall back then. Ambition ate at him. Consumed him. He *had* to get ahead of everyone else or he'd die."

"And Lucy was part of that," Kim said.

"She was indeed."

"But there came a night . . ." Kim said.

Penny shrugged. "When I look back on it, I see that it was inevitable. Randall and I were always together. Travis was just a year old, and I have to say that I was quite jealous of Lucy. I never had time for an outside life and never did find a man who'd put up with my constant working. Anyway, Randall and I stayed late at the office, we had sex, and I was pregnant."

"What did Mr. Maxwell say when you told him?"

Penny shook her head in memory. "He was thrilled. Lucy's pregnancy had been complicated and she couldn't have more children, so Randall was happy to have another child. He wanted to put the two kids together."

"You are kidding, aren't you?"

"Not at all. Randall doesn't live by other people's rules. But in the end I persuaded him to keep his mouth shut, but still Lucy always knew there was something going on between us. She always sneered at me and I never retaliated because I deserved it."

"And you and Mr. Maxwell?"

"We never slept together again, if that's what you mean. And he rarely slept with Lucy. He did what he was so good at and provided lavishly for all of us. I lived modestly but gave my son the best education there was."

"And Russell knows who his father is," Kim said.

"Always has. I never hid it from him."

"Did they spend time together?"

"Randall spent as much time with my son as he did with Lucy's. He's not a TV father who tucks the kids in at night."

"And you continued to work for Mr. Maxwell. Does he have any more children anywhere?"

"No. None. Randall's always had affairs, but he's never been serious about any of the women, and he was discreet."

Kim thought for a moment. "He had Lucy at home and you at work and two beautiful sons. I can see why he didn't want to mess that up."

Penny smiled. "I think you're beginning to understand Randall Maxwell."

"Why did he blackmail Travis into working for him?"

Penny's face became serious. "Now that is the clog in Randall's overall life plan. He assumed that when they grew up, both his sons would come to work for him, but neither one wanted anything to do with him. Travis was very angry at his father and Randall couldn't understand why. In his mind, he'd protected Travis all his life."

"And Travis saw himself as being held captive in a beautiful prison."

"That's right. Randall's much better at business than he is at life. I told him not to do it, but he threatened Travis to make him work with him. Randall thought that if Travis was in the office with him every day, he'd catch his ambition bug and that eventually his son would understand."

"But he didn't," Kim said.

"No. Travis had been sidetracked by a little girl who showed him how to have fun."

Kim smiled. "That was a turning point in both our lives." Her head came up. "So what happens now? How do we tell Travis that Russell is his brother?"

"I'm not sure he doesn't know."

"I've not seen any sign that he does."

"Both of them are half Maxwell and they don't let people see what they're thinking."

"Not even me," Kim said softly.

"You didn't exactly blurt out the facts when you realized the truth, did you? From what I've seen, you and Travis are well matched."

Kim thought about that for a moment. "So what now? Will it take Travis years of fighting his father to help Lucy get a divorce?"

"I don't know what Randall is up to right now. He's been very secretive lately. In fact, for the first time in nearly thirty years I don't even know where he is."

There was something about the way she said that last statement that made Kim's hair stand on end. "You wouldn't have a photo of Mr. Maxwell, would you?"

"I can bring one up on my phone," she said as she removed her cell from her bag. "Randall likes to stay out of the spotlight."

"Unlike Travis," Kim said, remembering the photos Reede had sent her. "So how's Leslie?"

"Paid off," Penny said as she handed the phone to Kim.

She wasn't surprised to see a picture of the man she knew as Red, but she wasn't about to say that Mr. Maxwell was here in Janes Creek. "He doesn't look much like Travis or Russell," she said as she returned the phone.

"The boys look like Randall's grandfather, and he was a handsome devil. Have you—?"

Kim stood up so abruptly Penny didn't finish her question. "Travis is going to think I've left him. I was supposed to meet him at the diner fifteen minutes ago. This has been . . . informative, and thanks for helping me understand Travis better." She gathered up her things and hurried into the antiques store. She hadn't wanted to answer Mrs. Pendergast's questions about whether she'd met Randall Maxwell or not. Yes, she had. Twice.

Outside the shop, she paused for a moment, trying to remember everything "Red" had said to her. Fishing in Edilean came to mind first. It looked like he'd known all along where Lucy was. And if he knew where she was, then he knew about Joe Layton. And if he did, and if he hadn't raised a stink, maybe that meant Travis wouldn't have to spend years helping his mother get a divorce.

"Maybe we can have a *life*," she whispered. Now. Not years in the future, but now. She went across the street to the diner, but she didn't walk fast. She had a lot of information running through her mind and the truth was that she didn't know what to do with it all. How much should she tell Travis? How much to keep to herself?

And what would be his reaction to what she did tell him? Anger? He was from a rich and powerful family, so would he jump on a private jet and go . . . Go do whatever fabulously rich people did when faced with stress?

The picture of Travis in a tuxedo with a blonde model haunted her. Was that his *real* life? Had Travis adapted to the glamorous New York life better than his father thought he had?

Kim knew that whatever happened she needed to keep her cool. She couldn't go running to the two sons of Randall Maxwell and gush about what she'd just been told. Would they smile at her in an indulgent way and say they knew all that? That they'd figured it out long ago? Kim didn't think she could bear that humiliation.

She stopped outside the door to the diner and took a deep breath. She needed to keep a straight face and do what the Maxwell boys did and keep secrets to herself.

There were few people in the diner, and Travis and Russell stood out. They were at a little round wooden table close to a wall, with their backs to her. There was a big bowl of popcorn between them and they were eating and drinking beer as they looked up at a TV screen. A soccer match was playing and both men seemed totally absorbed in it.

Yet again, Kim marveled at how alike the two men were. If they changed clothes, and she saw them from the back, she wondered if she could tell them apart.

Travis turned and saw her. For a moment he looked at her so hard she thought he knew where she'd been. But then his face relaxed, he smiled, and moved a chair out for her.

"You didn't buy anything?" he asked.

"Buy . . . ?" She had to remember that she did go to a store. "I didn't see anything I liked."

Russell was staring at her. "You look like something happened."

"Just looking forward to the company of two gorgeous men," Kim said quickly. So much for keeping secrets, she thought. "So what's good to eat here?" she asked.

"We waited for you," Travis said. He was still looking at her as though he was trying to read her mind. "Ol' Russell here has something to show us, but he wanted to wait until you were here."

Kim refused to meet Travis's eyes. She didn't want him seeing more than she wanted him to know. "That sounds interesting. What is it?"

Russell got up from the table and went to the side wall where there was a package, about two feet by three feet, wrapped in brown paper. As he picked it up and began to open it, he put his back to them so they couldn't see what he had. When he turned around, he was holding what was obviously a picture and from the look of the back of the canvas, it was quite old. He held it facing him, concealing it from them.

"Ever the showman," Travis said.

"You should talk, Maxwell," Russell said as he looked at Kim. "I was curious about these Dr. Tristans so I did a search and some photos came up. Distinctive-looking man is your cousin."

Kim couldn't help smiling. That was one way of putting it about her cousin's extraordinary beauty.

Still looking at Kim, Russell turned the picture around, and she gasped. The man in the portrait looked very much like her cousin Dr. Tristan Aldredge. "Is that him? The doctor who was killed in the mine?" she asked.

Russell leaned the portrait against the wall and took his seat at the table. They were all three facing it. "That's James Hanleigh, born 1880, died 1982."

"But . . ." Kim began. "He really does look like my cousin Tristan."

Travis looked back at the two of them. "Wrong side of the blanket?"

"That's my guess," Russell said. He started to say more but the waitress came to take their orders. Kim

ordered a club sandwich and Travis got crab cakes with
a triple order of coleslaw and a beer. She wasn't the least
surprised when Russell said he'd have the same. She
tried not to glance at him but she couldn't help herself. As she knew he would be, Russell's eyes were dancing with merriment. She wanted to kick him under the
table.

Their lunch conversation was about how the portrait had been found. It seemed that Russell's uncle
Bernie had discovered it.

"I needed to give him something to do to work off
all that food," Russell said. "He told me that last night
he'd run off some photos of the present Dr. Tristan
Aldredge that he'd found online, passed them around
to his mother's relatives, and told them to see if anyone in town recognized him. Sometimes blood relatives look like each other," Russell said—and again he
looked at Kim with a smile.

"And he found this portrait in one of the stores?"
Travis asked.

"No. That would be too easy. He found some old
man who said he thought maybe he'd seen a picture of
Dr. Aldredge but he couldn't remember where. Uncle
Bernie sent relatives out looking and asking and—"

"This all happened while we were at the Old Mill?"
Travis asked.

"Every bit of it. I think my relatives were like a
locust invasion on little Janes Creek."

"And where did they find it?" Kim asked.

"In the home of a little old lady who bought it at a yard sale thirty years ago for fifty bucks."

"How much?" Travis asked.

"Fifty—"

"No, how much did I have to pay for it?"

"Twelve grand."

"What?!" Kim said.

"She drove a hard bargain," Russell said, obviously enjoying himself, "and besides, she needed a new roof."

"I'll reimburse—" Kim began but stopped at the look Travis gave her.

"So how is he related and how does he fit in the family tree?" Travis asked.

"I haven't found that out yet. Give me the afternoon and at dinner I'll tell you everything."

"So you don't know if there are any Hanleighs still in town?" Travis's tone was that of a challenge.

"Not yet." Russell was calm, amused even.

Kim kept her attention on her food. Her mind was so full of all that Mrs. Pendergast had told her that she couldn't think about finding the descendant of some young man who may or may not be her relative.

When they finished eating, Travis asked if she was ready to go to the jewelry store.

For a moment she had no idea what he was talking about and stared at him blankly.

He smiled at her, his eyes alight. "I agree," he said in a voice that could only be described as seductive. Travis looked at Russell. "Kim and I are going to . . ."

"Take a nap," Russell said.

"Well put," Travis said as he backed his chair out, and held out his arm to Kim. "Thanks for lunch and we'll see you at dinner."

Travis led her out of the diner and to the car. The ride back to the B&B was silent.

Kim knew that Travis was hinting at sex. And why shouldn't he? It was a romantic little town, a charming B&B. They were young and by all accounts in love, so they *should* be spending every waking moment together in bed. Isn't that what she'd told her brother that she wanted? What had she said? *"I'll take all the passionate sex I can get. Days of it. Weeks if I can get it. Months would be divine."*

So now she had it and what she *really* wanted was to call her friend Jecca and spend about four hours on the telephone. Right now what Kim needed more than anything else was the release that discussion would bring.

So maybe I should find Red and ask him for advice, she thought. Ask the man who caused all the problems how to fix them? She gave a snort of laughter.

"What was that about?" Travis asked as he parked the car.

"Nothing," she said as she got out.

He held her hand as they went up the stairs to their connecting rooms. Once they were inside, he bent to kiss her, but Kim pushed back.

"Sorry," she said. "I have a . . . a headache and I think I should lie down for a while."

Travis stepped away from her. "Can I get you anything?"

"No, nothing," Kim said. "I just need some time . . . alone."

"Sure, of course," he said. He walked to the door to his room, opened it, went through and shut it behind him.

Kim looked at the bed. Maybe if she took a nap she'd feel better, but she knew she couldn't sleep. Mrs. Pendergast's words ran through her head. How much to tell? How much to hide? How much to—?

"No!" Travis said from the open door. "This isn't all right. None of it is. Something happened to you today and I want to know what it is."

"I can't—"

"So help me, if you say you can't tell me, I'll—"

"You'll *what*?" she shot at him, her voice rising with every word. "Leave? Walk away when things get too much for you? Disappear like you did before? Leave me alone, without a word? Let me search for you for *years* and all the time you were sneaking around at my art shows? Is *that* what you'll do?"

"No," he said softly. "I won't do that ever again. But right now, what I am going to do is stay in this room with you until you tell me what's tearing you up inside."

"I . . ." Her anger left her and she sat down on the side of the bed, her hands over her face.

Travis sat down beside her and put his arm around

her, drawing her head to his shoulder. "Does this have to do with Russell being my half brother?"

Kim hesitated for only a second. "How did . . . ?"

"I've not had a lot of experience with relatives, but I'm a good observer. Who else can look at you with the hatred Russ had for me that first day? It was like looking in a mirror, except that one reflection wanted to murder the other one."

Kim let out a deep sigh of relief that he knew. When her body relaxed, Travis turned her around on the bed so they stretched out together.

"So what happened while I was on the phone to Penny? You were fine while we were shopping, but when you came into the diner you were so white you looked like a vampire had drained you of blood."

"That's a more appropriate description than you know," Kim said with a grimace.

Travis kissed her forehead. "I want to hear every word of it. Don't leave anything out."

"But—"

He leaned over her and looked into her eyes. "No buts. No excuses. And most of all, no *fear*. Especially not of me. Did you murder anyone I love?"

She knew he was trying to lighten the mood, but to Kim all this was very serious. "No," she said, "but I'm considering running your father down with a lawn mower."

Travis's face lost its look of amusement and she saw the man who appeared in courtrooms. He fell back on the bed and pulled her to him so close she could hardly breathe. If she'd had her way, she would have moved even closer.

Where to begin? "Remember last night before dinner when I waited for you while you talked on the phone?"

"To that idiot Forester? Sure. What happened?"

"I met your father." Travis's hand tightened on Kim's shoulder, but otherwise he said nothing.

Once Kim started her story, Travis said little, and listened hard. She told him of her two encounters with the man who called himself Red, and she went over every word she could remember of their conversations. She told Travis of Red's little homily about children eating lead paint but only remembering being forbidden from doing what they wanted to do.

"That sounds like Dad. He thinks he can explain away every rotten thing he does."

She could tell that he wasn't shocked that his father had shown up in Janes Creek. But Travis drew in his breath when she told of Mr. Maxwell fishing in Edilean.

"I never asked Mom where she heard of Edilean in the first place. I never even thought about it, but Dad could have told her. It makes sense. Go on, please."

She told him of when she realized Russell was his brother. "They were giving me looks of pleading not to tell you."

"Penny was. Russ was enjoying every second of it."

"You knew?!"

"One of the things I've learned in being a lawyer is to watch as well as listen. None of you were subtle."

"Do you think Russ knows you know?"

"Of course. The kid is loving every minute of this."

"He's not even two years younger than you are, so he's not really a kid."

"Does your brother see you as an adult?"

"Not at all," Kim said.

"So what happened today while I was in the diner?"

"I met with your Mrs. Pendergast."

Travis was silent for a moment. "Now you're shocking me. What did Penny have to say?"

"She doesn't know your father is here. She—"

"No, wait. Tell me from the beginning. How she contacted you, what she said, you did, every word of it and don't leave anything out."

Slowly, Kim began to go over what happened. She started with the chairs and how she moved hers.

Chuckling, Travis hugged her and gave her a hard kiss on the mouth. "Good girl! I'm proud of you."

Kim liked his kiss so much that she returned it, but both of them wanted—needed—to talk about what she'd been told.

She started on the easier things, what she thought was least likely to upset Travis. She told him of how Russell was conceived. When Travis didn't reply, she said, "You don't seem surprised."

"I am, actually, but in an opposite way from what

you mean. The scuttlebutt around the office is that Dad and Penny were lovers for years. The surprise is that it was just once."

"A one time that produced a child."

"Big, ugly kid at that," Travis said, and Kim heard affection in his voice. "What else? And what are you holding back?"

"Will you let me tell the story in my own time?"

"I think I have, haven't I?" he said softly.

Turning, she looked at him, her eyes asking what he meant.

"I didn't take over."

"You mean like you did with Dave?" she asked.

"I . . ." He hesitated, as what he had to say was difficult for him. "I'm afraid I have more of my father in me than I want. When I took over Borman Catering, I was high-handed, and as you told me, I didn't believe that you could handle something like that on your own. I apologize. I'm not going to do that again. I'm not going to step in and take over your life, but I do think that if we're going to make this work that we need to do things *together*. As a pair, a team. I'm here and I can listen. Maybe if you tell me what is bothering you, together the two of us, can find a solution." He grinned. "That said . . . I admit that I have *never* been told off by anyone as *you* did. I had to check my eyebrows to make sure you hadn't singed them off."

"I wasn't that bad."

"Yes you were and I deserved it."

She snuggled back into his arms. "So this time . . ."

"This time I sat back and let you handle it on your own, and that wasn't easy for me. I can't tell you how much I wanted to let Russell know what I thought of the way he was smirking at you."

"Your brother."

"Yeah," Travis said with a little catch in his voice. "Odd thought, that one. Okay, so tell me more."

Kim took a breath. "You're not going to like this part."

"That means it's about Dad."

"Yes, it is," Kim said and began telling him Randall Maxwell's point of view of Travis's childhood. He didn't speak during the whole time and when she finished, Kim looked at him.

"I'd guessed some of it," he said. "Not that Dad would ever admit to me that he was bullied by anyone. My guess is that his mouth got him in trouble. He tends to order everyone around, and he was probably the same as a kid."

"You're not upset by this?"

"I . . ." Travis began, and smiled. "No, I'm not. This is hard to admit, but maybe I went to work for him because I wanted to know if I could cut it with my old man. It's not easy being the son of Randall Maxwell. Sometimes when I was doing stunt work the guys would ask me why I was risking my neck every day. They liked to tell me that if they were me, they'd be on a private jet sipping champagne."

"But not you," Kim said. "At least not then. I think you did come to like those things."

"I did. I had lots of champagne. Lots of—well, other things."

"Must have been nice," Kim said quietly.

"Not really. You know something? I received more actual *caring* from Joe Layton than I did from . . . well, from most anyone I ever met. Can I tell you a secret?"

"Please do," she said. She was smiling at his words about Joe, the man who was going to be his stepfather. Joe lived in Edilean, so maybe Travis would too.

"I want to open a camp."

"What kind of camp?"

"A free one," Travis said. "It's been in my mind for years and I thought I'd try it in California, but ever since I saw the preserve around Edilean, it's stayed with me. Joe could build it, Penny could manage it, and—"

"She wants to retire."

"After years with my father this would be a retirement."

"Your mom could decorate the place."

He pulled her up to face him. "How do you think you'd be at teaching kids how to make macaroni necklaces?"

"I taught you how to make a house for a doll, so I can teach anyone anything."

"Taught me? Ha! You ordered me around." He was unbuttoning her shirt.

"Please tell me you aren't going to ask me to shut down my business and work for you."

"I'd never dream of it," he said as his lips touched her neck. "But I can tell you that my secret plan is to take over managing your finances."

"Would you please?" she whispered as his mouth took her breast.

"Think I can get you to give me a recommendation to your local law firm?"

She drew back from her mouth on his ear. "Our very own McDowell, Aldredge, and Welsch? You have to be *born* into that law firm."

"Marriage not good enough?" he asked, but then his mouth was on hers.

An hour before, the last thing Kim wanted was sex, but now all she wanted was release.

"I think we have a future," she whispered.

Travis drew back from her. "What?"

"I think we have a future," she repeated.

"You . . ." He began, but stopped. "You really did think I was going to leave you?"

"Yes. I mean no. I just couldn't figure out where we were going to *live*."

"Your house, if I can get you to move your stuff out of the garage. Joe said—"

She kissed him to silence. "What about the divorce?"

"Joe can handle that. In fact I'm a bit afraid for my father when he goes up against Joe. Do you want to talk *more*?" His voice was full of exasperation.

"Yes!" she said. "Yes and yes and yes! I want to talk endlessly about us, about our future, about—Oh!" Travis's mouth was on her stomach.

"Go on, keep talking," he said as he moved his lips lower on her body.

"Maybe later," she said as she closed her eyes and forgot all about whatever she'd been worried about.

Fifteen

When Kim woke up, she could see that it was dark outside. The first thing she noticed was that Travis wasn't in bed with her. They'd made love all afternoon and she knew she'd never enjoyed anything so much in her life. She hadn't realized it, but from the beginning she'd had so many questions that she'd never fully relaxed. All the years of searching for him, of not knowing what had happened to him, were between them.

It wasn't that she'd completely forgiven him, nor did she fully understand his male reasoning, but for the first time since she'd seen him, a stranger standing in the moonlight, she saw the possibility that she *would* get over it.

There was a knock on the door into the hallway, and Kim looked about for her clothes. They were folded neatly on a chair, certainly not where she'd tossed them a few hours ago.

"Just a minute," she called, but then Travis came out of the connecting room. He was showered, shaved, and wearing jeans and a T-shirt. She thought about not getting out of bed.

"Hungry?" he asked as he opened the door and spoke to someone. He closed the door and turned to Kim. "They're going to set up dinner in my room. Or would you rather go downstairs and hear what the Pendergasts have found out about your relatives?"

He made the second choice sound so awful that she laughed. "Russell will miss you."

"He'll miss *you*," Travis said. "Do you think that kid has a girlfriend somewhere?"

"I'm beginning to wonder that too. I guess if he were a New York lawyer that you'd know it."

"Probably." Travis sat down on the bed beside her, and his face was serious. "I didn't realize that I hadn't made myself clear about my hopes for the future."

She knew he was referring to her outburst of fear that he would leave her again. "It's all right," Kim said. "We have . . ." She hesitated. "Some time to think about what we want to do."

The sound of a champagne cork being popped came from the other room.

"I think our name is being called," Travis said as he took her hand to pull her out of bed.

But Kim pulled the sheet close to her and didn't get out. "I'll meet you at the table *after* I've had a shower," she said pointedly.

Smiling, he kissed her hand and left the room.

Kim took a full thirty minutes showering and getting dressed. She put on a blue silk dress that she'd tossed in her bag as an afterthought. When she'd packed she'd thought it was over between her and Travis, that she'd never see him again. Smiling, she remembered that she'd thought he had given up. She had told him off and he'd run away. But Kim was learning that the three Maxwell men *never* gave up.

When she'd finished dressing, she took a breath, smoothed her skirt, and opened the door into Travis's room. It had been set up so beautifully that she stood still just to look at it. Cream-colored linens, blue-green dishes with little seashells on them, silver that glistened in the candlelight. But to her eyes, the most beautiful thing in the room was Travis. He'd changed into a tuxedo, and Kim was very glad of her silk dress.

"May I?" Travis asked, holding out his arm to her. He led her to a pretty chair done in blue-and-white-striped satin. "This is lovely," she said, looking across the table. But when she turned to him, he was on one knee beside her.

Kim's heart leaped into her throat and began pounding.

"Will you marry me?" he asked softly. "Would you be my wife and live with me forever?"

There wasn't any hesitation on Kim's part. "Yes," she answered.

Smiling, Travis bent forward to kiss her, and took

her hands and kissed the back of them, then her palms.

Still on one knee and holding her left hand, he reached under the tablecloth and pulled out a long, wide box covered in blue velvet. Kim knew what it was, as she'd seen the same box in her work.

Travis flipped up the lid, and inside were a dozen rings, each one different. Kim didn't need her jeweler's loupe to know that she was looking at world-class stones. Sapphire, diamond, emerald, ruby, they were all there. Each setting was unique, and she knew that each one was the work of an independent jeweler. She would never see the same ring on another person.

With her eyes wide, she looked at Travis in question.

"Mind if I . . . ?" He glanced down at his knee.

"Of course," she said and took the box from him to look at the rings. "I don't know what to say. They're beautiful. How did you . . . ? Oh. Mrs. Pendergast."

"No," Travis said as he filled their champagne flutes. "While Russ drove me here, I called places and had the rings sent. Each one was made by a different artist."

"That's what I thought." It wasn't easy to choose from among the rings.

"They're nonreturnable," he said.

At that she frowned. "You're not going to lavish me with gifts, are you?"

"Since you're supplying the house we live in, and the furniture, I think I have a right to add a few things."

Kim pulled a ring with a large square-cut emerald

from the box. Her jeweler's eye could tell that it was excellent quality. She held it near the light of the candle to admire the occlusions, the tiny imperfections that showed it to have been taken from the earth and was not man-made.

She held out the ring to him and extended her left hand. He slipped the ring onto her finger, kissed the back of her hand, and held it as he looked into her eyes.

"Kim, I love you," he whispered. "I have loved you since I was a boy and I don't want us to be apart again. I want to live where you do, with you."

Kim, ever practical, smiled at him. "I'd like to talk about where, when, how. You seem to have made a lot of plans and I want to know what they are."

"Good!" he said as he removed the lid from a silver platter, exposing two filet mignons. "I like women who know their own minds."

They talked and ate and discussed. Travis told Kim his ideas for the future, that he wanted to live in Edilean and open his camp for the summer. In the winter he'd do law work. "I like it better than I thought I would, so maybe what Dad told Penny is true, that there is some Maxwell in me."

"Do you think little Edilean could be enough for you?"

"Yes," he said, "and I promise that I won't do anything that we don't agree on." He leaned across the table to her. "But I think maybe you have some of your brother in you and your ambition is a bit more than your little town."

"I'm found out!" she said, and they began to talk about her future as she saw it. Dave's ideas of expanding her company hadn't been just his idea alone.

They talked of the coming divorce, and Travis told how he'd decided that Joe and his parents could fight it out themselves. "I'll get Mom a good lawyer."

"Forester?" Kim asked, and they laughed together.

It was while they were sharing a thick slice of chocolate cake that an invitation was slipped under the door. After they finished dessert, Travis and Kim had eyes only for each other and didn't see the heavy vellum envelope.

It wasn't until morning that Kim picked it up and showed it to Travis. It was addressed to both of them.

"Open it," Kim said to Travis. "I bet it's from Mrs. Pendergast and she wants to tell you that Russell is your half brother."

"Too late," Travis said. "You already blabbed."

"That's not how I see it. I think you—" She broke off at the expression on Travis's face. He was still in bed, the sheet just covering his bare lower body. "What is it?"

"It's an invitation to a picnic at one P.M. today, and there's a map of how to get there." He handed it to her, and it was Kim's turn to be astonished.

"It's from your father." She sat down on the edge of the bed. "He says he has a gift for us all." She looked up at Travis. "Think it's a box of pirate's loot? I could use some pearls. And some tanzanite. Of course I'm always low on gold."

He took the invitation from her. "You won't get any of that from Dad."

"Any of what?"

"Gold."

"I sure hope it's not more of his bits of advice about your eating lead paint. I think I'll ask him about his office romance policy."

"You do that," Travis said as he flung back the sheet. "I'd like to see that."

She leaned back on her arms to watch Travis stride across the room naked. "So what do you think he wants to give you?"

"Us. Give to *us*." Travis pulled up his faded jeans. "My hope is that it's freedom. To agree to give Mom an easy divorce."

"You're worried about her and Joe in a courtroom, aren't you? Will your father have half a dozen lawyers at his table?"

"More like twenty, and each one will have a different ethnic origin and race. It will be a global rainbow."

Kim laughed. "My money is on Mr. Layton. I think he can handle anything, and from the way he and your mom were dancing at Jecca's wedding—" She broke off at Travis's look. "All right. No stories of parents and the *S* word."

"Let's go to breakfast and see who else has been invited to this shindig."

Downstairs in the dining room, people had seemed to settle on which tables they were to sit at, so there were two empty seats by Russell and Mrs. Pendergast.

"Oh, how lovely!" Mrs. Pendergast said as she stared at Kim's ring.

Russell was smiling because his mother was looking at Travis in shock.

"You didn't think he could do something like that all by himself, did you? But he did," Russell said. "He even punched the buttons on the phone without any help from anyone. I was amazed."

"I think little brothers should mind their manners," Travis said, a sentence that silenced the table.

Kim looked at Penny and shrugged. "He figured it out."

Penny's eyes were on Travis and they were asking how he felt about all this. Travis put his hand over hers. "Dad should have divorced Mom and given us our freedom and married you," he said softly. "That he didn't shows that he has no common sense."

For a moment there were tears of gratitude in Penny's eyes, then she moved her hand away. "That's enough of that nonsense. What do you think Randall is up to now with this surprise gift of his?"

"I'm hoping he shows up with a sister," Russell said, and everyone laughed.

All through the meal, Kim noticed Russell and Travis sneaking looks at each other. There were so many new relationships being established! There were the usual—she was going to have to get to know his parents, and he hers. But Travis was getting the worst of it. He had a half brother who'd shown great hostility toward him, and a future brother-in-law who didn't want Travis to marry his sister.

Travis seemed to know what Kim was thinking. He looked across the table and winked at her, as though to say that he could handle anything that was thrown at him.

She smiled, letting him know that whatever happened, she would be there with him.

"You two cut it out!" Russell said. "You're fogging the glassware."

Kim looked away in embarrassment, but Travis just laughed as he clapped Russell hard on the back. "Someday it may happen to you," Travis said.

When Russ didn't reply, Kim said, "For all we know, Russell may have a wife and three children."

When Russell looked at her but made no reply, Kim turned to Mrs. Pendergast.

Penny put her hands up in surrender. "I have been sworn to secrecy."

"More like privacy," Russell said, and for the first time since Kim had met him he wasn't wearing his usual look of amusement. That his merriment had always been at Travis's expense didn't keep Kim from laughing.

Abruptly, Russell said, "If you'll excuse me," and left the table.

"But he didn't eat," Kim said as she started to go after him, but Mrs. Pendergast caught her arm.

"My son has his own demons to fight," she said, "and it's best to leave him alone."

Kim sat back down, but she looked at Travis. His eyes said he agreed with Kim. Without so much as a look at Penny, he followed Russell out of the room, but he was back in minutes. "Russ took the Jeep. I don't know where he's gone. Should we worry?" he asked Penny.

"I should, but not you," she answered. "Who wants to try the peach pancakes?"

Sixteen

❦

Russell knew he was being childish at leaving the table without eating, but he'd reached his breaking point. Besides, his invitation to the picnic had included a note asking him to meet his father at the Old Mill right after breakfast. No specific time given, just go there and wait. Between feeling like an intruder among friends and his curiosity about what his father wanted, Russ left.

As he drove, he couldn't help but think about the fact that Travis now knew Russell was his brother. But then Russ had always known about Travis Maxwell. He'd known that living in a big house, seeing his mother every day, being given anything he wanted, was a boy who was his part brother. When he was little and his mother told him he had a "half brother" Russ had started crying. His mother couldn't understand why until Russell had tearfully asked which half of the boy was missing.

After his mother explained that they had the same father but different mothers, Russell had become interested in his brother and often asked questions about him. It was something he and his mother shared.

Not that there was much. They rarely saw each other when he was growing up. She'd be gone for weeks at a time, traveling all over the world, never far from Randall Maxwell's side.

Russell was left at home with nannies, who changed rather frequently, and later tutors came to him. It hadn't been a shock to find out that they were the same men who'd taught his brother.

When Russell reached high school age he'd had enough of living in Travis Maxwell's shadow, and he showed his mother a brochure for a boarding school. She wasn't allowed to say no.

Russell wasn't sure when his curiosity changed to anger. And he didn't know why his animosity was aimed at his half brother and not at his father.

He only saw Randall Maxwell about a dozen times when he was growing up. When he was five, one rainy Sunday morning he was sitting in the room beside his mother's office drawing pictures when a man walked in. He wasn't especially tall and he didn't seem frightening in any way.

The man stopped at the doorway, didn't say anything, but then he turned back. "Are you Russell?"

He nodded.

The man came to stand by him and looked at what Russell was drawing—a picture of the big buildings outside the windows. "You like art?"

Again Russell nodded.

"Good to know." The man left and Russell wouldn't have remembered it except that later his mother said the man was his father. And the next Sunday that Russell went to the office with his mother there was a big box full of art supplies there for him.

His mother said, "Your father is a very generous man."

For years afterward Russell had kind thoughts about his father. It wasn't until he was about nine that he began to be aware of what other people's parents were like and what they did for their children.

Russell couldn't afford to be angry at his mother, as she was all he had. And his mother said they owed his father "everything," so he didn't dare aim his animosity at him. Instead, Russell took his anger out on his brother, the boy he'd never seen, the boy who had everything, including a mother who stayed at home *all* the time. And Russell never forgot that their father lived with *him*.

Russell went to the same college his brother went to, but by then his mind-set was different. He didn't study law. After school he traveled some, returned to the U.S., and studied some more. But he'd never been able to settle anywhere for long. Maybe it was the demons that raged inside him that made settling impossible.

When his mother had called recently and asked him

to help Travis, Russell had said no. He'd even laughed. Help a brother who had never contacted him? In Russell's mind it was up to the older brother to make the first move.

That's when his mother told him that Travis didn't know he had a brother. That had been such a shock to Russell that he'd agreed to sweet-talk some girl enough to find out information from her.

But when Russell was finally able to meet Travis, every bit of the anger he'd felt as a child came forward. He'd expected a spoiled, know-it-all jerk, but what he'd found was a man who made an omelet for him.

Since that first day the two of them had been nearly inseparable. But in spite of their ease together, Russell still felt the anger inside him. He'd liked besting Travis in negotiating the contract with Kim's greedy boyfriend. He'd even liked riding around with his brother. And later, when Kim told Travis off, Russell didn't think he'd ever enjoyed anything so much in his life.

But still . . . What had been difficult for him was seeing the way Kim and Travis loved each other. While it was true that they fought, it was easy to see that underneath it all they belonged together.

On the drive from Virginia to Maryland, Travis, nervous and upset, had told him how he and Kim had met as kids, and how she'd changed his life. For the first time Russell heard the full story of how Travis's life hadn't been the glorious adventure that Russell had always assumed it was.

This morning at the breakfast table had been all that Russell could bear. "Domestic bliss" was written all over the faces of Kim and Travis. And this afternoon Randall Maxwell was throwing a picnic, no doubt in honor of his eldest, number one son.

Russell was thinking so hard that when the car in front of him suddenly stopped he had to slam on the brakes. When he did, the blue velvet box Travis had handed him yesterday slid forward.

"Kim doesn't want them," Travis had said yesterday when he'd called Russ to his room. "Get rid of them."

Russell refrained from pointing out how much the rings cost. Nor did he snap that he wasn't Travis's servant. Russell knew this was brotherly bossiness and not business, so he shoved the box of rings under the seat of the Jeep, intending to give them to his mother to deal with.

Russell turned down the road to the Old Mill. He'd found out—or his mother's relatives had—that a descendant of James Hanleigh, Dr. Tristan Janes's first illegitimate child, still lived in Janes Creek. "She's a widow," he was told, and he envisioned a gray-haired woman with a bun at the back of her neck. No wonder she couldn't afford to renovate the old stone mill.

Russell needed a place and time to sit and think. He knew that it was time to point his life in the right direction, and to do that, he had some difficult decisions to make.

He parked the Jeep in front, wandered past the

herb patch—a Tristan garden, he thought—and went toward the back. He hadn't taken but a few steps when he heard a rumble that sounded like falling tile, then a half scream, as though someone had been injured.

He ran toward the sound, through a doorway, and into a room that was missing part of the roof. But he saw nothing and no one, just a stream of sunlight showing dust motes.

"Help?" came a small sound from above his head.

He looked up to see a young woman hanging by her fingertips from a rotting piece of wood that ran along the top of the wall.

"By all that's holy," Russell said under his breath as he ran forward to stand below her. "Do you have a ladder?"

"On the other side," she whispered.

Russell ran toward the doorway into the next room, but then he heard the crack of the old wood and he knew she was going to fall. There was time to do only one thing: put himself directly beneath her. His body would cushion her fall.

He leaped the few steps forward, his arms extended, and got to her just as the wood broke away. She hadn't looked very big as she hung from the top of the wall, but when her body hit his, he staggered backward. His feet tripped over some loose boards, and he went down. The weight and the momentum of the two of them made him skid backward. He felt skin come off his back as he slid across the rubble. Pain ran through him and he grunted—but he didn't let go of the woman he held. His arms were around her so tight it's a wonder she didn't break in half.

When he stopped moving, dust billowed around them. Russell was on his back, the woman on top of him. To protect them from the dust and falling debris, he put his hands over her head, hiding her face in his chest, and he buried his face in her blonde curls. As the dust engulfed them, he inhaled the fragrance of her hair. And when it settled, he still lay there, holding her tightly.

"I think it's okay now," she said, her voice muffled against his chest.

"Yes, fine," he said, his nose still in her hair.

"Uh . . ." she said. "I think I can get up now."

Russell's senses began to return to him enough that he managed to lift his head to look around, but he didn't release his hold on her. She was a small thing and her body felt good on his.

When she pushed against him, he reluctantly released her, and she rolled off to sit up beside him. Russell lay where he was and looked at her. Even with a streak of dirt on her face, she was extraordinarily pretty. Her dark blonde hair was short and rampant with soft curls, one of them hanging down over her left eye. Cornflower blue eyes, a little nose, and a mouth that turned up on the corners completed the picture.

She made a swipe at the dirt on her face but only succeeded in smearing it.

Russell pointed to the side of her right cheek. She pulled her shirtsleeve over her hand and wiped at it.

"Did I get it?"

"Not quite," he said as he reached his hand out. He was still lying where he'd landed, but he raised a hand toward her face. "May I?"

"Might as well. It's not like we haven't met."

Smiling at her joke, he cupped her chin—more than was necessary—and used his thumb to wipe away the smudge. When she was clean, he didn't let go and for a moment their eyes locked.

They might have stayed that way if a timber hadn't fallen to the ground behind them. Instantly, Russell rolled to one side and put his body between hers and the falling wood. Her arms went around him and stayed there even after the dirt settled.

"I think we better get out of here," she said and again had to push him away.

Russell pulled himself to a sitting position, his eyes on hers, and he was smiling. "Are you—?" He cut off at a gasp from her. She was holding out her hands and they had blood on them.

In an instant she went from sweetly smiling to all-business. She put her hand on his shoulder and twisted her body to look behind him. "Your entire back is bloody."

When Russell just kept smiling at her, she grimaced. "Okay, hero, get up. We need to get you cleaned up."

She stood and Russell saw that even in her loose

jeans and big shirt that covered a tee with MYRTLE BEACH written over the pocket, she was very nicely built. Nothing flashy, but trim and firm.

She put out her hand to help him up, but when Russell moved, the pain in his back brought him back to reality. But with her big blue eyes on him he couldn't let out the groan he was feeling.

When she saw him wince, she slid her arm around his waist and helped him pick his way through the rubble on the floor, out the doorway, and into the courtyard and the sunlight. She guided him to sit down on the low stone wall. "Sit here and don't move, got it?"

"But—" he began.

"I'll be right back. I have to get my medical bag."

Russell's face lit up. "You're a Hanleigh."

Pausing, she smiled. "I am. At least that's my maiden name."

Russell's face fell, but then the light came back to it. "You're the widow."

This time she laughed. "I am Clarissa Hanleigh Wells, I own this pile of rocks, and yes I'm a widow. Anything else you need to know before I get my supplies?"

"You're a Tristan," he said.

She shook her head. "I have no idea what that means. Just sit there, don't move, and I'll be right back." She disappeared around a wall.

Russell took his cell phone out of his pocket. He

saw that he had six e-mails and three voice mails, but he ignored them. He was going to text Travis that he'd found Clarissa Hanleigh, but on second thought, he turned his phone off and put it back in his pocket. He'd see the lot of them at the picnic, so the news could wait until then.

He looked up as Clarissa was hurrying back to him. She lithely leaped over fallen stones and rotten timbers, a heavy-looking red leather bag in her hand, as she returned to him.

He just sat there smiling at her in what he knew was an idiotic way.

She stood before him, looked at him for a long moment, and said, "Take it off."

"I beg your pardon?"

"Oh my!" she said. "Where did you go to school?"

"Stanford."

"I could have guessed. Take your shirt off so I can see the damage."

As he began unbuttoning his shirt, Clarissa moved around him, to see his back, and he heard her deep intake of breath. "Never mind. I have to cut this off, and if it's too bad I'm taking you to the hospital."

"No," he said. "I'd rather you fixed it." He heard her pull on sterile gloves, then felt her hand on his shoulder. He had to hold himself rigid as she began to pull the fabric from out of the scrapes on his skin.

"I think you should—"

"No," he said firmly. "You're a doctor, aren't you?"

She hesitated in the cutting. "I had planned to be."

"Wanted to be one all your life? You seemed to have been born to be a doctor? That sort of thing?"

"Yes, exactly," she said. "Is that what you call a Tristan? Named after my ancestor?"

"It's what they call them in Edilean."

"Never heard of the place."

"It's in Virginia, and you have relatives there."

She stopped, with her hands on his skin. "Jamie and I have no relatives."

"Jamie?"

"My son," she said.

Russell drew in his breath as she used tweezers to pull a strip of cloth out of a cut. "Oh. A son. How old?"

"Five."

"I guess he's the reason you didn't . . ." He was concentrating on his breathing because what she was doing hurt a lot.

"He's my reason for living, if that's what you mean. But yes"—she paused to pour water on a gauze to blot the blood away—"Jamie is why I didn't go to medical school. Well, actually, that's not fair. A good-looking football player, a few tequila shots, and the backseat of a Chevy are the real reasons."

"So you married the player?"

"Yes," she said softly, "but he got drunk and ran off a bridge before his son was born. Jamie and I have always been alone."

"Not any longer." He turned to look at her just as she was cleaning a cut, and he gasped at the pain.

"I won't think less of you if you scream. Or cry."

"And lose my hero status?" he said.

She stopped working, put her hands on his shoulders, and moved her face near his. "You will *never* lose your hero status with me. You saved my life," she said softly as she kissed him on the cheek.

Russell bent his head and kissed the back of her hand.

She removed her hands. "Lifesaving doesn't get you anything else. Who are you, why are you here, and what's this about having relatives?"

As Russell began to talk, he knew that what he was saying was slightly incoherent, but it was difficult for him to think clearly. Between the pain and the presence of this young woman, he wasn't quite himself. He started by telling her the purpose of his journey, how he'd come with his half brother, Travis, to help his fiancée, Kim, trace an ancestor in the hope of finding descendants.

"All of Edilean is related to one another," he said, "so I don't know why they need more."

"You sound envious."

"I . . ." he began. He was going to say that he had relatives, but those people his mother had booked in the B&B only called when they came up with some scheme that her rich boss could finance. Other than that, he and his mother were on their own.

"Go on," Clarissa urged him. "How did I suddenly acquire a family?"

"Shenanigans between Dr. Tristan Janes and Miss Clarissa Aldredge of Edilean, Virginia, back in the 1890s. They produced a child she named Tristan, and the name has been given to succeeding eldest sons."

"And they're all doctors?"

"I think so. You'd have to ask Kim for the facts."

"And she is going to marry your half brother?"

"Yes," he said, then couldn't resist telling her what he'd thought that meant when he was little.

Clarissa laughed and he liked the sound. "That sounds like my Jamie." She was bandaging his back.

"What were you doing here when I rescued you?"

She gave a groan of frustration. "Trying to repair this place, but I'm no good at it."

"I have to agree on that." Her hands were on his skin, smoothing the bandages, and for a moment he closed his eyes.

"There, I think you're done." She walked around him. He still wore the front part of his shirt, which she hadn't cut away, and she smiled at his comic appearance.

He started to pull the remainder of the shirt off, but at a sound from Clarissa he looked up. There were tears gathering in her eyes. It was a natural thing to pull her into his arms, his hands entangled in her hair, her head buried in his shoulder.

"I was so scared," she whispered as the tears began

to flow. "All I could think of was that my son would lose his mommy. He'd never recover from it. I'd ruin his whole life because of my stupidity. And it *was* stupid of me to be up there by myself every Sunday morning."

"Yes it was," Russell said as he held her close—and he suddenly remembered that his father had sent him to the Old Mill on a Sunday morning. "You have to swear not to do it again."

"But this is all I have," she said as she pulled away from him. "This old, rotten, falling down pile of rocks is everything in the world that I own. My job barely pays expenses and—"

"I'll help you."

"What?" She drew away to wipe her eyes and look at him.

"I'll stay in Janes Creek and help you."

"You can't do that. I don't know you. I don't even know your name."

"Oh. Sorry. It's Russell Pendergast. I'm twenty-eight years old and my father is Randall Maxwell."

"Isn't he . . . ?"

"Right. A mega big shot in the world. But I think he may have—" Russell thought that the story of whether or not his father had sent him there to meet Clarissa was for another time. "My mother works for him. Or for my brother at the moment, but he's about to move to Edilean, and my mother wants to live there too. Where's your son?"

"In Sunday school. One of the women I work with takes him so I can spend a couple of hours here." She glanced at the old place. "I think I need more than a couple of hours a week, don't you?"

"This place needs months, lots of machinery and materials, and at least a dozen workmen."

"Or women," she said, and he smiled.

"Right. Where do you work?"

"Guess."

"For a doctor? In a hospital? Something to do with medicine."

"It looks like you're not just a pretty face," she said, then turned red. "I didn't mean . . ."

Russell was smiling at her. "Is there someplace I can get a shirt? I don't want to go back to the hotel. And breakfast. I'm afraid I left without eating and I'm famished."

"I . . ." She hesitated. "In my attic I have a box of my father's clothes. He was about as big as you. I could throw one in the washer while I make you a pile of bacon and eggs."

"When does your son get home?"

"About eleven."

"I'd like to meet him," Russell said softly.

"And I'd like for him to meet you."

For a moment they looked at each other and there seemed to be an understanding that this could be the beginning of something real, something permanent.

Russell was the first to break the silence. "Would

you and Jamie like to go to a picnic with me today at one? I'm sure there'll be lots of food, and I think I can arrange to have some entertainment for Jamie there." His eyes told how much he wanted her to go with him.

"I think we'd both love that."

"Great!" Russell said as he stood up. But that crinkled his back and he winced in pain.

Again, Clarissa put her arm around his waist to help him.

"I may stay injured forever," he said as he put his arm around her shoulders. "So what does Jamie like? Balloons? Animals? Acrobats?"

"Fire engines," she said. "The bigger, the redder, the better."

"Fire engines it is," Russell said.

"I'm going to go get my car and bring it around," Clarissa said. "Stand here and don't move your back."

"Yes, ma'am," Russell said and watched her hurry away.

As soon as she was out of sight, he typed out a text message to his mother.

I'M BRINGING A FIVE-YEAR-OLD BOY TO THE PIC-NIC. HE LOVES FIRE ENGINES. I'M GOING TO MARRY HIS MOTHER. R.

Seventeen

When Travis drove into the pretty, wooded area that had been set up for the picnic, he was hoping to see Russell's Jeep, but it wasn't there. Instead, he saw a brilliant red fire engine and what looked to be an entire fire department of men and women in full uniform. They were standing around talking, laughing, and helping themselves to what looked to be a lavish spread of food and drink.

"What's this about?" Kim asked.

"I have no idea, but then for all I know, Dad's planning a bonfire."

She looked at the idyllic setting and let out her breath. It wasn't what she now realized she'd been dreading. She thought maybe there would be white-gloved waiters serving champagne in crystal glasses, and there'd be a hundred people there.

Instead there was just a red-and-white-checked cloth spread on the ground under a huge black walnut tree, with half a dozen red coolers to the side. There wasn't even a sign of a waiter.

The only oddity was the local fire department to the side.

"It's not what I expected," Kim said.

"Me neither," Travis answered. As he spoke, Penny drove up, quickly got out of her rental car, and ran to them. "Is Russell here?" she asked through Travis's open window.

"I haven't seen him. What's the—" He cut himself off as Penny hurried away toward the fire engines.

"Do you think something's wrong?" Kim asked.

Travis was looking in his side-view mirror at Penny as she quickly moved from one person to another. "I've never seen her lose her cool before," he said in wonder. "One time we had two sworn enemies in the office at the same time. Dad and I were worried there'd be gunplay, but Penny deftly moved the men in and around and they never saw each other. She saved a multi-million-dollar deal."

Kim was looking out the back windshield. "Whatever is going on has upset her. She looks frantic."

"Interesting," Travis said as he turned back and smiled at Kim. "Are you ready to go to this thing? I'm sure Dad—Holy crap!"

Kim looked up to see another car pulling off the road and into the little parking area. "It's . . ."

"Right. That is Joe Layton and my mother," Travis said and his voice lowered. "Speaking of sworn enemies . . ."

"Your mother and Mrs. Pendergast," Kim said as she collapsed back against the seat. "I have a suggestion. Just a little one, but I think you should consider it. How about if we leave here right now and go straight back to Edilean? Mrs. Pendergast can send our clothes to us. Or we can shop for new ones. What do you think?"

"I like the way you deal with a situation," Travis said as he started the engine.

But Joe Layton put his big body in front of the car.

"How about some race driving techniques?" Kim asked. "You could go around him."

"He's too big; he'd hurt the car. Let's get out on your side and make a run through the forest. Maybe we can escape."

Joe was too fast for them. He was standing by Travis's door, and his hand snaked inside to remove the keys from the ignition. "Come on, you two cowards. Get out and join the party." He opened Travis's door.

Travis squeezed Kim's hand and rolled his eyes skyward. "Give me strength."

Kim got out of her side of the car and stood back to look at Lucy, the pretty little woman who came to stand behind Joe. He was so big that she could disappear behind him.

Kim was curious to see this woman who'd so successfully hidden from her for four years. As Lucy came forward to stand on tiptoe to hug her son, Kim knew she would have done just that. Every minute of those weeks she'd spent with Travis when they were children was so burned in her mind that Lucy's face was there also. If Kim had seen her in Edilean, she would have done what Lucy feared and told everyone she knew. Lucy was the connection to Travis, the way to find him, and Kim would have thought only of that, not of any consequences.

Lucy's eyes met Kim's and there was apology there—from both women.

"Kim," Lucy began as she stood before her. "I never meant—"

"It's okay," Kim said. "I'm sure Mom told you I'd blab, and I would have. I so much wanted to find Travis that I would have sold my own mother into white slavery."

"From what I've heard she could have handled it," Lucy said, and the two women laughed together.

"It's all right between you and Travis now?" Lucy asked softly. Travis and Joe were a few feet away.

"Very, very all right. And what about you and Mr. Layton?"

Lucy gave a sigh that came from her heart. "It's nice to be loved, isn't it?"

"Yes, wonderful," Kim said. "Would it be impolite of me to ask what's happening with the divorce?"

Lucy gave a quick look at Joe and Travis, and leaned forward, her voice a whisper as she took Kim's hand in her own. "Randall has agreed to a peaceful divorce. No fighting. A fair deal. I told him I don't want Travis to have to so much as appear in court. I want you two to have all the time together that you deserve."

Kim couldn't help the tears of joy that came to her eyes. "Thank you," she whispered.

Lucy smiled, and the two women's hands just seemed to cling to one another.

"Hey, you two!" Travis called. "I'm hungry. Let's see what Dad sent us to eat."

Penny was still with the firefighters, and in spite of his professed hunger, Travis went to her.

Travis greeted the firefighters, told them that if they needed anything to let him know. They all wanted to shake the hand of the son of the man who'd just bought them a new engine.

It took Travis a while before he could make his way to Penny. "What's Dad up to now?" he asked. "It's nice he's contributing to the Janes Creek Fire Department but what's in it for him?"

"I did it," Penny said. Her eyes were on the road, not on Travis.

"You bought a fire engine?"

"I ordered it. Your dad paid for it," she said and stopped, as though that was all the information she was going to give.

"Penny?" he asked.

When they could hear a car coming down the road, she seemed to stop breathing. The car drove past and Penny let out her breath.

"What is going on?!" Travis demanded.

Penny, her eyes never leaving the road, handed him her cell phone. "Look at my text from Russell."

"Oh," Travis said as he read it. "He asked his girl-friend to marry him? Must be catching. I hope he used one of those rings I offered Kim. He—"

"Russell doesn't have a steady girlfriend."

"But he said he's going to marry the mother of a kid who likes fire engines. Who is she?"

Penny turned to look at Travis in silence.

It took him a few moments to get what she wasn't saying. "He just *met* this woman?"

"I think so," Penny said as she rubbed her hands together in nervous agitation. "Oh, Russell," she said under her breath, "what have you done?"

For the first time ever, Travis put his arm around Penny's shoulders. She had always been the one who remained calm through everything. When Travis and his father were at each other's throats, it was Penny's sensible comments, her refusal to let any crisis perturb her, that quieted everyone.

But now she was the one who needed a calm presence.

"Your mother will hate me even more," Penny said, her old self showing, but she leaned her head against Travis's chest for a moment.

He glanced over her head to see Joe and Kim and his mother sitting on the checkered cloth. They'd opened the cooler and taken out lemonade and glasses, and lots of cheese and crackers. Maybe the waiters were missing, but the food looked to be top-notch.

"My mother has eyes only for Joe, and when she sees Russell I think she'll like him."

Penny stepped out of Travis's embrace. "I hope so, but then he does look a lot like you. If there's one thing your mother loves, it's you."

Travis smiled. "Joe said Dad was going to give the divorce without a big court battle. Do you think he will?"

"I know he was quite taken with young Kim."

Travis couldn't help a grimace. "Bastard! Sneaking around like that! He knew where Mom was all these years. When I think of the trouble I went to in hiding from him I could—" He looked at Penny. "How do you know he liked Kim?"

"I talked to him. I showed her a photo of your father and she turned white. I knew she'd seen him somewhere."

Travis nodded. "She came into the diner looking like she'd seen a ghost."

"But she told you the story of how he pretended to be a caretaker?"

"Only after some persuasion."

"Good," Penny said. "Don't keep secrets from each other. Your father and I never—I mean . . ."

"I know what you mean. His life has always been more with you than with my mother."

Penny turned to look at Lucy and Joe sitting so close together on the cloth. "I've always disliked your mother. Not from something based on fact, but from what I assumed I knew about her. The old Travis family name made me think she lived in a world of garden parties and teacups. And I thought she'd like gentlemen who carried lace hankies."

Joe Layton was as far from being a stereotypical "gentleman" as was possible.

"I'm sure Russ will be here soon, so maybe now's a good time to brave it out with a face-to-face with my mother."

"Did she bring any weapons?" Penny asked.

"Only a couple of machetes," Travis joked, but when Penny took a step back, he laughed. "Come on, Kim and I will protect you."

Travis stayed close to Penny as they walked toward the picnic area and his eyes begged his mother not to attack. But then, he realized that wasn't fair. After all, Penny had had a child by Lucy's husband. On the other hand, it wasn't as though a happy marriage had been broken up. The truth was that Travis was so glad to have a brother that he didn't really care about anything else.

As Travis sat down between his mother and Kim, he looked at Joe for moral support. Joe took Lucy's hand and his eyes seemed to say that it would be all right.

"Is there any beer in there?" Travis asked as he watched his mother. She was refusing to look at Penny. "Mom," he said as Kim handed him a beer. "Kim told me you have a couple of brothers. Is that true?"

"Howard and Arthur," she said. "I haven't seen

them, well, since I got married. There were harsh words spoken."

Everyone was still, wondering if Lucy was going to say more, but she didn't.

"So what are they like?" Travis asked. He would say anything to break the awkward silence. "I'd like to meet—"

"They're here!" Penny said in a voice of relief and joy. She got up and started running.

"Who's here?" Kim asked.

"It seems that since my little brother"—he looked directly at his mother, but she didn't meet his eyes—"left us at breakfast, he has met a woman, fallen in love, and asked her to marry him."

The others paused with food to their lips.

"Who is she?" Kim asked.

"I have no idea. Everything about my brother is a mystery. Shall we go meet her? It seems that she has a five-year-old son who loves fire engines."

All of them got up and started walking toward the fire truck when they heard a squeal of delight, and a beautiful little boy was running toward them.

"Tristan!" Kim said, then she too started running. "He looks like my cousin Tristan!" she called over her shoulder. "Russell found my cousins!"

Her enthusiasm was contagious, and Travis, Joe, and Lucy hurried after her.

The little boy was already halfway up the side of the

truck, all the firefighters helping him up. The happiness on the child's face made everyone smile.

Behind the little boy, wearing a look of pure bliss, came Russell, and he was holding hands with a pretty young woman.

"I like the ring," Kim said to Travis.

He looked at her in question.

She nodded toward the woman's left hand. "It's the four-carat pink diamond from the tray you showed me. It was my second choice. She has taste."

Smiling, Travis nodded. As he'd hoped, Russell had used one of the rings he'd offered Kim for their engagement.

Russell stopped in front of his brother. "Dad said he wanted to meet me at the Old Mill this morning. Seems that Clarissa goes there to work every Sunday morning."

"If Russell hadn't shown up I'd be dead now or at least broken into bits," Clarissa said and everyone looked at her.

"You two have to tell us everything," Kim said, "and I think we're cousins."

"Second cousins once removed," Travis said.

"I need to see to my son," Clarissa said. "Jamie will—"

"He has a grandmother now," Russell said softly, and they all turned to look. Penny was on the ground, but her arms were extended over her head. As they watched, two big firefighters lifted her to the top of the truck to sit beside Jamie. He smiled at her, and when the engine started, Penny put her arm around the child.

"I think he's going to be fine," Russell said as he smiled at Clarissa. "Shall we all sit down?"

"And eat," Clarissa said. "I'm sure you're hungry again."

Like the lovebirds they were, that inside joke seemed to amuse them greatly.

It was three hours later before they were all sated with food and drink and news. The fire engine had returned and they'd all listened to Jamie's excited description of everything he'd seen and done. He'd been given a hat and a bright yellow coat, both of which he wouldn't take off.

After he'd eaten he wore down and snuggled on his mother's lap. When he fell asleep, Russell took him and stretched him out, his head on Russell's lap, his feet in Penny's.

Everyone had listened in silence as Russell and Clarissa tripped over each other as they told of their meeting. Travis looked at Penny, and communication based on years of working together passed between them. Randall Maxwell had found the Aldredge descendant they were looking for and he'd set his son up to meet her.

When Clarissa told of her brush with death from trying to renovate the Old Mill, Travis again looked at Penny, and she nodded. Randall Maxwell was going to give his son a wedding gift of a renovated building.

But what everyone was most interested in was the first encounter between Russell and Clarissa. They were both shy and reticent when telling that part of the story, but the looks on their faces told it all.

Several times Travis looked at his mother, and her expression showed that she was as fascinated as they all were by the story. Twice Travis caught her looking at Russell in wonder. He really did look like her son.

At about four they were all winding down from the excitement of the day. Travis and Kim were looking at each other as though they wanted to be alone, as were Lucy and Joe, and Russell and Clarissa.

The odd man out, the only one unattached, was Penny.

"Maybe we should go back to the hotel," Kim said. "We could all meet later for—" She broke off because a long black limo had pulled into the area beside their cars. The back door opened but no one got out and the engine wasn't turned off. Inside they could vaguely see the shadow of a person, but he or she didn't get out.

"That's Randall," Lucy said and she sounded like the party was over, but then her face lightened and she looked at Penny directly. Not with the sideways looks she'd been giving her all afternoon, but full into her eyes. "He's here for *you*."

Penny shrugged. "He probably wants me to pick up his dry cleaning."

Everyone continued to look at her.

"Mother," Russell said, "you have been in love with that man for nearly thirty years. Don't you think it's time you showed it?"

Penny looked at Lucy, and her eyes were asking permission. In answer, Lucy snuggled up to Joe. "I have what I want right here."

Penny took only seconds to make her decision. Looking as though she was finally going to get to do what she wanted to in her life, she got up, smoothed the front of her skirt, kissed Russell, then Jamie, then Clarissa on the forehead. She turned her back to them and started a slow, sedate walk toward the open limo. But when she got closer, she broke into a run. They saw her smile when she got to the door. She didn't hesitate as she stepped inside and pulled the door closed behind her. The limo drove away.

The stunned silence of everyone made Jamie stir. He looked up and saw Russell, and smiled that he was still there.

"You gave me a fire engine," he said and slipped his arms around Russell's neck.

"I think we should go," Russ said to Clarissa, and they stood up.

The others stayed seated on the cloth, looking up at them. Russell with the little boy clinging tightly about his neck, holding him in one arm while helping Clarissa with her bags with the other. It was impossible to believe that these people had just met that morning. If ever there were three people who were a family, it was them.

"So what are your plans?" Travis asked.

Clarissa looked up at Russell. As she folded a blanket, the big ring sparkled on her finger. "It's a little early to say yet."

Russell said, "I guess it depends on where I get a job."

"All right, little brother," Travis said, "we're all waiting. What *is* your vocation?"

Russell smiled in a way that said he wasn't telling.

Clarissa looked confused that these brothers didn't know such an elemental thing about each other. "Russell is a Baptist minister."

That silenced everyone.

Russell shrugged. "I trained to be, but I haven't had much practice at it. I was told that I have some, uh, anger issues, and it was strongly suggested that I deal with them."

Travis looked like he was about to laugh, but Kim gave him a look that warned him not to.

Kim spoke up. "You know, half of Edilean hasn't forgiven our current pastor for stealing my brother's girlfriend. Besides, he's been there for years now and . . ." She let the rest of that hang in the air.

"What my dear wife-to-be is saying is that there may be an opening in Edilean for a minister." Travis was looking at his brother with wide eyes, but he managed to recover himself. "I think we should talk about a camp I want to set up. There's a place for you."

"Gladly," Russell said, "but first Clarissa is going to med school. She wants to be a doctor."

"She's a real Tristan," Kim said, and they all laughed. She looked at everyone smiling, then up at Travis. At last she had what she'd wanted since she was eight years old.

"Ready to go?" Travis asked softly.

"Yes," she said. "Always yes."

Epilogue

It was late when Kim's cell phone buzzed. She and Travis were in Paris on their honeymoon and she thought about not looking at the e-mail. But Travis heard it.

"Go on, see who it is. I'm hoping to hear from Mom and Joe."

Kim clicked the phone and read in disbelief. "It's from Sophie."

"Who?"

"My other college roommate, besides Jecca."

"Oh yeah, the blonde bombshell."

As Kim kept reading, she collapsed on the bed.

"Is it bad news?"

"Yes and no," she whispered. "Sophie says she needs a place to hide and a job."

"To hide? From what?"

"She doesn't say," Kim said.

Travis sat down on the bed beside her and put his

arm around her shoulders. "If you want to go home, we can."

"No," Kim said. "Sophie said I wasn't to do that. I—" Her head came up. "I'm going to call Betsy."

"Who's that?"

"My brother's office manager. Reede doesn't know it, but he's getting a new employee." She held the phone to her ear.

Travis stood up. "Sounds to me like you're match-making."

"Heavens no! Reede and Sophie? It could never work. She's too smart, too *nice* for my brother. How-ever, I think I'll send my cousin Roan an e-mail and ask him to look in on Sophie."

Travis shook his head as he sat down in a com-fortable chair and opened a newspaper. It looked like his wife was going to be a while in organizing her friend's life.

Behind the paper he smiled. He was sure he was the happiest man on the planet. "Take your time," he said. "We have a lifetime ahead of us."

Read on for a preview of the next novel

in the Edilean series by

Jude Deveraux

Moonlight Masquerade

Coming soon!

Sophie tried to control her anger, but it wasn't easy. She could feel it rising in her like bile, traveling upward from her stomach.

She was driving her old car and she was about twenty miles from Edilean, Virginia. The scenery was beautiful, with trees sheltering the road, the fading sunlight playing on the leaves. She'd heard about Edilean from her college roommate, Kim Aldredge. The two of them, with their other roommate, Jecca, had laughed at Kim's portrayal of the little town as a cross between heaven and . . . well, heaven. "Everyone knows everybody!" Kim said with enthusiasm.

It was Jecca who'd asked for further explanation of that concept. Kim told them of the seven founding families who came to America in the seventeen hundreds and created the town.

"And they're all still there?" Jecca asked in disbelief.

"Enough of us are descendants of those seven families that we're related to one another, and yes, we still live there." There was so much caution in Kim's voice that Jecca pounced. They were told there were "others" in town and they were called "newcomers." Even if the family had moved there in the eighteen hundreds, they were still "newcomers."

When these lively discussions about the merits—or lack of them—of small town living took place, Sophie stayed out of them. She covered her silence by taking too big a mouthful of food and saying she couldn't speak. Or she would suddenly remember that she had to be somewhere else. Whatever she needed to do so she didn't have to participate in the discussion about growing up, she did.

But then, Jecca and Kim didn't notice for they had always been so very trouble free, with few worries. It was a state of being that Sophie had tried to imagine, but she hadn't succeeded. It seemed that her life had always consisted of running either toward something or to get away from a lot of things.

She glanced at the big envelope on the passenger seat of the car and the Treeborne logo seemed to leap out at her. It was like a flashing neon light going off and on.

The sharp sound of a horn brought her back to reality. Her distraction had caused her to drift across the line and into the left lane. As she jerked to the right, she saw what looked to be a gravel road disappearing into the trees and she took it. She only went a few yards before stopping, her car hidden from the main road. She turned off the engine and for a moment bent her head against the steering wheel as her mind filled with images of the last five years.

The death of her mother had changed everything. There'd been a job offer when Sophie graduated from college, but she'd turned it down. Oh, how noble she'd felt on that day! She'd called the nice older man who'd asked her to work for him. "It's not much to begin with," he'd told her, "but it's a start. You're talented, Sophie, and you have ambition. I think you'll go far." When she'd called him to turn the job down she'd felt like a saint. She was sacrificing herself for others, giving up what *she* wanted to help her sweet, innocent, vulnerable twelve-year-old sister.

The man had made an attempt to change her mind. "Sophie, you're too young to do this. Isn't there someone else your little sister could live with? An aunt, a grandparent? Someone?"

"There's no one, and besides, there are extenuating circumstances. Lisa needs—"

"What do *you* need?" the man had half shouted.

But nothing he'd said had dissuaded Sophie from putting her life on hold so she could spend the next five years protecting her sister. Protecting her, providing for her, trying to teach her about the world. But somewhere in there Sophie had begun to want things for herself, like love and family. At that she had failed.

Sophie got out of the car and looked around. Through the trees she could see the highway. There wasn't much traffic, just a few pickups, some of them with boats attached to the back.

She leaned back against the car, closed her eyes, and held her face up to the light. It was warm out but she could feel autumn in the air. Other people were raking leaves and ordering cords of firewood. Maybe they were thinking about Thanksgiving and what candy to give out this weekend at Halloween.

Would Carter spend the holidays with his fiancée? she wondered. What would he buy her for Christmas? A perfect little diamond tennis bracelet for her perfect little blueblood wrist? Would they go sledding in the snow?

Yet again, Sophie felt anger surge through her.

Carter had a right to his own . . . Sophie put her hand over her mouth as she had an almost uncontrollable urge to scream. He'd said, "You must know that you're the kind of girl a man—"

No! She was never again going to let herself remember the things he'd said to her on that last night. But then, it was the *way* he'd said it all that had hurt as much as the words. He'd acted surprised that she didn't know what to him was a given. His face—that she'd thought she loved—looked at her in innocence, as though no blame could be attached to him. According to him, it was all Sophie's fault because she hadn't understood from the beginning. "But I thought you knew," he said, his brow furrowed in puzzlement. "It was just for the summer. Aren't there books written about summer romances? That's what we had. And the good part is that someday we'll both look back on this with fondness."

His words sounded so sincere that Sophie began to doubt herself. Had she known but not let herself admit it? Whatever the truth was, she'd felt crushed, defeated. She'd truly believed that she loved Carter—and that he felt the same way about her. He'd made her feel good about herself. He'd listened to her complaints about her jobs, about how she often felt that she'd missed out on life, then he'd kissed her until she quit talking.

It had taken Sophie nearly a year after graduation to figure out that putting her own life on hold to help someone else was easier said than done. She'd gone from being a laughing college student to having two jobs. She was always on her feet, always having to smile at customers, at bosses, at coworkers, then having errands to run after work. It had all worn her out. When she got home, Lisa would help her with dinner, but she had schoolwork to do. And then there was their stepfather, Arnie, drink in hand, always nearby, always watching, always looking as though he couldn't wait to get away from Sophie's ever-vigilant eyes. Sophie had wanted to take Lisa away from that town but Arnie was the legal guardian so they'd had to stay there. Since college, Sophie's life had been endless stress—until Carter came in to it.

She stepped away from the car and looked at the wooded area around her. She'd like to think all that was behind her now. Two days ago she'd driven Lisa to the state university, and she'd felt good that she'd put enough money in the bank to cover the first year. There were hugs at good-bye, lots of tears, and Lisa's thanks. Sophie loved her sister and would miss her, but Sophie couldn't help but feel that she was at last free to start her own life. And that life centered around Carter Treeborne, the man she'd come to love.

As she drove the two hundred miles back to her step-father's house she'd been jubilant, feeling the best she ever had in her life. She would go back to her art, what she'd studied in school, and she and Carter would spend their lives together. That he was a Treeborne would cause some problems at first, but she could adjust. She'd met his father several times and the man had listened atten-tively to all she'd had to say. He seemed to be a very nice man, not at all intimidating, as people in town said he was. But then, the enormous Treeborne plant was where everyone worked. Of course they'd be in awe of him.

Sophie couldn't help comparing him to her alcoholic, lazy stepfather. He was the man Sophie had had to pro-tect Lisa from. That night after she'd dropped Lisa off, as soon as she entered the house—the one her mother had bought and that Sophie had paid the mortgage on since her mother's death—his greeting was to ask her what was for dinner. With a smile, Sophie said he could eat whatever he cooked for himself.

Ten minutes later, she was at Carter's house. After they made love, he told her that next spring he was marrying someone else, that he and Sophie had just been a "summer romance."

There are times in a person's life when emotion takes away the ability to think. Carter had taken full advantage of Sophie's stunned state as he shoved clothes at her, then had half pushed her out the front door. He'd placed a chaste kiss on her forehead and closed the door.

She'd stood there for what could have been ten minutes or an hour. She couldn't seem to make her eyes focus or her mind work. Somewhere in there she decided that Carter was playing a prank on her, a sort of belated April Fools' joke.

She opened the door of the big house and stepped inside. The huge entrance hall with its curved, double staircase loomed before her, silent, even menacing. Quietly, slowly, she went up the carpeted stairs, her heart pounding in her throat. Surely she'd misheard what Carter had said.

She stopped outside his room and looked through his open door. He was on the phone, lounging on the bed, his back to her. The tone he was using, so soft and seductive, was one she'd heard many times. But this time his words were being cooed to someone named Traci.

When Sophie heard a voice from downstairs, she came to her senses. She was sneaking around inside the home, the mansion, of the richest family in town, and coming up the stairs was Mr. Treeborne himself.

Sophie only had time to step behind the open door of Carter's room. She pulled her toes back into her shoes, praying she wouldn't be seen.

Mr. Treeborne stopped in the doorway and his big, powerful voice—the one his thousands of employees at Treeborne Foods knew well—rang out. "Did you get rid of that town girl?"

"Yeah, Dad, I did," Carter said and Sophie didn't hear a drop of regret in his voice.

"Good!" Mr. Treeborne said. "She's a pretty little thing, but that family of hers isn't something we can associate with. We have a status to uphold. We—"

"I know," Carter said, sounding bored. "You've said it all from the day I was born. Do you mind? I'm talking to Traci."

"Tell her father hello for me," Mr. Treeborne said, then went down the hall.

Sophie nearly fainted when Carter closed his bedroom door, exposing her to the hallway. Her first thought was to get out of the house as quickly as possible. She was at the first step down when she halted. Suddenly, it became crystal clear to her what she should do. She turned back and confidently strode down the hall, past Carter's room, and into his father's office. The door was open, the room empty, and there on the big oak desk was *it*. The recipe book. Two hours before, Carter had taken it out of the safe in his father's office.

The Treeborne cookbook was legendary in their little town and was used in all the company's advertising. It was said that the entire line of frozen foods was based on the secret family recipes passed down from Mr. Treeborne's grandmother. A stylized drawing of her graced every package. Her face and the Treeborne logo were familiar to most Americans.

When Sophie had arrived at the Treeborne house tonight, she'd been talking so much about her future plans, all of which included Carter, that she'd been unresponsive to his lovemaking. He'd become quite frustrated after just a few minutes. But then, he'd known that this was going to be their last night together.

Finally, he gave up trying to get her attention and said he'd show her *the book*.

She knew exactly what he was talking about and the

thought that he'd show it to *her* made her stare at him in stunned silence. Everyone in town knew that only people named Treeborne—by birth or marriage—had ever seen the recipe book. But Carter was going to show it to Sophie!

He'd been right that even the thought of such an honor would take her mind off everything else. Carter held her hand as he led her into his father's paneled office, moved aside a portrait, and opened the safe. Reverently, he pulled out a large, thick envelope.

Sophie waited for him to open it and reveal the contents, but that didn't seem to be part of the deal. He let her hold it in its envelope on her outstretched palms. When Sophie made a move as though she meant to look inside, Carter took it from her and started to put it back in the safe. He never made it because Sophie began kissing him. To her, being allowed so near something so precious was an aphrodisiac—and it seemed to be an indication that what was between them was permanent. In their urgency, Carter dropped the envelope on top of his father's big desk and they ran to his bedroom.

It was afterward that Carter told her it was over between them and pushed her out the door. But after Sophie heard Carter and his father's dismissal of her, as though she didn't matter as a human being, she walked down the lushly carpeted hallway, her shoulders back, her stride firm. She picked up the envelope containing the precious recipe book and tucked it under her arm. As she turned, she saw that the door to the safe was still open. Inside was a lot of cash, stacks of hundred dollar bills. It was tempting to reach inside and take a bundle, but she didn't. With great insouciance, not caring who heard, she shut the heavy little door hard. The resounding *bam!* made her smile. Still with her shoulders back and the envelope clutched to her chest, she went down the stairs and back out the front door.

By the time she got home, so much anger was surging

through her that she felt strong and sure of herself. She fell onto her bed and slept heavily. She awoke early the next morning and knew exactly what she was going to do. It didn't take her but minutes to throw her every possession into suitcases, plastic bags, and two cardboard boxes.

Her stepfather followed her out the door, already with a drink in his hand. "You don't think you're leaving here, do you? Lisa will be back for the holidays so I'd advise you not to go anywhere," he said with a smirk on his thin face. "So you'd better get back in here and—"

She told him precisely what he could do with his threats. As she opened the car door, her cell rang. The caller ID said it was Carter. Had he discovered the missing book already? She wasn't going to answer to find out.

She tossed the phone to her stepfather. He didn't catch it and it landed in the brown grass in the front of the house. As he fumbled for it, mumbling angrily, it kept ringing. Sophie got in her car and started driving. When she stopped for lunch, she bought a disposable phone and texted Kim. I NEED A PLACE TO HIDE AND A JOB, she typed out. She knew her friend well enough to know that the message would intrigue her. And she knew that even though she'd had no contact with her for years, Kim would help.

Instantly, Kim wrote back that she was out of town at the moment, but she'd take care of everything. An hour later, Kim called to say that it was all arranged—and it was so good to hear her voice. With her usual efficiency, Kim said Sophie could stay at Mrs. Wingate's house in Edilean, and she could have a temporary job working as a personal assistant for her brother. "Reede needs someone to manage his life, but I don't think he'll stand for it," Kim said. "I'll find you another job soon because I should warn you that my brother's temper isn't pretty. Nobody deserves what he shells out. The three women who work in his office all want to quit, but Reede keeps giving them raises to get them to stay. I think they make more money than he does."

Kim was happy and chatty, and at no time did she pry into Sophie's problems. In fact, when Sophie started making a weak, hesitant explanation about why she'd been out of contact for so long and why she needed to hide, Kim saved her by interrupting. "I'm just glad you're back in my life. When I get home we can talk and you can tell me as much or as little as you want to. But for now, I think you just need to feel safe."

Her words had been so exactly on target that when she hung up, Sophie allowed herself her first quick tears. But she knew she couldn't indulge herself that way.

She spent the night in a motel, paid for with cash she'd taken from where she'd hidden it from her stepfather, and was on the road just after sunup. By the time she neared Edilean, she'd calmed down some, but not much. She couldn't help comparing herself to Kim and Jecca. They were the same age as Sophie but both of them now had fabulous jobs and she'd learned via the Internet that both of them were married. Sometimes Sophie felt that her roommates had been given fairy godmothers while Sophie had been overlooked.

She shook her head at the absurd thought. Years ago when her mother had said she was going to marry Arnie, Sophie had seen the future. By then she was in her third year of college and her mother was ill. "He's only marrying you to get custody of Lisa when—" Sophie broke off. "When I die?" her mother asked. "Go on and say it. I know it's happening. As for Lisa, she can take care of herself. It's *you* who has the problems." Sophie resented that statement. Hadn't she fought like a demon to get herself into college? But when she pointed that out to her mother, she'd only scoffed. "You're a dreamer, Sophie. I mean, look at the facts. You go to college but what do you study? Art!

What use is that? Why didn't you learn something that could get you a job? Be a doctor or a lawyer, or at least work for one." Again, Sophie had no reply to give her.

Her mother died two days before Sophie graduated from college, and she'd raced home for the funeral. When she got there, she saw her stepfather leering at her pretty little sister. Sophie decided to stay for the summer, and she never left. Until now.

She walked to the other side of the car and opened the door, but paused before even touching the big envelope. Did she really have it in her possession? *The* book? The one the whole Treeborne empire was based on? Were there police after her? She had her laptop with her, but she hadn't checked the Internet. Her cheap phone had no Web connection, so she didn't know what was going on. Would federal agents be brought in? If so, how far back would they look to find out where Sophie was? There'd been no contact between her and Kim since college graduation, so they wouldn't find calls to Edilean.

Sophie shut the car door and told herself that she had to return the book. She'd go to Edilean and send the package back to Carter. Maybe if they got the book back he'd drop the pursuit. If there was one.

She got into the driver's side and turned the key, but nothing happened. Dead. "Like my life," Sophie muttered. Whereas before she'd thought the surrounding countryside was lovely, now it looked scary. She was down a gravel road that stopped just a few feet ahead, blocked from view of the main highway. It would soon be dark and if she stayed in the car she'd never be found.

She looked at her cell phone. No signal. She went outside, walked around, holding her phone aloft, but there wasn't even a hint of a signal.

There was only one thing to do: walk. She opened the trunk and rummaged through bags and boxes until she found her running shoes. Not that she ever ran. The last thing she was, was athletic. In the last few years, the most she did was walk from her desk to the water cooler.

She removed her pretty gold sandals, put on some ankle socks, and tied on her big shoes. She thought of changing into jeans but decided against it. All she needed was truckers hooting at her. She kept on her summer dress but pulled out a pink cardigan. It was going to get cool before she reached Edilean. She went to the front, got her handbag, and at last picked up the big envelope. She'd left her tote bag hanging on a kitchen chair so she didn't have anything to carry it in.

She tried the car again but nothing happened, so she locked it and walked back on the gravel road to the highway. The shade of the trees had changed to a deeper hue so that it was almost dark. A burst of wind rustled the leaves and Sophie pulled her sweater closer. When she heard a car coming down the road, she instinctively stepped back into the shadows and waited for it to pass. Every horror story of hitchhikers and the mass murderers who picked them up went through her head.

After the car passed, she started walking again and told herself she was being ridiculous. According to Kim, Edilean was the safest place on earth. Nothing bad ever happened there. Well, except for some major robberies in the last few years that Sophie had read about online, but it was better not to think about those.

Two more cars went by and each time Sophie stayed under the trees and waited. "At this rate I'll *never* get there," she said aloud, and shuddered as she had a vision of walking along the road at midnight. Every few minutes she stepped onto the pavement and checked her phone but there was still no signal. But then, she hadn't gone even a mile from her car.

She was so absorbed in maneuvering her phone around that she didn't hear the approaching car. It had come around a curve, headlights glaring, and for a second Sophie felt like a deer mesmerized by the lights. The car was coming straight at her! She could clearly see the BMW symbol just a few feet away. Survival was the only thing on her mind. She threw up her arms and, like a diver heading into the water, she dove straight for the side of the road. She landed facedown in the sharp branches of a clump of scrub oak, her mouth full of dirt. Quickly, she turned to look back toward the road. She was just in time to see a sleek little silver blue BMW drive over both her phone and the book. Thankfully, she'd been wearing her handbag cross-body so it was still with her. The car kept going; it didn't stop.

All of Sophie hurt as she got up, hobbled onto the road to retrieve the remains of the phone, and picked up the envelope. There were tire tracks across it and one edge had been torn open. There was little light but she could see that the book inside was frayed, the pages bent. She didn't know if it had been that way or if the damage had been done by the reckless driver in the BMW.

Sophie carried everything to the side of the road and for a moment she fought back tears. Maybe she wouldn't have been prosecuted if she'd returned the book in pristine condition, but now it looked to be nearly destroyed. She was going to prison because of some jerk in a Bimmer.

As she pulled leaves out of her hair, raked dirt out of her mouth, and brushed at bloody scrapes on her arms and legs, she knew her logic was flawed, but if she didn't give her anger an outlet she'd fall down into a ditch and never get out.

She started walking again. This time she didn't step aside for the cars, but kept going. Three cars, each with a single male driver, asked if she wanted a ride. The anger in her was increasing with every step and she had glared at the men as she said no.

Her legs ached, the cuts and scrapes on her arms and

legs hurt, and her feet were blistering. In fact, it seemed that every inch of her was in pain. But the image of the expensive car driving over the book kept her going. In her mind, it was just like Carter driving over her. He'd never looked back either. She put one foot in front of the other, each step so hard it jarred her body. But she kept going, never slowing down—just as the driver had done.

She heard the noise of the tavern before she saw it. It wasn't particularly loud but when the door opened, the music, a mixture of rock and country, floated out.

Sophie's steps began to slow down. Here at last was civilization. She'd be able to call a cab. Or maybe her landlady, Mrs. Wingate, could come and get her. If this town of Edilean was as good as Kim had said it was, there would be help.

When Sophie stopped and waited for a car to pass, she saw it. In the far left of the parking lot was the silvery BMW that had nearly run over her, had destroyed her phone, and was probably going to cause Sophie to spend a few years in prison. She put her head forward, set her sore jaw in a hard line, the recipe book in its torn envelope under her arm, and strode across the street.

Inside the restaurant, the lights blinded her for a moment so she stood in the doorway to look around. It was a quiet place, with booths full of people eating huge amounts of fried food. Very American. To the left was a big jukebox, a dance floor, and some tables with men and women drinking beer from pitchers and eating great bowls full of chicken wings.

Sophie had been sure that she'd be able to pick out the person who'd nearly killed her. Over the last several miles she'd conjured an image of a long face, close-together eyes, even big ears. She imagined him to be tall and thin, and of course he was rich. Carter's family was rich. If he ran over a woman, he'd wonder why she didn't get out of his way. Would he call it his "summer hit-and-run"?

She walked to the bar along the wall and waited for the bartender to come to her. He was a young man, blond and blue-eyed.

"Hey! What happened to you?" he asked.

"I was nearly run over."

He looked concerned. "Yeah? Want me to call the sheriff?"

Sophie tightened her grip on the stolen book. "No," she said firmly. "I just want to know who owns the silver BMW."

The young man's mouth opened as though he meant to say something, but a woman sitting at the bar spoke first. "See the guy over there in the blue shirt?"

"Is that him?" Sophie asked.

"Yes it is," the woman answered.

"Mrs. Garland," the bartender began, "I don't think—"

"Take it from me," the woman said to Sophie, "that guy's a real bastard. Thinks he knows more than anybody else in town. I'd like to see him taken down a peg or two."

Sophie didn't answer, just nodded and walked straight to the table. He had his back to her so she couldn't see his face. There were two other men sitting there and when they saw Sophie their eyes lit up in appreciation. Ignoring them, she walked to stand in front of the man in the blue shirt.

Her first impression was that he was strikingly handsome, but he looked tired—and sad. She might have felt sympathy for him, but when he saw Sophie he grimaced, as though she were someone he was going to have to do something for. It was that look that broke her. All she'd wanted to do was talk to him, tell him what she thought of him, but she'd be damned if anyone was going to look at her as though she were a . . . well, a *burden*. She'd not been a burden since she got her first job at sixteen. She prided herself on carrying her own weight.

"Can I help you?" the man asked, his deep voice sounding as though Sophie was going to demand something dreadful of him.

"You own the BMW?"

He nodded once and that look that Sophie was a great bother to him deepened.

She didn't think about what she did. She picked up a full pitcher of beer and poured it over his head. Not dumped, but poured it so it took several seconds to empty the contents. While cold beer was running down his face, she was aware that every person in the tavern had stopped talking. Even the jukebox was silenced, as though it had been unplugged.

As for the man, he just sat there, blinking up at Sophie, nothing but surprise on his face. When she finished, the restaurant was totally silent. Sophie glared at him, his face dripping beer. "Next time, watch where you're going." One of the men at the table took the empty pitcher, and Sophie walked across the room and went out the front door.

Outside, she stood still for a moment, not sure what to do next. Then the door behind her opened and one of the men who'd been sitting at the table came out.

"Hi," he said. "I'm Russell Pendergast, the new pastor in town, and I think maybe you might need a ride."

When Sophie heard noise returning to the tavern, she didn't give herself time to think. "Yes, I do," she said and got into a green pickup beside the man. They started the drive into Edilean.